DRIVING ON THE LEFT

Jeep Tour, Too

GAIL WARD OLMSTED

JERICHO ROAD PRESS

Edited by Kathryn F. Galán
Cover design by Brenda Gonet
Published by Jericho Road Press

This is a work of fiction. Names, characters, places, brands, media, and incidents are either the product of the author's imagination or are used fictitiously. Any resemblance to similarly named places or to persons living or deceased is unintentional.

PRINT ISBN 978-0-6927-1487-4

Dedicated to the sweetest woman who ever lived, my mother Anne Brennan Ward, who passed away on May 30, 2015.

Mom, you were my first and biggest fan. You loved us unconditionally, and I miss you all the time but especially on Sundays!

CHAPTER ONE

JACKIE

NO MATTER HOW OFTEN you travel, let's face it: packing is a real pain in the ass. It's always a struggle—what to pack and how much of it. Easy enough to over-pack, that's for sure. But then you're stuck dragging everything around the whole time you're gone, and you have no room in your luggage for souvenirs and gifts. Under-packing is also pretty easy, I guess. "If I really need it, I can get it there" could be an effective approach, depending on where you are headed.

My best friend, Suze, sent me a link a few years back chock full of packing tips. I printed it out and promptly lost it, but, from what I can remember, it was mostly commonsense advice: roll your T-shirts, stuff corners with socks, pick items that are multi-use, blah, blah, blah. Unfortunately, common sense is in short supply this afternoon. My brain is mush, and my bedroom looks like it was hit by a tornado.

Tomorrow morning, my daughter Rebecca and I are flying to Ireland! We will be there for three weeks. She graduated from college earlier this month, and we're celebrating. My husband Rob was scheduled to go with us, but his business partner needed an emergency appendectomy and will be out of commission for at least another week. They own the largest advertising agency here in the northern Verde Valley of Arizona, and there is just too much going on for both of them to be out of the office at the same time. I hope Rob can join us fairly soon. I will miss the hell out of him, but maybe a little time apart is what we need right now. It's been really tense around here lately.

What I'm getting ready for was supposed to be a relaxing vacation, but I've got to do some serious soul-searching over the next couple of weeks. Rob wants an answer, and I promised him one. Why I am convinced that the solution to our problem will come to me in a foreign country, when I haven't been able to figure it out here at home over the last several weeks? Well, that's beyond me. But I live in hope. The future of my marriage depends on it.

The last couple of weeks have been busier than usual, tying up loose ends at work and finalizing travel arrangements. Even though Amy, my business partner, is more than capable of running Encore without me, I'm still a little anxious about leaving.

We are going to take a guided tour of Ireland, but not the kind of tour bus that you are probably thinking of. It's more of a van, and there will only be eight or ten of us, plus the tour guide. Becca found it online. It promises to take us "off the beaten track to discover the real Ireland." A chance to see some amazing sights, hit all the top attractions, have our own tour guide, and not be saddled with fifty or sixty other travelers? Sounds good to me.

Wait, are you thinking about that other time I took a guided tour…? My girlfriend Suze has been cracking up about this upcoming Ireland trip ever since I told her about it. And when I mentioned that Rob was not going to be able to join us at first…. Well, let's just say she had a field day. Rob's ex-stepmother joined in to laugh, as well. Typical Edie.

"Be careful, doll face," she said. "What with your track record..."

Yeah, simply hilarious. My *track record*? It's not exactly common knowledge. Many of my current friends, employees, and clients have no idea what first brought me to Sedona more than two decades ago. But Rob knows, of course. Even Becca has heard that her sedate, middle-aged mom had a romantic fling with a sexy tour guide, sandwiched between two marriages to her father.

Okay, let's back up. Here's the story, starting back nearly twenty-four years ago in Massachusetts…

* * *

My marriage to Rob had ended in divorce, but we were still romantically involved. Well, *sexually* involved, that is. Long story, but one for a different day.

I was a marketing professor at the time, on the tenure track at a local college. A couple of my colleagues and I went out to Phoenix to attend a conference. It was a totally forgettable few days, but we had decided beforehand to tack on some time at the end and drive a couple of hours north to Sedona. My co-worker Kate had heard Sedona was a great place to visit, so we booked a triple room for two nights and headed up there for a little R and R.

Well, Kate had heard right. Sedona *is* spectacular. Red rocks, bright blue skies, vistas galore. For our one full day in town, we scheduled a Jeep tour of the desert. Kate packed her camera, and the three of us showed up at the appointed time, ready to be amazed. Rick, our tour guide, was also pretty spectacular, if you like tall, bronzed, blond hunks, that is. And I did.

We had a really great day exploring the desert. Rick was knowledgeable, entertaining, and kind of flirty. At the end of the tour, he gave me his number, scribbled on the back of one of his business cards. *Call me,* it read.

I laughed it off at the time, but a small part of me was intrigued. Kind of excited. Like I said, I was recently divorced, and, although Rob and I still had sex on a regular basis, I was living alone and couldn't escape the feeling that something was missing from my life. So yeah, it felt kind of good when a sexy younger guy found me attractive.

A couple of days later, back at work, I finally heard the decision on my tenure bid. It was a no-go. I was floored. My ass-hat boss droned on and on about timing and budgets and enrollment trends, and then he told me that I had a couple months left to finish out the spring semester. After that, I was done.

I went through all of the stages—you know: denial, anger, acceptance, etc.—and somehow decided that the time was right to pack up and head west. It was an opportunity to start over, surrounded by red rocks. A pair of bulging biceps factored in, for sure. But I couldn't actually admit that Rick was the real motivation for my move. Not even to myself.

I did know that I needed a change and saw the tenure committee's decision as a sign. So why not, right? It's not like there was anything keeping me there. My parents had died while I was in college; Rob and I had sold our house after the divorce, and most of my things were still in storage. At the time, I was living in a tiny apartment and working like a demon at the college. Over those last few years, I had taught extra classes—all the ones that my tenured co-workers avoided—and served on so many committees, I could barely keep track of them. All in the hopes of getting tenure so I could have summers off, while sharing my love of marketing and consumer behavior with a new crop of fertile young minds every semester.

When I heard that it had all been for nothing, I was really pissed, maybe even bitter. I had sacrificed a lot for that job. I can't, in all honesty, blame my crazy workload for imploding my marriage, but it certainly hadn't helped, either. Rob and I had both been putting in tons of overtime the last few years of our seven-year marriage. He had been bucking for a partnership at the ad agency where he worked. That partnership never materialized.

So yeah, there I was, treading water and going nowhere. Falling in love with a desert community and falling in lust with one of its sexy residents wasn't what I had expected. But I did.

Before I left New England, I spent lots of time with my ex, much of it between the sheets. We didn't talk much about our future and how a few thousand miles might affect it, but Rob promised to visit me once I was settled. I hugged Suze goodbye, got in my new car, and arrived several days later in Sedona. I looked Rick up immediately. Although he had no clear recollection of who the fuck I was (in his defense, nearly three months had passed; if he met fifteen tourists on an average day, well, he couldn't be blamed for failing to recognize me, right?), we started seeing a lot of each other. Rick was light and breezy, fun to be around and easy to talk to.

But I wouldn't exactly describe our physical relationship as hot and heavy. After a couple of weeks of some fairly energetic sex, we quickly fell into a pattern: a couple of sleepovers a week preceded by dinner at either of our places; plus, once or twice a week, we met for lunch or dinner out, depending on Rick's crazy schedule. That was about it. Fun, sweet, and easy. Those were the hallmarks of our relationship. Nothing at all like the sizzling, sexy thrill of my first few years with Rob, but what can you do? I thought at the time that Rob had been "it" for me, and maybe I wasn't going to have another chance at a passionate love life.

Besides, I had other goals back then. Sedona was not the easiest place to start a new life. Actually, it was kind of an insular community. I made some new friends, including my landlord Coop (Edward Cooper) and the dealer of coffee (my drug of choice), barista Mo (Maureen). She and I bonded over lattes and laments about our failed relationships.

My best friend, though, was a stray tiger cat that I named Jagger. He was the coolest cat ever, with more swagger than most felines can even dream of. For the first couple of months, Jag would come and go as he pleased. He showed up to eat and sleep but spent most of the nighttime hours prowling the neighborhood. One morning, he limped in with a torn ear, looking much the worse for wear. I put my foot down and started barricading his cat door when I went to bed at night, forcing him to stay in. He didn't appear to mind his transition from alley cat to house cat, and he never strayed out of the yard after that. The day he failed to wake up from one of his long naps on our sunny patio was one of the saddest days of my life. I miss him to this day.

After taking a couple of months off to get settled, I started my own business and found it really satisfying to put my marketing skills to good use. I named my company Encore, because I offer all kinds of classes, training, and resources for midcareer types looking for a do-over, as well as those just starting out.

So there I was, trying to build a new life for myself, when my ex-husband decided to make good on his promise and pay me a visit. I think he was curious to see what I was up to and with whom, but it was immediately clear that Rob and I had unfinished business and lots of it.

The old physical attraction was still there, and, out here in the desert, our friendship was able to flourish, as well. I loved having him back in my life, and, once again, he became my biggest supporter, my best friend, and my oh-so-passionate lover. And Jag adored him, too. So I told Rick that we were not going to be hanging out any more, and Rob and I began a long-distance romance that lasted for several months.

We finally admitted to each other that there was no good reason to be anything other than totally committed, so it was his turn to pack up and move west. He bought into an ad agency out here and moved in with me, which was a good thing, as I was several months pregnant by then with our daughter.

I was skeptical at first. *I can't really be pregnant, can I?* I was nearing the age when perimenopause was just as likely the reason behind a couple of missed periods. Rob and I had talked on and off during our years together about having a child but had never gotten around to it. I had stopped even thinking of parenthood as an option.

The day Becca was born was the happiest day of my life. After nearly thirteen hours of sweaty labor, I was a mother to a wriggly, healthy bundle of joy. We named her Rebecca Sullivan Colby. I like to think that she represents the best of both me and Rob. She looks a bit more like me, with her reddish-brown hair, green eyes, and freckles, but she's got her dad's easygoing disposition and quick wit.

Once, a friend of a friend stopped me in the grocery store when Becca was about three months old. Totally sleep-deprived and running on autopilot, I was pushing Becca's stroller up and down the aisles, desperately trying to remember what had been on my grocery list, which, of course, I couldn't find. Small pieces of paper and I, we never manage to stay together very long.

"Who does she favor?" I was asked after the prerequisite *oohing* and *ahhing*.

"Oh, I think she likes both of us about the same," was my response. It wasn't until I shared the conversation with Robbie that I realized why she had looked at me so strangely.

Becca was a happy baby who grew into a happy young woman. Other than a brief period of time when she was fifteen and I was certain that aliens (horrible, pissy ones) had taken up residence in my daughter's body, I love being her mom. Robbie kept his promise of a manageable workload, and, since I run my own business as well, one of us was usually with her during those early years. In a period of just six months, I went from living solo to having a very active family life. It was spectacular!

* * *

Right now, however, I have a spectacular mess on my hands, and I am still not finished packing. One of the problems is weather, as Mother Nature can be a real bitch. Unless you're going someplace with the same climate as where you're coming from, you need to pack all kinds of extra things.

Since we're travelling to Ireland, I am packing plenty of wool socks, the type of rainproof jacket I rarely if ever need in sunny Arizona, hiking boots for those "off the beaten track" trails, and lots of tanks, tees, yoga pants, and comfy stuff for long hours in the van and hanging around in our room.

Lost in thought, I jump when I hear my husband's voice. "You know, if you forget something, you can just tell me, and I'll bring it with me next week, Jaxie."

"Rob, you scared me. I hate when you do that," I complain. He crosses the room and wraps me in his arms.

"When I do what?" he asks, the picture of innocence with a devilish grin.

God, after all these years, this man still does it for me: makes my heart race, my palms sweat, weak in the knees—the whole nine yards. How can I even imagine a future without him?

"How about when I do this?" he asks, planting kisses that start at my neck and work down my arm. "Or this," he continues, taking my hand and placing it…

"Oh, gross. You two are at it again. How am I ever supposed to have a chance at a normal life with you two cavorting around like a couple of horny teenagers?" Becca plants herself firmly in the doorway and looks at us both with mock disapproval. It is true that she's grown up witnessing countless scenes like this one. She should know better, but she walked right in on us. She is obviously out of practice, as she usually calls to us from at least twenty yards away, in case anything is brewing. Her dad and I? Well, let's just say that we've never lost that lovin' feeling.

"What do you think has gone on here for the last four years, while you've been away at school, Bex?" Rob asks with a smirk. His arms still around me, he nods in my direction. "This one here? Your mom? Let me tell you, honey, she is one hot..."

"Dad, no! My ears," Becca shrieks. "I don't want to know. What happens between you two needs to stay between you two. You had to sleep together the one time, to make me, and that's it. Yuck. Anyway, I just want to ask her if she's planning on bringing any makeup remover." I just love when my two favorite people in the whole world are able to carry on a conversation like this, like I'm not even here.

Time to weigh in.

"*Her*, huh? I'm right here, my darling daughter, and yes, I just bought a new package of oil-free wipes for the trip. If you're nice to me, I'll even share them with you." I pull away from Rob. "And as for you, my darling husband, I'm going to take a rain check on whatever *this* was, okay? Right now, I need to pack." I shoo them both out of the room. First things first. A travel umbrella or something larger? Binoculars? A "real" camera? Or will I just use my phone? Decisions, decisions. Maybe more socks?

"Coop's on his way with Thai," Rob calls over his shoulder. I groan.

Crap, it's Friday. Make that Aloha Friday. We've been getting together with our friend Coop on Friday nights since forever. We take turns hosting and alternate between a few of our favorite takeout restaurants; there's a different music theme each week. I love the tradition, and I absolutely adore Coop, but Aloha Fridays are meant to kick off a relaxing weekend with good food and great music. There is nothing relaxing about the coming weekend: twelve hours of flying, three airports, customs, etc.

I will have to limit myself to a single glass of wine tonight. I'm a bit of a lightweight when it comes to drinking, and flying is *not* my favorite pastime. Flying with a hangover would really suck.

"Okay, Rob. I'm just about done here," I assure him. And I am.

A few more pairs of socks and a shawl for my carry-on. Airplanes can be pretty chilly at times. Power cords for my phone and e-reader, and I am finished. Tomorrow morning, I will pack my makeup and toiletries and head out for a wonderful trip, during which I need to make a decision that will impact the whole rest of my life. *Yikes!*

But right now, it's time for Aloha Friday!

BECCA

My mom always stresses out before she goes on a trip. The packing alone just about does her in. I mean, please. What's the worst thing that can happen? You forget something you need, like, let's just say, a phone charger. Not a tragedy, people. You pick up a spare at the airport or any number of shops spread across the whole world. If you were going on an African safari and forgot your phone charger, I guess that would be a different situation. But then, you probably wouldn't get cell coverage anyway, so who cares about a missing charger? Anyway, I have bigger issues to deal with today. Like, oh, I don't know, *my life*?

My mom and I are going on a tour of Ireland to celebrate my recent college graduation, and, in about a week and a half, my dad will be joining us. We'll head up to Northern Ireland for a few days and then fly back here to Sedona. So I have definite plans for the next few weeks.

Once we return home, I'll divide my waking hours between working for my mom, my dad, and my Aunt Mo. Hopefully fit in some time to shop and read. Get a couple of pedis and drink gallons of iced coffee. That will take me right through the summer. Yeah, and one more thing: I have a class to make up. Well, complete, actually.

I *know* I said I graduated, but, technically…? I dropped the ball during the last semester, and my final paper, well, I never turned it in. I threw myself on the mercy of the professor. Thankfully, I'm not usually one for excuses and she knew that. So when I said, "I blew it. I'm sorry," she was cool. I could have flunked the course, but she gave me an incomplete. As long as I turn in the paper by mid-July, she'll adjust the grade at that time.

But I haven't told my folks yet. A couple weeks back, when they called my name at commencement and I marched up to get my diploma, I received the same empty envelope that all my classmates did. The only difference? Everyone else received real diplomas in the mail last week.

My mom has been hounding me and keeps telling me to call the school and find out where mine is, and I can't keep putting her off. She's been real distracted lately, and there's definitely something going on with her and Dad. They're having some sort of disagreement, and they're doing their best to keep it from me. I am going to have to figure out a time to tell her during the trip. I know she'll flip out, so I may have to wait until she's all mellow after a day of sightseeing and a couple glasses of wine. As soon as we get back to Sedona, I'll get to work on the damn paper. So it's going to be a super busy summer. After that, things are not so clear.

I plan to go to grad school back in Boston, at the same school where I've been doing my undergraduate degree in psychology. I love the university, love Boston, and I'm excited about the idea of going back there. To the city; not back to school. I've been thinking I should probably take a year or two off. Get out there in the real world before hitting the books for a few more long years. My academic advisor suggested it months ago, and my parents did, too.

I'm toying with the idea of holding off, but I keep coming back to the same old question. *What the hell am I supposed to do, if I'm not in school?* Who is Becca, if she's not a full-time student? It's part of who I am. Hell, it *is* who I am. I've always been a good student, but I've had to work hard to get the grades that put me on the honor roll and the Dean's List.

One semester, I got the opportunity to intern at a teen center. What a great experience *that* was. I dished out dating advice and condoms like a champ. I really connected with those kids, I think. During my senior year, my classmates started to talk about internships and full-time career type jobs. We were encouraged to draft cover letters, practice our interviewing skills, and build our "network." I was freaking out. My mom teaches people how to do all that, so I know what it entails, but still. The whole process was overwhelming and the thought of finishing college felt scary. Maybe that's why I blew off the paper.

And it's a lot harder to work on all of those things if you haven't narrowed down where you plan to live. And I haven't. Don't get me wrong, I love Sedona. It's beautiful and friendly and familiar. But I keep telling myself that it's time to spread my wings and fly a little. Boston is a great place to live. It seems like there are lots of opportunities, and I've gotten used to the snow and the cold after four years. I can see myself moving there, but what will I do?

I can work in an office doing something or other, or work in retail, I guess, like some of my classmates. But those jobs don't pay very well, and Boston is an expensive place to live. I would end up sharing a tiny walk-up with two or three roommates and barely breaking even.

I can live free of charge, if I move back home, I guess, and I know that I can find work. Ever since I was fourteen, I've spent breaks and weekends working in my mom's consulting business or my dad's advertising agency or my Aunt Mo's café. But with graduation looming, I decided to apply to grad school and got accepted for this fall. Seemed like a good idea at first, but I am starting to have second thoughts.

If I back out now, I'll probably lose my deposit, and I don't know if they would hold a seat for me for next semester or next year. I've committed to being a resident advisor for the upcoming academic year, as well. Free room and board and a stipend that will keep me in lattes and Netflix, but very little else.

Aaarrgghh. The decision is really starting to weigh on me. I am looking forward to a relaxing few weeks in Ireland. I need to clear my head and finally decide what I want to do with my life. Take in the sights, and catch up on my sleep. And come clean with my mom. So yeah, worrying about packing an extra pair of socks or a spare charger? Not sweating that.

CHAPTER TWO

JACKIE

I AM BARELY AWARE of the droning noise that would normally bug me during airplane travel, as I am totally preoccupied with watching Becca sleep in the seat next to mine. She is so much like her father. They can sleep practically anywhere, and neither has a problem falling asleep, whereas I tend to toss and turn for hours. The only time in my adult life that I've been able to get a solid eight hours a night was when I was pregnant with Becca. What an amazing time that was…

* * *

Rob had moved in with me, and although it was a bit of a tight squeeze, it was fabulous to be living under the same roof again. We planned to stay for a few more months in the Sedona guesthouse I had been living in for the past year. I felt like we should take our time, looking for a new house. There was no rush, and continuing to live next door to my landlord Coop had its advantages, in the form of his dry wit and fresh produce from his garden.

I decided to share the exciting news that we were pregnant through our cat, Jagger. The afternoon of Robbie's first day in town, I printed up a little sheet of paper that read *I'm Going To Be A Big Brother,* rolled it up, and stuck it in Jag's collar. Never the most cooperative of felines, he hightailed it out through his cat door, leaving the note behind. Before I could stop him, Robbie picked it up off the floor. He read it and turned to me, looking a bit confused.

"Hey, Jax? What's this?" he asked, waving the note as he spoke.

"Oh, *um...* It's Jag's. *Uh,* you should ask him."

"What do you mean it's Jag's? Wait, what? Oh my God, are you serious?" He raced over to me and hugged me close. "This is amazing. But how?"

I pulled away just long enough to cast an appraising glance at him. "Second time's the charm, lover-boy," I drawled, right before I burst into tears. He pulled me back into his arms.

"Jaxie, don't worry. We're gonna be great at this," he assured me. He was all choked up, too.

We hugged, and I started getting really excited. *This is really happening.*

We decided not to tell anyone until I really started to show. Maybe in another month? Women were having children later and later, but I didn't want to take any chances. But within an hour, I had spilled the news to my best friend, Suze, as well as Robbie's ex-stepmother Edie. Both phone calls produced ear-splitting shrieks and more tears. Then I couldn't *not* tell Coop, so Rob and I accosted him in the yard a few minutes later. His response, though not as enthusiastic as the ones I had just received, was typical Coop. He shook hands with Rob and swept me up in a bear hug.

"I'm happy for you, Jackie. This is the life you were meant to live," he whispered in my ear. Then he broke out a bottle of bubbly, and the guys toasted with champagne, while I opted for a delightful glass of seltzer.

Rob called his partner Joe next, and, before long, I was on the phone with Joe's wife Meg. Her twin boys were four years old, and, as they had no intention of adding to their family, she promised me all of her baby furniture and everything that had been languishing in her garage for the tag sale that was *never* going to be scheduled.

"Whatever I don't have, we'll just have to go shopping for," she promised. Yeah, an excuse to go shopping—as if I had ever needed one!

Even though it was the middle of the summer, Sedona had been cool and comfortable that year. It was a beautiful day to stroll into town with Rob and enjoy an iced latte with my friend Mo at Caffe-

Nation. "Better make mine decaf, Mo," I told her after I ordered our drinks. At her surprised expression, I mimed rocking a baby in my arms.

"Oh my God, that's great!" she yelled, running around the counter towards me. She hugged me, and then Rob. "You stud," she teased. My grinning-like-a-fool baby daddy.

Yuck, I hate that expression. But what? My ex for sex? My partner? The father of my unborn child? I would have to give it some thought, but it was official: we were having a baby!

* * *

So here I am, twenty-one years later, watching my baby sleep beside me on a plane. My five foot ten "baby" with both a larger shoe size and cup size than mine. She is really such a joy, and I am so excited to be taking this trip with her. It's wonderful to have girl time, before she goes back to school. I'm certain that the more Becca lives in Boston, the more likely it is that she will remain there after she finishes her education. I can envision her getting a job, falling in love and building a life for herself out there. Isn't that what all parents are supposed to want for their children?

And now Rob seems ready to make a major move, as well. He's got this crazy idea of us selling both of our businesses and travelling around the world. Don't get me wrong. Part of me thinks it sounds amazing, to be footloose and fancy free. But the practical me panics at the thought of handing over my business and living out of a suitcase.

Lots of changes on the horizon, and I'm not at all sure that I'm ready for any of them.

BECCA

Wow. I almost never sleep on planes, and yet, I was out… almost three hours?

I'm not sure if the time on my phone will update automatically or wait until we get to Dublin, but from what I can tell, we boarded the flight nearly four hours ago. Mom and I chatted a bit and had a snack, then we both started to read, and that's the last thing I remember.

I look over at her. She's out cold: her head back, and her mouth open just a little. A bit of a mouth-breather, my mom.

I brush the hair out of her eyes. She has pretty reddish-brown hair recently threaded with silver. All of my friends adore her. And my dad, as well. Over the last four years, while I have been going to school in Boston, I have brought countless suite-mates, friends, and even a couple of boyfriends out to my childhood home in Sedona. Everyone loves coming to my house, and my parents enjoy it, too.

"Your parents are so cool, Becca," my best friend Lily marvels whenever she comes over. "You're soooo lucky. My parents are so lame."

Yeah, my folks are pretty cool. There is always enough food for a last-minute guest or three, always room at the table. Mealtimes in the Sullivan household are usually quite joyous. My Uncle Coop frequently joins us, along with his girlfriend, my Aunt Edie, when they are both in town. My mom introduced them to each other before I was born, and, for the last twenty years, they have gone back and forth from Edie's home in Florida to Coop's in Sedona. They spend a month together at one place, then one of them returns home solo for a few weeks before they get together again.

I like to tease Edie. (She's not really my aunt; she's my dad's former stepmother. My dad's dad, my Grandpa Robert, divorced Edie years ago. I barely know him, but he has to be crazy to let someone like Edie go.) So I tease her that she and Coop must have expiration dates, and, after a few weeks together, it's time to go their separate ways for a while. Time to reboot.

"Keeps the sizzle in the relationship, doll face," Edie tells me with a wink.

I love her to pieces. She is so sassy and such an excellent match for Coop (who isn't really my uncle, either; he was my mother's landlord back in the day and an old family friend). He tends to be a man of few words, but when he speaks, believe you me, you want to hear what he has to say.

My mom's business associates don't really drop by, but they are frequently invited, and we also see a lot of my dad's business partner, Joe, and his wife, Meg. They are currently empty nesters, as their twin sons, Alex & Max, chose to attend colleges back east and, when they graduated, both found jobs in Boston.

I had a crush on Alex at one point and decided to look him up when I moved to Boston, four years ago. I grew up with the twins, and although a five-year age difference is a lot when you are thirteen and they're eighteen, the difference between eighteen and twenty-three doesn't sound all that bad, right? But after a few dates and a not-so-memorable hook-up during my freshman year, we decided to just remain friends. Facebook friends.

* * *

I inch my seat back just a little further. Airplanes really are not built for us tall people. As I struggle to get comfortable again, I begin to feel really excited about this trip. I haven't given it much thought before now, after the whirlwind of activities relating to graduation and moving back home, but now that we are on our way, I'm psyched. I've been to Europe before, but now I am an adult. I can hang out in pubs and raise a pint or two. It will be a blast.

I hope some of the others on our tour are young like me. Or at least fun. My mom's idea of living on the wild side is splitting two desserts, not just one, or going full-caff after four p.m.! My dad is a little bit more of a partier, but they are both fairly tame. I mean, so

am I, actually. But when in Rome…
My mom suggested this trip to me last winter. I guess there had been talk of her going to Ireland with her mom, when she graduated from college, but my grandmother died during my mom's senior year, so no trip. This is a terrific opportunity to spend one-on-one time with her, at least before my dad joins us next week. Something is going on with those two, I know there is. I sensed it when they were in Boston with me a couple weeks ago, and it's been even worse since I got home. There's a tense vibe or something. I don't know. It's probably my imagination. Maybe I'm projecting because I'm scared to come clean about not graduating. If I open up to her first, she'll probably tell me if there's anything wrong.

She has a great job and lots of friends and is very much in love with my dad, but I know she's not really thrilled about my staying in Boston for a couple more years. I want to make this a really special time for us both, before we get separated again.

I pat her hand as she sleeps beside me. "Love you, Mom," I whisper, right before I recline my seat a bit more and close my eyes again.

CHAPTER THREE

JACKIE

IT WAS AN uneventful flight—just the kind I like. No screaming babies, no delays. A little time to chat with my girl, read, and sleep. We arrive at the Dublin airport on schedule, make it through customs in record time, and catch a cab to the hotel. We are only going to be staying here for one night, before meeting up with the rest of the "Nomads" in the morning. I could easily take a nap right after we check in, but, as it is mid-morning, Becca is starving and wants to go for a full Irish breakfast and do some sightseeing first.

"The sooner we acclimate to the local time, the less jetlag we'll have," she informs me. *Hmmm. When did she get so smart?*

I agree, and, after dumping luggage in our room, we set off on foot. Becca is so excited, she's just about skipping down the street.

"Their bacon's not like ours," she tells me. "I think it's more like ham, but I want some anyway. And eggs, too. And Mom, they grill their tomatoes. Can you imagine? But what's up with that black pudding? I bet it tastes even grosser than it sounds."

She starts walking even faster, and I hurry to keep up. That is one thing I really love about my daughter. When she gets into something, it's 110%. Her enthusiasm is contagious, and now I'm looking forward to our first meal together in Ireland.

We find a little coffee shop promising the "best" breakfast in town, sit down at an empty table, and order. When I ask for some skim milk for my coffee, the middle-aged waitress shakes her head at me.

"American, I'm guessin'?" she teases. At my nod, she continues. "You eat a heapin' platter of bacon and sausage and fried potatoes, but you're afraid of a little cream for your coffee?"

I have to agree with her logic, but I like things the way I like them. It's the same as ordering a Diet Coke with a big, greasy cheeseburger. She brings a little pitcher of what looks like milk, maybe 2%, and I am happy.

After breakfast, we stroll around the neighborhood. Since we'll be spending the next week on the tour and doing lots of sightseeing, there is really no rush to try to see anything on our list. Becca suggests starting the search for the limited-edition bone china teapot that Edie requested, but I assure her that we'll have plenty of time to find it on our travels.

Rob's ex-stepmother has been collecting teapots for years and asked us to be on the lookout for one that is rumored to be in short supply and only available here in Ireland. I'm certain we'll find one in the first gift shop we visit, and, anyway, we're returning to Dublin next week and staying in Ireland for almost two more weeks. Plenty of time to find a simple teapot!

It feels good to just wander aimlessly. We find an empty park bench and relax for a bit. The sun is shining brightly, and I close my eyes and lift my face up to catch a few rays. You always hear about how overcast and cloudy it can be in Ireland. Gorgeous days like this apparently draw everyone outside. Becca enjoys people watching as much as I do, and, for a while, we entertain each other by telling stories about the passersby.

"She's doing the walk of shame," Becca advises me, referring to a young woman who is a bit overdressed for a Sunday morning. "Bet she never planned to be hiking back home in those heels, when she went out last night," she adds with a grin.

"They're on their first date." The young couple that I point out is walking along, looking awkward and totally out of sync with each other. He seems too shy to take her hand, and she is so busy looking at her feet, I figure she wouldn't know what to do, if he did.

After a while, we return to the hotel and play cards in the lobby with a deck that I carry in my tote bag. We are a cards-and-games-loving family, often playing gin rummy or setback for hours on the odd rainy Sunday at home. I keep looking around the bustling lobby, wondering who else will be on the tour with us.

"What do you suppose Dad's up to?" Becca asks me. "It just sucks that he's not here. I miss him, don't you?"

I smile at my daughter. "You know your father," I console her. "He's probably chilling over at Coop's or working around the house.

"Dad's hardly Mr. Fix-it, Mom." Becca chuckles, and I have to agree with her. Rob is an amazing man in so many ways, but home repair is just *not* one of them. We have built up a long list of handy professionals on speed dial to keep our small suburban home in tip-top shape.

We play a few more hands of rummy, but Becca is getting kind of antsy. I'm ready to fall asleep right there in the lobby, and neither of us is hungry for a big dinner, so we opt to check out the hotel's café. We pick a few different appetizers to share, and I order a glass of wine. Becca asks for a Diet Coke.

"You can have a drink, you know," I tease to my "just turned legal drinking age" daughter.

She shakes her head. "No, I'm good. We're gonna be in pubs all week. I'm pacing myself."

Probably a solid plan. When our drinks arrive, I offer up a toast.

"Slainte, my girl. It means 'cheers' in Gaelic." We clink our glasses together. "To an amazing time in Ireland and making lots of wonderful memories."

"And to taking lots of pictures and finding Aunt Edie's special teapot," Becca reminds me with a grin.

After gorging on a selection of yummy "starters," we head back up to our room and finally collapse in bed at around 8:30. I can't keep my eyes open for another minute. This gives us twelve hours to sleep, shower, eat breakfast, and check out before we're due to meet up in the lobby with the rest of our fellow travelers.

Becca is sound asleep shortly after her head hits the pillow. I take my usual time to wind down and quiet the thoughts whirling through my brain. Tonight, my thoughts are on Rob. I miss him. He's my best friend and the love of my life. I wish I could just give in, give him what he wants, but I don't know if I can. What if I hate it? Will I resent him for making me choose?

I'm thrilled to have this time alone with my daughter, but it will be amazing to have Rob here, too. Plus, he can drive the rental car that we have reserved for next week. I have way too much respect for the good people of Ireland to risk their lives and ours by attempting driving on the left.

Becca

It isn't looking too promising. I am trying not to judge, but so far, I am the youngest person in this hotel lobby by at least a decade. It's kind of hard to tell if anyone is part of the Nomad tour. Everyone looks like a tourist waiting for a tour guide and hoping for a big adventure, just like us.

Wait, some of the luggage tags are starting to make sense to me. There is a whole group of senior citizens who seem to have luggage marked with a big "Celts Tour" logo. And that new group that just arrived? The "Irish Wanderers" are young, too young. Looks like a middle school group.

My mom and I came down to the lobby with our bags about twenty minutes ago. While I dug around, looking for the luggage tags we were sent, she paid the bill and took off for the ladies room. Again. That woman has a bladder the size of a pea, I swear.

I strain to see other travelers with the Nomad logo that our tags feature. Maybe that young couple over in the corner? If he will just move out of the way, I can check out their backpacks. Yes, they are Nomads.

Wow, she is definitely pregnant! Tiny little thing with a baby bump stretching her North Face hoodie. She's barely five feet tall and can't weigh more than ninety pounds, bump and all. She's kind of pretty, with big brown eyes and short, spikey black hair.

Whoops, she catches me staring. I smile at her, and she smiles back and rests her hands on her bump. I check out the guy she is with. Her husband? Or boyfriend? He looks to be about her age, tall and really thin. I think he might be trying to grow a mustache, but it looks pretty wispy from here. He's probably doing it to look older. His short brown hair is slicked back, but I bet it's just wet from a shower. He doesn't look like a guy who would use his wife's hair gel.

Now they are both smiling at me. I give a dorky little half wave and smile back. *Oh crap*. Now they're walking over to me, still smiling. He reaches me first.

"Hey, I'm Ollie. It's Oliver, but everyone calls me Ollie. This is my wife Carrie, and she's carrying Peanut, our soon-to-be baby. So, you're a Nomad then?" He points to the luggage tag on the large duffel bag at my feet. Before I even nod, he's rambling on again. "Are you all rested up and ready to be jammed in a van with a bunch of total strangers for the next seven days?"

"Yes. Hi. I'm a Nomad. *Um,* I'm Rebecca. Becca. Nice to meet you." I reach out to shake hands, but Carrie pulls me into a hug instead.

"Don't let my husband scare you. We're gonna have a ball, Becca. Are you on your own?"

Out of the corner of my eye, I see my mom crossing the lobby on her way over to us. I wave her over. *Yes*! She is much better around new people than I am. I point her out to Carrie.

"No, that's my mom. We're traveling together."

"Hi, Becca's mom," Carrie calls out, and, next thing you know, my mom is getting a hug, as well. "I'm Carrie and this is my husband Ollie. Where are you gals from?"

"Hi, Carrie. Hello, Ollie. I'm Jackie Sullivan, and it looks like you've met my daughter, Becca. We're from Sedona, Arizona. Have you ever been there?"

"No, but it's on my bucket list, right, Ollie? I've always wanted to go. We're from Atlanta. Well, near there, anyway. It's kind of a small town, so I just say Atlanta, 'cuz no one has ever heard of the actual town. But everyone knows Atlanta, am I right?" Carrie beams at my mom, who smiles right back at her. While Carrie and my mom get better acquainted, Ollie focuses his attention on me.

"Well, I hope we're not *it*, Becca. There have to be a few more Nomads in this bunch, wouldn't you say?" He surveys the room with a critical eye. "I'm hoping for a couple more guys to join us, you know? 'Cuz Carrie? Ever since she's been pregnant, she's been turning in at like eight o'clock every night. I need to find some 'mates' to hang out with in all of those pubs I keep hearing about. How 'bout you? Are you looking to ditch your mom and hit the town or what?"

"*Um*, yeah, sure, I guess. I mean, it'll be fun to go out. I hear all of the places have live music, right?"

"I know all the best pubs with the best craic. Stick with me, kid."

I look up in surprise at a guy who has joined our conversation. *God, he is cute.* Where did he come from? Wait, *crack*? Is he offering me drugs?

Ollie smacks the new guy on the back. "Hey, Sean, good to see you man. Have you met Becca?" Ollie turns to me expectantly and, at my blank look, explains, "Becca, Sean's our tour guide. He's the head Nomad. Sean, Becca, and her mom are from Arizona," he adds. "Carrie and I ran into Sean after breakfast this morning. And don't worry. Craic's a good thing."

Sean, the absolutely gorgeous tour guide, looks down at his clipboard. "Right then, Jackie Sullivan and Rebecca Colby from Arizona. Welcome to Ireland, Rebecca. Glad you're joining us." He shakes my hand and starts to move on to my mom.

"It's Becca," I mumble. *Wow, he is seriously handsome.*

"Craic's like the atmosphere in a pub, Bex," my mom explains with a smile. "Good craic means the place is lively, full of fun. Right, Sean?"

"Exactly right, Jackie. I'm like a magnet for good craic," he boasts. "Sounds like someone's been reading their tour book," he teases.

My mom gives him a big, goofy grin in return. *Oh Christ, is she flirting with him? He's young enough to be your son-in-law*, I chastise my mother silently. Sean looks to be in his mid-twenties, give or take a few years. He is tall, even taller than Ollie, with broad shoulders and kind of a rangy build. His brown hair is fairly short, and he's clean-shaven, except for a reddish-brown chinstrap. He's wearing khakis and a dark green button-down shirt featuring the Nomad logo above his first name in black script. No piercings, no visible tats. Dumb ass cap, though. But that accent! I could listen to him all day, and I will be.

Wow, the tour is looking really good again. Even if there are no other travelers my age, Sean will make it fun. I'm suddenly hoping that I am the only young, single female in our group. Wait, is Sean talking to me?

"So, how's the talent then?"

What? My mom is still chatting up the young married couple, and I'm the only one within earshot. I guess he *is* talking to me.

"Huh? The talent? I don't know what you—"

"The other Nomads? Have you met any of them? Checked them out?" I flush and hold back the answer that I want to give him, that I don't really care and probably won't notice anyone else but him on the trip. But I hold back. Too much information, for sure.

"No," I tell him, hoping that my tone is all casual. "Just Ollie and Carrie. And you," I add. He is watching me closely, I realize. He grins and then jots something down on his clipboard before getting all business-like again.

"All right then," he says briskly. "It's time to head out." He takes off through the lobby, and within minutes, the rest of the Nomads are clustered around him.

There's Elaine, an older woman from Denver; Richard and Geoff from England, who tell us that they are celebrating their ten-year anniversary; and Tracie, a well-dressed woman I imagine is in her early thirties. If she mentioned where she is from, I must have missed it. So it's two couples, two women travelling on their own, plus Mom and me. And Sean. Ready for our Nomad adventure!

Like sheep, we follow Sean out to the van. It is a damp, dreary day, and I consider pulling my hood up, as my hair gets wicked frizzy in this kind of weather. As soon as we take off, I figure I'll pull it into a messy bun and not have to deal with it for the rest of the day.

"Ladies and gents, I would like to introduce you to your home away from home for the next seven days. Meet Bertha!"

Bertha is a fairly standard twelve-passenger van, dark green with a map of Ireland and the now familiar Nomad logo plastered on each side. She's towing a rickety-looking trailer that has a worn plastic tarp stretched over it.

"That'll be reserved for your luggage," Sean tells us, indicating the trailer. "And don't worry, there's plenty of room in the trailer for anyone who gets voted off the van," he adds with a menacing tone.

I am feeling a bit frisky. Maybe it's that third cup of coffee I consumed this morning.

"What do you have to do to get voted off the van, Sean?" I ask in a teasing voice.

Our tour guide casts me an appraising glance, before answering. "Asking foolish questions, for one." He grins. "And not obeying the rules. Let's get the luggage loaded and get you all settled in. I'll go over the rules, once we're on the road." He begins tossing our assorted duffle bags, suitcases, and quilted totes into the trailer. Someone is a big Vera Bradley fan, I note. Geoff and Ollie pitch in, and, seconds later, we are climbing in the van.

"I've got my eye on you, Becca," Sean warns, but he is smiling as he says it.

I feel a warm tingle. *God, he's cute*. He can eye me all he wants.

"Oh, yeah. You, too," I mumble, as he grips my elbow and helps me into the bowels of Bertha. I suck at flirting, by the way.

Richard already clambered into the front seat, and Ollie and Carrie are stretched out in the last row. That leaves Mom, me, Elaine, Tracie, and Geoff in the middle two rows that face each other. I find myself sitting between Mom and Elaine for the first leg of the journey.

We all buckle in as Sean's amazing voice comes through the loudspeaker.

"All right then, we're off, Nomads. I'm Sean Donovan, and I'm looking forward to getting to know each and every one of you," he begins in a practiced tone. Mom, Elaine, Geoff, and Tracie all beam at the idea of getting to know Sean. *What a charmer*! "So, a few rules before we get too far out of town. Just in case one of you has a problem with authority, Becca..."

My cheeks flush at the sound of my name.

"What'd I do?" I murmur. My mom pats my hand.

"Sean's just teasing, sweetheart," she whispers.

I know that, okay? It is just kind of weird, yet exciting, to be singled out by Sean. I am already attracted to this hot guy who I am going to be spending a whole lot of time with this week.

I shiver and hug my arms to myself.

"Do you need a sweater Bex? Are you cold?"

My mom thinks everything can be fixed with a sweater. Or a

bowl of ice cream. She's right no more than half the time.

"I'm good, Mom," I tell her, just as Sean starts talking again.

"So you've met me and Bertha, and I'll thank you not to be abusing the ole girl. Or me, either," he adds. "You need to stay buckled up anytime the van's in motion. I'll control the temperature from up here, so tell me if you're too hot or cold, okay? I also have control of the music, so if you have any preferences, let me know, and my co-pilot here," he says, indicating Richard, "will play your requests. Since every one of you should have the pleasure of riding shotgun, let's plan to switch up the seating after every couple of stops."

The thought of sitting up front with Sean makes me shiver again, but this time, my mom doesn't notice. She has the strangest look on her face, a little smile curving up her lips and a faraway look in her eyes.

What is she thinking about? Probably Dad, I reckon. Those two are like a couple of honeymooners, instead of an old married couple who have gotten hitched twice. I often wonder if I will ever meet anyone who looks at me the way my dad looks at my mom. They are really something. I hope I'm just imagining that there's some sort of rift between them.

I tune back in to listen to Sean, as I would hate to break any of his rules. Or would I?

"Whenever we stop for a break, I'll tell you how long we'll be stopping for and what time we'll be taking off again. So no wandering away, okay? It's not cool to make me or your fellow Nomads wait for you, so allow enough time to pay for your souvenirs or queue for the loo."

Queue for the loo! The expression makes me giggle.

"And that means you, Becca."

How did he hear me? The guy must have bat ears. My mom smiles and pats my hand again as Sean continues.

"And on the subject of breaks, there's no food or drink allowed on Bertha. That's a company-wide rule. We have to keep the ole girl looking sleek and shiny, so enjoy your crisps and your Cokes before you board. Water's okay," he relents, as if he could actually see a few of the Nomads looking longingly at their plastic bottles.

I glance around and see a few of my fellow passengers nodding off. Sean told us there wouldn't be too much to see that morning, as we head southwest towards Cork. The countryside is full of green meadows dotted with cows.

Maybe I should close my eyes and rest up a bit. I want to have all the energy I need to scramble up some of those hills the tour promises. Right behind Sean. Awesome!

CHAPTER FOUR

JACKIE

THAT FIRST DAY on the van? We get off to a fairly quiet start, but by mid-morning, most of us are chattering away. A lot of getting to know you's. We all share our stories as we pass through the lovely countryside: Elaine is a widow with grown kids; Tracie is single and travels a lot for work; and Richard and Geoff run a consulting firm in London, specializing in logistics. I tell the group that Rob, Becca, and I live in Sedona, but that I grew up in New England. Carrie pipes up.

"How long have you been married, Jackie?"

Sounds like a simple enough question, right? You would expect a pretty straightforward response from most folks. Not from me. Robbie and I first got married almost thirty years ago. We split up and divorced after seven years, then got back together two years later. We remained in our blissful unmarried state for years and probably would have stayed that way forever, until Becca came home one day from school. She was about seven.

"When's your 'versary, Mommy?" she asked me.

"What?" I had to ask her to repeat the question, so she did.

"Your 'versary? When is it? Lily's mommy and daddy are having a party for their tenth 'versary. When is yours?"

Uh oh. How to explain?

"*Um*, well, I guess it's in late December." We hadn't celebrated it for years. "Yeah, that's it. December twenty-eighth, honey-bun." She looked at me suspiciously.

"How many, Mommy? How many 'versaries?"

Whoops.

"*Um*, I guess it's about seventeen years." Becca wasn't going to let this go.

"Why didn't you and Daddy have a party?"

"Well, not everyone has a party, Bex."

"We should have one. Okay, Mommy?"

I agreed that we would have a party (someday) and celebrate our 'versary. I thought that was it. The next day, however, Lily's mom Cindy called me.

"Well, congratulations are in order I hear, huh, Jackie? Seventeen years—wow! Becca is thrilled. I think she's invited everyone in her class. What's the exact date? You're brave to have so many families over. Can I bring something?"

Oh crap.

"*Um*, I think my daughter jumped the gun on this one, Cindy."

"Oh, wow, is it a surprise for Rob? Don't worry. I won't say a word."

Okay, this was officially awkward. "No, Cindy, that's not it. You see, Rob and I aren't, well, married, exactly."

There was silence, then, "Oh, sure, that's cool. I mean a lot of people…"

"*No*, we were married. We got married seventeen years ago. Honest. But it didn't last, and then we got back together, and I got pregnant, and we just never bothered to...you know, go through it all again."

"Sure. I mean lots of people stay together because of an unplanned pregnancy. I'm not judging. Live and let live, that's what I always say."

Seriously?

"No, we were getting back together *before* I found out I was pregnant." I was starting to feel really defensive.

"So you're *not* having a party to celebrate?"

"No, but I understand you are. Ten years, huh? When is the big day?"

"*Um*, it's on Friday. This Friday."

Wow, that was just three days away, and we had not received an invitation. No big surprise, however, as our families weren't all that close, but still.

"Well, I hope it's a great party. And hey, congratulations."

"Thanks, Jackie. Well, take care. Best to, *um*, Rob."

"You, too. Give Len a hug for me."

A hug? I am not a hugger, and even if I were, Len Burton would probably not be included on the list of men I actually wanted to hug.

So we convinced Becca that we would plan a big party soon, and for several years after that, we celebrated our anniversary between Christmas and New Year's Eve.

When Becca was thirteen, she flew down to see Edie in Florida for a few days right after Christmas. When she told Edie that she was going to call and wish us a happy anniversary, Edie got confused, then she spilled the beans and Becca found out that her parents had gotten a divorce before she was born. She was pissed.

"So, I'm a bastard, Mom. Wow, nice. That's just awesome." Did I mention that Becca could be a bit of a drama queen at times?

I assured her that her dad and I were the most committed of couples, and she challenged us to prove it. So that's how, a few days later, on New Year's Eve, Rob and I got re-hitched by a justice of the peace in Boca Raton in a simple ceremony, witnessed by our daughter, Edie, and Coop. We let Becca have a couple sips of celebratory champagne at a very festive brunch and then spent the afternoon at the beach. That was eight years ago. So, yeah, I hate the whole "how long" question.

"Oh, since forever. How about you two?"

Carrie tells us they were high school sweethearts who went their separate ways when they attended college in two different states. It wasn't until their fifth high school reunion that they got back together.

"I saw her from across the room and told my buddy Skip, 'I'm not letting her go this time. I'm gonna marry that girl,'" Ollie tells us with a big grin.

"And he did. Took him a few more years, but he did," Carrie says, beaming at her husband. They married three years ago and just bought their first home. Carrie is a human resources administrator for a pharmaceutical firm, and Ollie is an IT technician. They are thrilled about the upcoming birth.

"I told Ollie, I said, I want to have the first one by the time I'm thirty. And I'll just make it, too," Carrie squeals as she hugs her husband.

"How many kids are you planning on having?" asks Elaine. Ollie smirks in response.

"The house we just bought has four bedrooms. A face in every window, huh?"

Wait 'til you find out just how much work they are, I think to myself. But so worth it. I pull Becca close. "You're about to embark on an amazing journey, you two," I promised them. Rob and I talked about having a second child, but, despite all of our efforts, I never got pregnant again.

Not all of the Nomads have happy marriages, however. Elaine tells us that she was married for nearly forty years to a man she describes as "difficult." She finally served him with divorce papers and the next day, he dropped dead of a heart attack. Her two grown children never forgave her, blaming her for their father's untimely death.

"He was at least thirty pounds overweight, and he smoked two packs of cigarettes a day," she confides. "But it's *my* fault that he died." She admits that she speaks to her son only once or twice a year and that she hasn't even seen her latest grandchild who was born last year.

"They'll come around," I assure her.

She just smiles sadly at me. I can't imagine Becca not talking to me. What on earth could I possibly do that would be so horrible as to cause a split that deep? Elaine just booked the Nomad excursion last week, right before she purchased every piece of Vera Bradley luggage she could find. It's the fifth anniversary of her late husband's death.

"I just needed to get out of Dodge, you know?"

Yeah, I knew.

"We're gonna have a great week," I predict with a smile.

Tracie is not quite as forthcoming about her background. She apparently travels solo quite a bit, and Ireland was the next place to cross off her list. I am a list-maker, myself, but my lists tend to be of the "call this person" or "buy this or that" variety.

"I don't usually do the whole *group* thing, you know? It's easier to be on your own. I can do whatever I please, eat where I want, switch plans at the last minute," she boasts.

Hmmm, maybe this one doesn't play that well with others. Her last comment got our tour guide's attention, and he turns towards us.

"Not on this trip," Sean tells her with a smile. "We have a strict schedule to adhere to. There'll be no lollygagging. Not on my watch." He grins as he says it, so I can only imagine that he is teasing. But still, there *is* an itinerary to follow. I hope he will allow us some flexibility, but we will have to watch Tracie. The last thing we need is to be waiting on her after every stop.

Sean, our tour guide: now there is an interesting young man. Extremely good looking, taller than most of the men I have seen over here, with reddish-brown hair and, *hmmm,* maybe green eyes? Or hazel? Similar coloring to mine. Becca's, too.

And, speaking of coloring, I notice my daughter's cheeks go pink whenever Sean addresses her. The same with Elaine's and Tracie's. Only Carrie and I are seemingly immune to the charms of our handsome guide. He is too old for Becca, I decide, but maybe Tracie?

Get your mind out of the gutter, I tell myself. The only hooking up on this trip will have to be between Geoff and Richard, but they aren't openly affectionate with each other, so who knows? I imagine that Geoff is at least ten years younger than his mate. Neither of them is particularly chatty, but it's only the first day. Plenty of time to hear their story. As far as the other couple on the trip, Carrie tells us that she and Ollie booked rooms with twin beds for the entire trip, so they each could get a decent night's sleep.

"No bow-chicka-bow-wow for us," Ollie says, with a hangdog look on his face. Carrie smacks his arm.

"Thank you, Captain Obvious," she tells him. "Everyone knows that pregnant women shouldn't be having sex anyway."

I smile to myself and catch Elaine's eye, and we simultaneously wink at each other. I recall the last several months of my pregnancy. It was like a second honeymoon for Rob and me. We were living together again, and, well, let's just say we were frequently eager to show the other just how glad we were about that. The fact that I was pregnant was just the icing on the cake.

We stop to check out the ruins of an ancient castle, and, as we're strolling around the grounds, Elaine tells Sean that she is on the hunt for a four-leaf clover.

"I can use all of the luck I can get," she says without a trace of self-pity. We all help her to search as Sean explains the meaning of the shamrock.

"The shamrock is more than the unofficial symbol of Ireland," he begins.

"It's also one of the tasty marshmallows in a bowl of Lucky Charms," Ollie interjects. "They're magically delicious." He attempts an Irish accent but fails badly. Carrie swats at him as Sean continues.

"Nearly all of the historic cultures of Ireland place a great deal of meaning in those green leaves. The Druids believed that they could ward off evil spirits, and the Celtics, who believed that three is a sacred number, held that the shamrock had mystical properties. Early Christians felt that the three leaves represented the Holy Trinity."

After a few more minutes of searching, we conclude that finding a four-leaf version of the little plant is probably not going to happen today and head back to Bertha. Now it's my turn to sit up front with Sean. He is a great conversationalist, and although most of what he says while we travel is meant for everyone's ears, it's great fun to experience a private conversation with him.

That accent. Wow, he is easy on the ears. And on the eyes, too. *Oh, grow up*. I am old enough to be...

"So, Arizona, huh, Jackie? Is it all desert out there?"

I tell him a little about Sedona and the red rocks that surround it. "It's just spectacular," I boast.

"Sounds grand, but when we get to the coast, well, you'll see some pretty great rocks, too. And we have an ocean! Does, *um*, Becca live at home with you and your husband?"

"Yes, for now." I explain that she will be returning to college in Boston for her master's degree.

"Her master's? So she's pretty smart then?"

"Yes, we're really proud of her. She's always been a good student."

"So, does that come from you or your husband?" he teases.

"Well, actually, I used to be a college professor."

"A professor? What'd you teach then?"

"Marketing. My favorite course was consumer behavior."

"Well, I'm kind of an expert on that myself," he brags. "Four years on the job and I know just which shops to stop at and when. Who would be looking for Irish lace, and who would be wanting to score some whiskey."

"That sounds about right. It's all about satisfying needs and wants." We grin at each other, and a thought crosses my mind.

"So, I have a special request. My husband's former stepmother collects teapots. Becca and I want to bring her back a certain one." He looks amenable to the idea, so I hurry on. "There's a limited edition one that I know she would love, but I hear it's next to impossible to find." Sean brightens at the challenge.

"No worries. You leave it to me. I guarantee that, if that teapot exists in all of Ireland, we will locate it and your husband's.... Wait, former stepmother?" I nod and shrug my shoulders.

"It's complicated. Let's just call her Edie from now on."

He nods vigorously. "We'll find that pot for Edie," he promises with a grin.

"Well, enough about me. How about you? Do you live in Dublin?"

"Yeah, my brother Declan and I share a two-bed on the quays. It's kinda pricey, but it's convenient, and we have a pretty good view of the Grand Canal. I might be moving soon, though."

"It sounds ideal. But why would you want to move?"

"Well, Dec, he's probably going to ask his girl, she's called Sarah, to move in with him one of these days. It would be great to have a third person to split the rent with, but Sarah, well, I can't see her livin' with two brothers, you know? She's a graphic designer, and she works from home. She needs her space, I guess. I came in the other day after a long week and saw a scrap of paper on the counter. She had measured my bedroom, trying to decide if it was big enough to suit her needs for a home office."

"That's not fair," I protest. "Have you told your brother?"

"Nah. What would be the point?" He shrugs. "I mean he could deny it, or he could say he'd talk with Sarah, but either way…it is what it is."

"But what will you do?" I press. "Rents in Dublin are really high, aren't they?"

"Yeah, and getting higher all the time. If I had my way, I'd bag Dublin all together. I'm thinking Dingle, out on the coast. You'll see in a couple three days for yourself. It's the most beautiful country you've ever seen," he promises.

"Can you still work for Nomad? Based in Dingle?"

"Nah, I think it's about time for a change, you know? Time to try something new."

I laugh at that. Yes, I know. I tell him about Encore and that it's a one-stop shop offering all kinds of trainings and resources to help workers in transition. Sean seems intrigued.

"So, maybe I'll pick your brain a bit this week, if you don't mind. I mean I hope that's not a conflict or anything. Seeing as how I'm your guide and all," he adds.

Now I really have to laugh. The last time I got involved with a tour guide? Well, that was Rick, and meeting him was at the root of my decision to move cross-country in the first place.

"Don't worry. We'll keep it all on the up and up," I assure him. At his confused expression, I clarify. "Strictly professional and off the record, okay?"

"Thanks, Jackie." He gives me a thumbs up. "We're gonna have a great week."

The morning flies by, broken up by two stops to stretch our legs, use the loo (Elaine, Carrie, and I are the most vocal about that), view the beautiful countryside, and drink coffee. Turns out we are a java-loving group, and our fearless leader Sean is determined that we make at least a couple of coffee stops each day.

"The pints are for nighttime. During the day, it's all about the coffee. But not in the van," he reminds us. And only smoke in designated areas, okay guys?" Geoff and Richard are the smokers in the group, and they both nod their assent.

We stop at a lovely inn for lunch. After making sure that there is a table for us, Sean announces that he will see us back at the van in an hour and strides out of the dining room. There will be a full Irish breakfast provided each morning, but lunches and dinners are not part of the package. I assume that the group will split up for most of our evening meals, provided there are a couple of options. Sean wouldn't be joining us. He was fairly clear that both lunch and dinnertimes are a bit of a break for him and that he usually makes other plans.

"As soon as I've got you lot sorted away," he promised us, "I'll be off. Gives you a break from all my yakking."

I check out the menu. There are a few things that look appealing, but I know there will be plenty of opportunities to sample some of the more traditional fare—shepherd's pie, fish and chips, and lamb stew. Today, I will keep it fairly light.

"Chef's salad," I request when it's my turn to order. "Dressing on the side, light on the egg and cheese, and all turkey instead of half ham and half turkey, please."

"Americans," our server retorts, shaking her head.

Hey, what can I say?

"What sounds good, Bex?" I ask my daughter then laugh at her goofy grin. Just like her father!

Rob has hardly ever opened a menu in his life and always ends up with the best meal of anyone at the table. Wait staff trip over themselves to recommend the very best dishes, even things that aren't on the menu, in their efforts to please him. Becca has apparently just negotiated something special for herself.

"Coming right up, dear," our server says briskly, before racing off to personally ensure that my girl's food is cooked to perfection.

And it is. As I enjoy my yummy salad, Bex chows down on a grilled sandwich several inches high and a tureen of sweet potato fries. She has a very healthy appetite and a speedy metabolism. Just like I used to, I think sadly. Mine has started to slow down over the last few years, and, for the first time in my life, I have to be careful about what I eat, so as not to pack on extra weight.

"I didn't see these on the menu," Ollie complains, as he reaches over and snags a handful of fries. Becca just laughs, but Carrie swats at her husband.

"You can't just take food off someone's plate, you jerk," she tells him sternly.

"There's no way I can eat them all," Becca admits. "Dig in."

And they do. Husband and wife polish off the fries in a matter of minutes, despite Carrie's concerns that "they'll be repeating on me tonight."

All in all, it's a nice meal, and I feel fortunate to be part of a friendly, social group of people.

When we're all chattering away, the topic of packing comes up. Becca shares my struggles with the group, exaggerating how I was rushing around at the last minute, while Rob sat in the driveway, beeping his horn. Of course, I need to jump in and defend myself, and I imitate my chill Millennial daughter texting away, thumbs flying, while her dad and I load the luggage into the car. Soon, we're all laughing, and I notice Elaine watching me and Becca with great interest.

She smiles as she leans towards us. "It's like seeing double with you two. You look alike, but even more, you sound alike. If I close my eyes, I swear I can't tell which of you is talking."

"Yeah, we get that a lot." I hug my daughter to me as we finish our coffees and prepare to depart.

Separate checks were requested, and most of us pay with euros or travelers' checks. Tracie uses a black American Express card, I notice. Business must be good. She keeps to herself, but I figure that we will draw her out after a bit. All five of us women visit the loo after lunch before we amble down the street, where the guys are waiting for us by the van.

"Let's go, ladies," Sean calls out. "It's gone two, and we've still got a few hours before we're done for the day. Gorgeous salmon, am I right, Elaine?" He winks at Elaine, who had let it be known that she was going to eat salmon at least twice a day for the entire trip.

"My husband hated fish," she announced with a sly grin. "I've got to make up for lost time."

I give up my front seat to Tracie and settle in between Carrie and Becca. Within minutes, both girls have fallen asleep with their heads resting on my shoulders. I look over at Elaine, who is watching me with the oddest expression on her face. Sad and almost envious, as if she is longing for physical contact like that.

Edie told me once that several of her friends complained frequently that, as widows or divorcees, it wasn't just the sex that they missed. It was the hugging, the handholding, the daily touches that those of us in a relationship often take for granted. I am not a big hugger, myself, but maybe I can mention something to Becca or Carrie.

"Just give her hand a squeeze or pat her shoulder as she goes by you next time," I'll suggest.

Problem solving must be in my DNA. I obsess over fixing problems that people don't even know they have! Time to relax and enjoy the craic!

Becca

From my current vantage point, I can just about make out what Sean and Tracie are chattering on about. She took the desirable front seat right after we stopped for lunch, and, nearly two hours later, she's still there. Their conversation seems pretty tame; they're exchanging stories about growing up, jobs, and siblings.

Sean's deep baritone is very discernible, but his strong accent is causing me to miss a few key points. Sounds like he was born and raised in Dublin, has a couple of brothers, and has been working as a tour guide for almost four years. Tracie is harder to hear, as she speaks more softly and has an annoying habit of raising her voice at the end of a sentence in kind of a breathy way, almost childlike. And she keeps flipping her blonde hair around as she speaks. Bitch, please! I gather that she is in compliance (whatever that means) in the banking industry and is currently living in Chicago.

Sean announces that we are heading to Cobh, a quaint harbor town favored by the Nomad organization over Cork City. After a quick stop at the Waterford Crystal Factory Store, we will be arriving in time for drinks and dinner.

We pass through Kilkenney and learn that "Kil" means "old church." Sean's voice is deep and rich, like melted chocolate, and that accent of his!

I groan, knowing that I just compared our tour guide's voice to chocolate, for God's sake. I need to snap out of this. Mooning over some guy I barely know, and fantasizing about all kinds of ways that I might end Tracie's dominance over the prized seat next to him is, well, silly, right? My best friend Lily always told people that she got carsick, which usually meant that she got to ride shotgun, up front with the driver. Maybe...

"But Sean. Oh my God, are you seriously kidding me right now? It's really *no* harder to drive on the left side of the road? It looks really challenging to me. You must be really clever…"

Blah, blah, blah. Freaking Tracie. And that dumb ass laugh.

Sean seems to be eating up all of the attention. I can only see the back of his head most of the time, but every once in a while, he turns towards Tracie just a bit. Like right now. He's laughing at something she said. More like he is just being polite, though. Not like laugh-out-loud or anything.

What a nice profile he has. Straight nose, kind of patrician looking; firm jawline; reddish chinstrap thing going on. He keeps his hair short; it's nice and neat around his neck. He is very well groomed, and I approve. I hate when guys have a hairy neck or too much facial hair. His skin is pale, especially around the neckline of his collared shirt. A lot of the young men I saw in Dublin have a number of piercings or tattoos. But not Sean. I wonder if that's a company policy or something.

His uniform shirt appears clean and well pressed. Does he carry a week's worth of shirts for every trip? Or does he hit the laundromat every couple of days? And does he iron his own shirts, I wonder? My mouth goes dry at the sudden image of Sean, naked from the waist up, competently ironing a shirt. Testing the iron first to make sure it sizzles, then dragging it smoothly over the cloth, back and forth, slowly and again…

I reach for my water bottle. Is it getting hot in here or is it just me? Just then, Tracie turns around and winks at me. And not a "hey girl" kind of wink. More like, "Don't you wish you were sitting where I'm sitting?" I swear she sees the way I was looking at Sean and can tell what I am thinking.

I manage a tight little smile and close my eyes, like I am ready to take a catnap. I slow my breathing down. Getting all worked up is ridiculous. But seriously, I have to get my turn up front and soon.

CHAPTER FIVE

JACKIE

AFTER A FULL DAY in the van, I am happy to relax in our room for an hour before we meet the rest of the group for dinner. Right after we check in to a lovely little vine-covered inn, Becca and I drag our bags down the narrow hallway and into our room. Tiny by American standards, there are two twin beds, a dresser topped with lace doilies and a little coffee maker, and an en suite bathroom. It is simple, clean, and looks like it has been freshly painted. Perfect!

"Do you have a preference, Bex?" I ask, indicating the two beds.

"Huh, what? No, whatever. I don't care."

Hmmm. My usually enthusiastic daughter is staring out the large window with a frown on her face. As our room overlooks a green pasture surrounded by a white picket fence, I can't see what there is to frown at. Now, if we were overlooking a parking lot maybe…

"This one is fine," she calls out. Dropping her bags in the middle of the tiny room, she flops down on the bed closest to the window with a loud sigh. She pulls the pillow over her head and lies, sprawled out like that, her long legs extending over the foot of the bed by several inches.

That can't be comfortable, I decide, and am about to point that out to her, but I stop myself. She's just tired. Of course, that's it. We have been here less than thirty-six hours and haven't adjusted to the time. After all, it's… Wait! How many hours' difference between here and Sedona? Seven? Or is it eight? Either way, the time change has thrown her off, and the catnaps she caught in the van probably haven't helped any.

I resist the urge to cover her up with a blanket and instead let myself in the bathroom. A shower would be good, and a bath even better, but I am starting to run out of time. We all agreed to meet in the lobby and eat dinner in the pub next door. Sean isn't going to be joining us, but he promised to reserve a table for the eight of us. I have only about forty-five minutes left to relax, freshen up, and change my top.

I briefly imagine letting Becca sleep for a bit and ordering a tray from room service, but it is the first night, and we should probably all stick together. I will have to settle for splashing cold water on my face and, *aarrgghh,* the faucets are switched. Hot water! I will have to get used to that.

I dry my face off with a tiny towel and, after a final look in the mirror confirms that I do, indeed, look the worse for wear, go back into the room and perch on the edge of the bed. It is sometime in the morning back home, so maybe I can call Rob and catch him between meetings. Hopefully he'll be too preoccupied with work to ask me if I've thought any more about his proposal.

I dig my phone out of my bag and decide to text him instead, so that I won't wake our sleeping daughter.

Hi, sweetheart. How r u?

In less than a minute, I get his response.

Great, Jax. Where u at?

Just checked in. Going to dinner soon.

Sounds good. How's the group?

Interesting. And I'm not the oldest one, either.

Wow! How is that even possible?

Oh you r a riot. Should I tell you about our sexy tour guide?

Wait. Too much?

Yes pls. Tell me all about how you're traveling around the country in a van with a hot guy. Insert groan emoji here.

Just kidding. He's way too young. Anyway…

Don't let him near Becca, okay? Promise me.

He's kidding, right?

Too old for Bex. No worries. We're in Cobh. Find Cork City on the map, and we're right nearby.

Yeah, I see that. I have your itinerary right here. Sounds fun. What's Bec up to?

Right next to me, sleeping soundly. All the travel and the time change wore her out.

Surprised you're still standing.

I won't be for long. Dinner and maybe a glass of wine and I'm going to crash.

Okay honey. Take care of our girl. I wish I were there with you.

I feel a lump growing in my throat. Yeah, I wish he were here, too.

Me 2. Love u. I'll call tomorrow.

Love u 2. G'night.

Phew. No mention of his grand plan. I'm safe for another day. I shut my phone off and shove it back into my bag, and then decide to let Becca sleep for a few more minutes. I prop my pillows up against the headboard and settle in with a smile on my face. It feels heavenly to put my feet up for a bit.

Dinner is going to be right next door, so, after a couple of hours, we will be back in our room. Sean told us we could "sleep in" and that he'll join us for breakfast at half past eight. That should allow us plenty of time to get a good night's sleep. Lucky Becca is just getting a bit of a head start.

Becca

After dinner the first night, Mom and I go back to our room. A short while later, I look up from my book and chuckle when I hear her scream. I shake my head in amazement. Some people never learn.

"Mom, it's been two days since we landed. It's not that hard," I call out to her. She yells back at me from behind the closed door of the bathroom.

"I'm left-handed, Rebecca. And yes, it *is* that hard.

I want to say something childish, like, "That's what he said," but one of us has to be a grownup. I decide to hold my tongue and wait for her. I don't have to wait long. She comes out wrapped in her favorite pink terrycloth robe, rubbing lotion into her hands.

"You and your dad are both right-handed. You have no idea how difficult it is sometimes. And don't roll your eyes at me, young lady."

I decide to cut her some slack.

"I'm sure you're right," I reassure her in what I hope is a sincere voice. She narrows her eyes at me.

"Don't patronize me, Rebecca. Left-handed people have a real challenge when it comes to figuring things out. It's a right-handed world, that's for sure."

"It must be horrible. No one should have to put up with *all* that. But just remember, what doesn't kill you makes you stron—

"All right, you." Mom chuckles at me. "So, are we reading for a bit or is it time for lights out?"

I pick my book back up. My mom loves her e-reader. I love mine, too, but I cheat with print books sometimes.

"How about a couple more chapters first?" I ask. My book is getting really good. I enjoy reading all of my assignments for school, spending hours on topics like cognitive reasoning and human development. But for pure pleasure? It's chick lit all the way. The heroines are always smart and sassy, and the heroes are strong and dashing. Works for me! Before we left, I downloaded all the latest titles and tossed a few paperbacks in my carry-on for good measure. As soon as I go back to Sedona and start working on my paper, time to read for fun will be non-existent.

Tonight, Mom is only too quick to agree with me. She is big reader, too, although her tastes tend more towards mysteries and suspense novels.

"Okay, but lights out in twenty minutes," she says with a grin. Already curled up, she is quickly engrossed in her current whodunit. But after a couple of minutes, I decide to call it a night. I've read the same page several times and nothing is registering.

I call goodnight, switch off my bedside lamp and slip between the sheets. Just as I close my eyes, Sean's handsome face pops up. *Oh, great!* This is something I don't need right now.

I am going to have to seek out some male companionship when I return to Boston in the fall. I haven't dated anyone regularly for quite a while. The women in my stories tend to ultimately end up with their Mr. Right. Why not me?

I flush thinking about our sexy tour guide. Sean is sweet, funny and gorgeous. And totally off limits, I remind myself. *Damn.*

CHAPTER SIX

JACKIE

THE FIRST COUPLE of days on the tour have been really enjoyable. As a group, I think we work well together. No drama queens, except Tracie once in a while, and sometimes Richard gets a little whiney. But, for the most part, everyone gets along really well. Sean runs a tight ship, and I mean that in a good way. He's really clear about what he expects, and he's always reliable. Fifteen-minute stops mean just that, and if he says we'll do something or see something, we do. Also, he's so passionate about the stories he shares.

This morning's story was about Finn MacCool, a mythological warrior from Irish legends. Apparently, Finn decided to eat a salmon reported to possess all of the world's knowledge. While cooking the fish, juice squirted out and burned Finn's thumb. When he stuck his thumb in his mouth to stop the pain, he got all of the fish's knowledge, and, from then on, he sucked his thumb whenever he wanted to know something.

Ollie laughs at that and outs his pregnant wife as a latent thumb-sucker. She vehemently denies the accusation and attempts to change the subject.

"How about Finn, if it's a boy?" she asks us, patting her baby bump.

"Finn is a fine name for a little guy," Sean assures her and launches into another story about Finn and his bravery on the battlefield. Even Ollie listens with interest.

Sean reminds me a little of Rick, my Sedona tour guide from

back a million years ago. Not like *that*.... Just in the way he is able to draw people together. Maybe it's a confidence thing. Although I discovered Rick did have a few insecurities, he always appeared calm and unruffled. He was probably paddling like crazy, but he gave off an air of confidence and ease, like everything was smooth sailing.

Maybe that's how Sean is, too. The more I think about this, the more Sean seems like Rob, at least my young Rob. When we first met, he was only a few years older than Sean is now. A little cocky. Well, a lot cocky actually. Smooth, really good-looking. Charming and funny, never at a loss for words. It took me only a little while to discover the smart, sensitive, warm, and wonderful man I've never stopped loving all these years. Maybe there's more to Sean than meets the eye, as well.

But who would find it? Take the time to really get to know the man inside? Tracie? No, I fear that, with her, what you see is what you get, and what you see is a shiny, attractive shell. From the little I've seen, there's not a lot going on below the surface. She's intelligent. That's really clear. But let's just say that empathy isn't her strongest character trait. Case in point: Tracie almost took the head off the poor girl at the reception desk tonight. We were getting checked in, and the young woman was a bit frazzled. She asked Tracie if she needed two room keys. I honestly think she thought that Tracie and Geoff were together as a couple, standing side by side as they were. It was an honest mistake. But Tracie flipped out, demanding to know why she would want two keys and why it was so expected that a woman couldn't be traveling alone. The poor girl almost cried.

Geoff was smooth and jumped in before things got any worse. He assured young Margaret that while Tracie would undoubtedly be thrilled to share a room with him, he was, alas, committed to another. He really vamped it up and had us all laughing. Even Richard, and I've rarely seen him laugh.

Tracie grabbed her single key and flounced away, dragging her collection of designer bags behind her. She could have used that article on packing smarter that I lost. We're all tired, and checking in to a different inn every night kind of can get old after a short while.

But suck it up, would you?

There are other things, too. Tracie is a miser when it comes to tipping. She keeps trying to tell the rest of us that ten percent is considered a generous tip in Europe. But even Ollie and Carrie, who are on a really tight budget, aren't buying it. The rest of the Nomads keep to the American standard of fifteen to twenty percent. Even Richard and Geoff, who are British. They seem to be generous with their tips, especially Geoff, if the waiter is a good-looking younger male.

I just report the stories; I'm not here to judge.

Anyway, why am I ragging on Tracie tonight? She's always pleasant enough to me. Maybe she's really shy and covers it up with that snooty attitude. Or maybe she's just cheap and bitchy! I guess time will tell.

I think she's interested in Sean, but I don't really see anything happening. I think she's a little too worldly for him. Or maybe, just not nice enough. I think he deserves a really nice girl. If only Becca were older. Ha-ha! Can't see that happening either. My daughter is too sensible to get caught up in some fling with a guy like Sean. Irish, I mean. He lives here, and she doesn't.

Sean probably already has a girlfriend, anyway. Although he told me he's rarely home long enough to even do laundry, so maybe not.

But back to tipping. It's customary to tip your tour guide, and guidebooks state that the norm is ten to twenty dollars per day per guest or whatever the equivalent is in euros. Wow, with eight guests for seven days, that's between six hundred and a thousand dollars. Not bad money, plus whatever the company pays him.

I sit up in bed just enough to flip my pillow over. The new side feels cool against my neck. I am having a hard time sleeping on this trip and have been lying here for well over an hour, trying to fall asleep. Although the narrow twin bed is comfortable enough, I miss my own bed, and Rob's solid presence next me in that bed.

I can count on both hands the number of nights that Rob and I spend apart each year. A couple girls' weekends away with Becca, and, once or twice a year, I fly to Boston, combining visits with my oldest friend, Suze, and Becca at college. I hope that Rob and I can work things out, as I have no intention of making sleeping alone a habit. But the thought of sleeping in a new bed each night is only slightly less appealing. I'm just not ready. Why can't he see that?

I glance over at our daughter. Flat on her back, sleeping soundly. Just like her dad.

Oh, this isn't working. Maybe I can throw on some clothes and go down to the lobby.

And do what? Count the number of cabbage roses on the peeling wallpaper? When the Nomad crew promises to take you off the beaten path, they aren't kidding. Other than the diehards at the pub next door, I bet not a soul is still awake in this little burg. Just me.

Tomorrow promises to be another busy day, with lots to see and do. I will require my own personal trough of coffee at breakfast, if I stay awake much longer. I need my ZZZs!

BECCA

First impressions of Ireland? Green, damp, and beautiful. The people we've met have been just lovely: friendly, helpful, and super-psyched to be living here. It's everything that the Nomad website promised and more.

Sean has been just great. He's shown us all around, and his energy level? Well, it's tough to keep up with him. He is super-knowledgeable about so many things—the history, the culture, lore, and legends. He is a born storyteller, and I think we're all half in love with him. I mean it, he's just this freakishly handsome, super-charming guy.

Elaine and my mom want to *mother* him, Ollie seems to want to *be* him, and Geoff, Tracie, and me–I think we would like to be *with* him. I can't speak for them, although I guess I just did, right? I know I would. Like to be with him, that is. He's smart, funny, gorgeous, and that accent is just to die for.

I think Richard and Carrie are the only ones on the trip who seem immune to his obvious charms. I've certainly seen the way Tracie looks at Sean, like he's a tempting dish on a buffet table that she just has to have. Geoff is a little more discreet, especially when Richard is around. And he almost always is.

What must it be like to be in a relationship with someone so much younger and better looking than you are? I'll probably never know, but I do feel for Richard. He's kind of annoying at times, but he seems to be very protective of his young, dashing mate.

Geoff is actually really funny and good looking. Too short and dark-haired for my tastes, but I can see why someone would be attracted to him. He gets pretty flamboyant at times—really struts around and hams it up. But, most of the time, he seems sweet, and I think he's quite devoted to Richard, although he doesn't get the opportunity to show it much. At least not in front of us. Richard won't even hold his partner's hand in public but gets super-clingy if he feels threatened at all.

Like this morning. The busboy who cleaned off our table was kind of smiling at Geoff, who smiled back. Richard got all kinds of pissed and just about dragged Geoff out of the dining room.

Tracie smirked and continued to push her eggs around her plate. Why she orders a full Irish each morning is beyond me. She barely makes a dent.

On the other hand, I have an appetite like a farmhand, and, except for the disgusting black-pudding pellet, I clean my plate and sometimes even finish my mom's bacon, if it's not crispy enough for her. Sean usually joins us for a cup of coffee after most of us have eaten our breakfast. Today, he walked into the dining room just as Richard and Geoff were rushing out.

He raised his eyebrow as he sat down and asked, "Do I want to know?"

Everyone kind of grunted, and the subject was dropped. Twenty minutes later, Richard and Geoff appeared together in the lobby all smiles, and Richard even carried one of Elaine's bags out to Bertha. And off we went.

Today we are going to engage in one of the most iconic Irish tourist activities ever. We are heading to Blarney Castle and will be queuing up to climb to the top of the tower and kiss the Blarney Stone! According to Sean, the tower was built nearly six hundred years ago by one of Ireland's greatest chieftains, Cormac MacCarthy.

Carrie asks Sean about the whole "gift of gab" legend, and he is happy to tell us all about the Irish goddess of beauty, Cliodhna, the Fairy Queen of Munster. The man who built the castle was involved in a lawsuit and asked Cliodhna for help. She told him to kiss the first stone he laid eyes on that morning as he went to court. He did, and his speech was so persuasive, he won his case. In gratitude, he took the stone home with him and put it in the castle wall.

"And that's why anyone who kisses the stone is granted the gift of eloquence," Sean finishes with a twinkle in his eye.

Well, legend or not, I'm actually pretty excited. Maybe it's in my DNA, but this whole Irish experience is really meaningful to me. I feel like I am meant to be here, and not just because I have the hots for our handsome tour guide, either. Tracie tells us that she's going to remain in the gift shop down below, as nothing could be more disgusting to her than climbing up a dark tower and kissing some filthy rock.

But the rest of us are looking forward to it, and we're all planning on taking lots of pictures, too. I really want someone to take a picture of Sean and me. *Just* Sean and me. Someone like Ollie or Tracie always seems to be in the photo with us, no matter how carefully I try to stage it.

I do have several shots of Sean, mostly when he wasn't aware that I was taking his picture. He's pretty animated most of the time, but I've managed to capture him looking quite pensive. I wonder what's going on in that handsome head of his. I guess I'll never know, but I get the feeling that there's more to Sean than meets the eye. I would love to find out more, but for now, I just have to be content with the sight of his chiseled jawline and the way that his eyes get all crinkly when he smiles.

God, what a sap I am. I'm not sure that I can take five more days of this. It's torture, I'm telling you.

But we're here at the castle. Just before Tracie makes a beeline for the gift shop, Mom reminds her to be on the lookout for Edie's teapot. Elaine, Carrie, and my mom rush off to the ladies room, leaving me alone with the guys. Sean is busy giving out tickets to get us into Blarney Castle and instructing us to meet back here at Bertha afterwards. I decide to make my move, lame as it is.

"So, are you joining us then?" I ask Sean in as casual a tone as I can muster, like I don't care what his answer is. He looks up from his clipboard with a grin.

"What, me? No, Becca, I've kissed that Stone one too many times already, and besides, who could handle more of my gabbing anyway?"

I'm not giving up that easily.

"C'mon, Sean. You're always saying that it's all about the journey, right? Not just the destination. You should put your money where your mouth is." And if it's not on mine, then your mouth should at least be used to kiss the Blarney Stone, am I right?

"So you have been listening to me, heh?" He is looking right at me, like he is really seeing me for the first time. He appears to be weighing something over in his mind, like his decision on the matter really counts for something. Then he speaks up again. "All right, you're on. I'll go to the top with you. Guess Tracie's ticket shouldn't go to waste, am I right?"

Am I imagining it, or is he flirting with me? I kind of suck at picking up on this sort of thing, but, either way, Sean will be joining us on our climb to the top of the Tower.

"Oh, great!" I gush.

But before I have a chance to say anything else, the ladies return, and next thing I know, the eight of us are climbing up the staircase towards Blarney Castle. I somehow end up leading the way for our little group, with Sean falling behind.

We join hordes of tourists all intent on accomplishing the same goal and move en masse, onward and upward. I look over my shoulder to catch my mom's eye. We are growing farther part as the lines of people merge, but she gives me a smile and a thumbs up, so I am able to relax.

Mom gets a little claustrophobic at times, like the time we went below ground to a silver mine in Idaho. My dad had to practically carry her out of there, and that image of my brave, ballsy mother just about paralyzed with fear has stayed with me. But she nods at me and smiles again, right before I turn a corner and lose sight of her.

I refocus my attention on the task at hand and plod on up the winding stairs until at last we emerge back out into the fresh air. I gulp in a lungful and watch with interest as the group directly in front of me approaches the Blarney Stone. Apparently, you have to crouch down and then lay back in order to make contact with the Stone.

Hmmm. I thought it would be bigger.

Suddenly Sean is right beside me, leaning down and whispering in my ear. "So, are you going to go for it?" he asks suggestively.

Well, two can play at this game.

"I was just thinking that it would be *bigger*, you know?" I try to arch my eyebrow. Sean's eyes widen in surprise, then he chuckles.

"Bigger, huh? Are you sure you could handle it?" A quick flick of his tongue over his top lip tells me that I might be getting to him.

Maybe making him a little nervous, even. Or, he has dry lips.

"Oh, I can handle it," I assure him. "I've kissed things much bigger." Sean bursts out laughing.

Yeah, that sounds really gross. But I'm pretty sure I had him going for a moment there. He rolls his eyes at me and takes my arm.

"C'mon. Let's get you and our famous stone properly introduced." And he leads me over to where the guide is assisting the next willing tourist.

Sean and I are up next.

CHAPTER SEVEN

JACKIE

I COULDN'T WAIT to text Rob!

I kissed the B stone! Climbed up the tower & everything.

I wait for his response. Nothing. That's odd. Usually… Oh, wait! We're seven hours ahead. It's only 6 a.m. in Sedona. Rob's an early bird, but not this early.

Well, at least my text will be the first thing he sees when he gets up. After letting Brenda and Eddie out for their morning constitutional, that is. And brewing a pot of coffee. Strong, the way he likes it. When it's for both of us, he'll compromise with a breakfast blend. But it's full-scale Colombian when he's solo.

I can just picture him, moving around our compact kitchen, scooping up fresh kibble for the dogs, filling their water dish so that Eddie will have no real need to drink from the toilet, maybe grabbing the newspaper off the front porch, if he has time to peruse the headlines and enjoy a second cup of coffee in the sunny dining nook. After more than twenty years in the same house, it is easy to close my eyes and imagine Rob anywhere in it. I love living there, and I don't understand why he's willing to leave it all behind.

"Did you get hold of your husband, Jackie?"

I jump when I hear Elaine's voice.

"You're a million miles away." I look up and smile at her sweet face. I can't imagine anyone giving this dear woman a hard time. She is so pleasant and easy to be with. I pat the faded cushion next to me.

"Plenty of room, Elaine, if you want to join me," I offer. I think she might pass, but then she nods and plops down on the other half of the loveseat.

We arrived right after an early lunch today, and, after depositing my bags and splashing water on my face, I came back down to the lobby. I love traveling with my daughter, but I think it's a good idea to give each other a little space sometimes. I figured I'd take an hour to enjoy my book and a cup of tea, maybe post an update on my Facebook page, then meet back up with Becca and explore the town on foot.

"So, did you reach him?" Elaine asks again. I had told her I wanted to let Rob know that, despite my silly worries, I was able to handle the confines of the tower at Blarney Castle and kiss the Stone.

"It's the crack of dawn back home," I remind her.

"So, what's he like, your husband? You said he's in advertising?"

She seems interested, so I tell her all about Rob: his creativity, his outgoing nature and his zest for living, All the while, she sits there, not saying a thing, and it hits me: sounds like I'm bragging. Especially when my audience is a woman whose marriage and family life were far from ideal.

"So, yeah, he's pretty, *um*, great," I finish weakly. "I'm sorry if I got carried away. I mean it's not…"

Elaine shakes her head vehemently. "No, Jackie. Never apologize for sharing something so good with anyone. I wish I had asked for more, expected more, you know? You and Rob, what you have is a real partnership. You've built something together. You run your own businesses…" She stops mid-sentence as my eyes fill with tears. "Jackie. What's wrong?"

Suddenly I feel the need to confide in someone, even a near stranger. I haven't shared Rob's plan and my hesitation towards it with anyone, not Suze or Edie or Becca. But I have to talk about it. The pressure of keeping it all in is killing me.

"It's not all a bed of roses, Elaine. We have a problem, a big one. Rob wants us to sell our businesses and probably our home too. Buy an RV and travel the country. Buy a boat and sail around the world.

Live out of a suitcase. I just don't think I can do it."

Elaine has been watching me closely. She leans towards me and pulls me into a hug and I collapse against her.

"What do *you* want Jackie?" *Wow, good question.*

"I want…I want it all, I guess. I want to travel with my husband, see all of the things we've been putting off, but I want to wake up in my own bed too. Putter around my little house, hang out with our friend Coop. I just don't know how to make it all work, you know?"

"Talk to Rob. Tell him what you told me. He wants to be happy and he wants you to be happy too. Baby steps, Jackie. Keep your house. Go on a trip, then maybe plan a longer one. Take your time. You can do this," she finishes with a grin. I take a deep breath. I feel strangely relieved, lighter somehow. "So do you have a picture of this husband of yours?" she asks me with a twinkle in her eye.

I fumble on my phone, skimming through hundreds of photos. "Oh, yeah, here's one. That's Rob with Brenda and Eddie." She smiles at the photo of my puppies clambering over Rob shortly after we brought them home.

"Oh, Jackie. So cute, and that hubby of yours! Wow, he's really good looking."

I get that a lot. Rob is an exceptionally handsome man, while I am, even on my best day, no one who would win any beauty contests. I've held up pretty well, better than most, but I am a low-maintenance woman with a no-fuss hairstyle, and I rarely wear much makeup. I prefer flip-flops to stilettos and jeans to dresses, but I watch my weight and use gallons of moisturizer and sunblock to stave off damage from the hot desert sun. "I bet you make a really lovely couple," she adds.

Well, enough about me, I think. *So, do I dance around this or jump right in?*

"What was your husband like?" From the little she has shared with me, I understand her marriage was much less idyllic than mine. And now he's dead, so…

"Ronald was, well, difficult, I guess. Always a bit of a prickly pear, you know?" I didn't, but I nod anyway. "Well, that's not really fair. He wasn't always that way. When we first met, he just about swept me off my feet." She closes her eyes, and a slight smile plays over her lips. I wait, and she continues. "We met at work. I was an administrative assistant at an insurance company, and Ronald was one of the computer techs. Kind of a nerd, I guess you'd say. We had this mutual friend, a girl named Cindy. She kept telling me, 'Oh, you should meet my friend Ronald. Come out with me and my friend Ronald some night for a drink after work.' I kept thinking, if he's so great, why don't *you* go out with him?"

"But she already had a boyfriend, so, one night, I agreed, and I went to meet them at this little bar near the office. I show up, and there's Ronald, but no Cindy." She chuckles at that and smiles again. "We had been set up all right. He was pretty easy to talk to. Well, he actually listened a lot. I was a chatty little thing back then. One thing led to another, and six months later, we were engaged."

"Then I got pregnant, so we moved up the date and put down a down payment on a little house. Before you know it, we're raising two kids and living on just the one paycheck, and now, I'm not so chatty anymore, and turns out, he's not such a good listener, anyway." Elaine's smile disappears, and her cheeks get all blotchy.

I start to tell her that it's okay, that she doesn't have to continue, but she cuts me off.

"No, Jackie, I need to tell you this, okay? He was always just so angry, you know? Like nothing I did was ever good enough. He belittled me, in front of the kids, in front of his family. According to him, I was dumb and boring, couldn't cook worth a damn, couldn't keep up a house. Back then, I felt like I deserved the crappy life I had made for myself. Even my kids knew it. They always went to their friends' home for dinners and sleepovers. Never asked anyone over. 'Why don't you invite so and so once in a while?' I'd ask. My son would just ignore me. And my daughter? She'd roll her eyes at me. 'Why would I want to do that?' she'd ask. 'Who would want to come here?' And she was right. No one in their right mind would choose to spend any time there, unless they had to. It was such an unhappy place." Elaine shakes her head and looks so sad. Her eyes have this faraway look to them.

I have to at least try to bring her back to the here and now, which in my opinion is looking pretty damn good.

"I'm so sorry you had to go through all that, but look at you now. You've got friends. Every one of the Nomads loves you. You're in a really happy place, here in, well, wherever the heck we are, and, most important, you don't have to listen to any negative complaints about who you are or what you can or can't do."

She smiles and pats my hand.

"Thank you for that, Jackie. I *am* in a much better place today, and you're right, I don't have to listen to anyone complaining or criticizing me anymore." She stands up and suddenly seems quite satisfied with herself. "I'm going to go across the street and check out that little gift shop I saw on our way in. And I'm likely to buy some bauble or trinket that I don't really need, just because I feel like it. Any problem with that?"

I respond to her mock defiance by assuring her that I have no problem whatsoever with her plan, and then remind her to look for Edie's teapot.

As she grabs her bag to leave, her eyes twinkle mischievously, and she says, "But you know, my late husband was right about one thing." I look up at her. "I really can't cook worth a damn." And with that, she sweeps through the lobby. "See you at dinner," she calls out.

BECCA

Another wave of nausea hits me. My whole body feels like it's been hit by a truck. I try to roll over but immediately regret it. My head is pounding, and my throat is dry, raw feeling. I will myself to keep from puking. Through blurry eyes, I try to see the little clock on the nightstand. 5:35 a.m. *This is not good.*

I can barely make out the shape of my mom in the bed next to mine. She is sleeping soundly, or so it appears, with her back towards me. I try to look around our little room but have to shield my eyes from the rays of sun that are starting to make their way through the curtains.

I struggle to sit up in bed and prop myself up on the pillows. I groan with the effort. I am a lightweight when it comes to booze. Oh sure, I went to a few keg parties in high school, with everyone milling around, gripping their red plastic cups of foamy beer, passing a bottle of whiskey or whatever, smoking weed. I went through the motions like everyone else but rarely finished even a single beer.

On Monday mornings at school, it was like a badge of honor. "Oh man, I was so wasted." Or "Dude, what happened? I don't remember anything." I had enough trouble navigating the social scene with my classmates when I was sober, so getting wasted was a hurdle I chose to skip. I loosened up a bit during my four years in Boston. Mine wasn't a big party school, but frat parties, tailgating, and pub-crawls were a big part of college life. I learned to pace myself and rarely got shitfaced.

But last night? *Oh God, just how much did I drink?* What would Sean think? We spent the night dancing and drinking and…did he really kiss me…? Or did I kiss him? How am I going to face him this morning? Spend the whole day with him and all the others, acting like nothing happened.

But how much did Ollie see…?

* * *

The night started out innocently enough. We arrived at our bed and breakfast for the night, and, after making sure that our accommodations were sorted out, Sean took off on foot. I am sure he needs a break from all of the questions and concerns posed by the motley group of eight tourists in his care. He told us that the pub next door had great food and that the music started about 9 p.m.

"It's good craic," he assured us. "Save me a seat," he added, as he left the little lobby. Did he look at me when he said it? "I'll be back later."

The eight of us dispersed to drag bags to our rooms after agreeing to meet back in the lobby at 8 p.m. to go to dinner. You would think that, after a full day sharing the close quarters of our van, we would want to go our separate ways, but no. We always ate dinner together. Sean never joined us, but often mentioned that he would be in the closest bar later in the evening.

I would have loved to trail after him. But instead, I followed my mom down the hall and into our room. She was chattering on about the quaint little town we were in and all that we had seen that day.

"Bex? Becca? Are you okay?" She sounded concerned.

"Huh? I'm fine. No, really, I'm just tired. Kind of antsy." Normally, Sean broke up the travel with stops in little towns for homemade ice cream or a hike through the meadows or to climb a hill to visit a 500-year-old castle. But today, he'd warned us that we would be driving straight through, in order to check in early. Ollie slapped him on the back and teased him about having a hot date. My cheeks flamed, and my heart started pounding at the thought of Sean rushing off to meet some girl. But I have no right to think like that. He is single and a flirt; however, I'm certain that after-hours fraternizing with the paying customers is a real no-no.

I mumbled something about wanting to pick up some postcards. Mom was already running a tub, which she planned to relax in for the next hour or so. "Be careful," she called out to me as I left. "Make sure you have your key."

I wanted to snap back, "Of course I'll be careful. I'm always careful. And I have my damned key, okay?" But this is my mom, after all. It had been a long day, and she loves me. It isn't her fault that her daughter has the unrequited hots for a certain long and lanky tour guide.

"I'm fine, Mom," I assured her as I wiggled my key in her direction. "All set. I'll see you soon. Enjoy your bath." And I ambled back down the hall, through the little lobby, and out onto the street.

The tour promised accommodations "off the beaten track," and they nailed it. We are smack in the middle of a postcard-cute village: cobblestone streets and shops with brightly colored doorways. Several pubs and a couple of churches. Yes, this is a typical small town in Western Ireland.

Is Sean in one of those pubs? I wondered. *Does he have a girlfriend that he promised to meet?* I looked up and down the street but didn't see a familiar face, not even any of my traveling companions. I poked around and looked in at the little shops but was too restless to do any serious browsing. No sign of Edie's teapot, either. *Damn.*

A short while later, I let myself back in the room and flung myself down on the nearest of the twin beds.

"Bex, is that you?" my mom called out.

"No, I'm a serial killer."

"What? Bex?"

"Yes, it's me." *God, who else would it be?*

Wow, I was in a totally crap mood. I decided to relax for a bit. I figured, maybe when Mom finished her bath, we could play cards or something. We still had a couple of hours until dinner. Next thing I knew, Mom was sitting on the bed, rubbing my back.

"Sweetie? Bex? C'mon, honey. Time to get up. We're heading out for dinner. C'mon, sweetheart."

Crap. I felt groggy and disoriented. For some, a power nap is just the ticket. Not for me. I couldn't nap for…wait, it was five minutes 'til eight? I had slept for almost two hours!

"I can't believe you let me sleep so long. I still need to shower. And my hair! I have to find my clothes. Iron a top. God, why didn't you wake me?" I was hollering at her as I raced around our room.

Where is my makeup bag? My mom cast me an appraising glance. I thought she was going to snap back at me, but she softened slightly when she saw how upset I looked.

"It's not a problem. Hop in the shower, and I'll find you a top to wear. Just twist your hair up. It looks adorable like that. Slap on some blush and you'll be good to go. I'll save you a seat. We're just going next door. Sean says the food is..."

"Sean says, Sean says. That's all I hear anymore," I snapped as I headed for the bathroom.

"What's gotten into you, Rebecca? He *is* our tour guide after all. Here's a shirt. It doesn't need ironing. I'll see you next door in a few, okay?" She left quickly and closed the door behind her.

I let the hot water cascade over me. I really needed an attitude adjustment. Aiming the showerhead away from me, I tried to keep my hair from getting wet. It is thick and wavy; just a little bit of hot water makes it swell right up. I dried off with one of the postage-stamp-sized towels and checked myself out in the mirror. *God, what a sight!* My eyes were ringed with dark circles and there was a fresh crop of freckles on my sunburned nose. I was relieved that at least it would be dark in the pub tonight.

I kept hoping that Sean would join us. I really wanted to see him. *God, he is cute,* I thought, as I slipped into a pair of skinny jeans and a black tank top. I wondered what he thought about me, or *if* he thought about me. I am the youngest on the tour, but maybe he prefers older girls, like Tracie. She is so sophisticated, with her black American Express card and fancy luggage. Note to self: act older!

I pulled on the shirt Mom found for me, but left it unbuttoned. I don't have much going on upstairs, if you catch my drift, but the jeans showed off my long legs, and the tank top clung to me in all the right places I decided. I twisted my hair up into a messy bun and, at the last minute, added a pair of dangly earrings. *Why not, right?*

If anyone noticed the extra care I took to get ready for dinner—besides my mom, that is—I wouldn't know. As I walked into the crowded pub five minutes later and slipped into the empty chair next to her, she looked at me and grinned.

"Don't you look nice," she teased. "That must have been some shower."

I just smiled back at her and took a long pull on the Diet Coke she had waiting for me. "Did you order yet?" I asked. "I'm starving."

Our server was already circling the table, pad in hand. My mom and Elaine both ordered the salmon, but the rest of us went with the pub's special, fish and chips. Thirty minutes later, I pushed my plate away from me. I couldn't eat another bite. I had plowed through my entrée and finished the mash-and-veggie mix off my mom's plate, as well. At the rate I'm eating my way through Ireland, I will be lucky to still fit into my jeans by the time I get home.

We all passed on dessert, except for Carrie. At five months pregnant, she vowed to enjoy sticky toffee pudding every chance she got. Her husband Ollie put his arm around her and hugged her close to him.

"My little baby-making machine," he bragged. "What a champ!"

They are a seriously cute couple. I wonder if anyone will look at me the way Ollie looks at his wife. The way my dad looks at Mom. Pride and joy with a touch of "how the fuck did I get so lucky?"

Richard and Geoff headed outside for a cigarette and the rest of us got comfortable, scooting our chairs around to face the little makeshift stage. Several of the night's musicians were warming up and the bar was filling in. I looked around anxiously.

Where is Sean? I wondered. A few minutes later, I saw him. He strode in like he owns the place. So comfortable in his skin. Where did he get all that confidence? I wondered. Still wearing that silly hat, he'd changed into a pair of jeans and a striped button-down. He is thin but has such a great pair of shoulders and a really nice butt.

I flushed at the sight of him and watched as he made his way across the bar towards our table.

"Got room for one more?"

Wow, I thought, *did his accent get even stronger?*

"Sure," I squeaked. "I mean, yeah, I'm sure there's an extra chair around or whatever." My mom was looking at me strangely. So was Sean. *Must act calm!* He slipped into the empty chair next to Elaine. I thought he may have winked at me, but it happened so fast.

"How was your dinner?" he asked. Elaine and my mom gave a glowing review of the meal, punctuated by high voices and lavish praise. Sean has that effect on women, I'd noticed.

The guys came back, and Sean told us about tomorrow's itinerary. Driving, beach, horseback riding (optional), lunch, then a hike or a sea-kayaking lesson. Our choice.

"What sounds good, Bex?" my mom asked me. "A hike would be good, but we can do that at home, right? Maybe the kayak? I dunno, what do you think?"

I thought, *I want to go wherever Sean goes,* and wondered which activity Sean would take part in. Or maybe he gets both groups settled and takes some time for himself? Off to see some local girl…?

"Earth to Becca," my mom teased. "Honey, what sounds good?"

"I don't know. Either. Whatever. Can't we just play it by ear for once?" Her face fell at the sound of my sharp tone. Her penchant for planning is legendary. My dad and I often tease her about it, but I went too far. I hurt her feelings, I could tell. *Take a deep breath and chill out.* "Mom, I'm sorry I snapped at you. If it's warm tomorrow, maybe the kayak, okay? Sounds fun, huh?"

"Sure, sweetheart." She patted my hand. "Let's wait and see."

A few minutes later, the band started up in earnest, and it was hard to talk much after that. They were really good and got the crowd clapping their hands in time to some of the more familiar tunes. A few couples got up and danced. *Would Sean dance with me if I ask him?* I wondered. Of course, that would require me to be able to dance, which is not the case. Other than playing field hockey, I have two left feet.

Then I heard the opening sounds of "Galway Girl." Sean had called our attention to the catchy tune earlier that day, when it played on the radio, so I turned to him just in time to see him getting dragged onto the dance floor by Tracie. *Bitch.* Damn, I'd missed my chance.

Then Ollie pulled me up on the floor, and next thing I knew, I was being spun around by a very enthusiastic partner. His wife cheered us on as she sat by the sidelines. I lost track of Sean and really got into the music. Ollie wasn't a great dancer, either, but what he lacked in skills, he more than made up for in enthusiasm. For once in my life, I was dancing as if no one was watching.

Hot and sweaty after all that dancing and jumping around, I

collapsed back into my seat. I gratefully let Carrie pour me a beer and started to gulp it down.

"Hey, slow down there, hot stuff," she warned. "The beer's not like back at home. But if I can't drink," she relented, patting her tiny baby belly, "at least *someone* should have a good time."

I started to sip more slowly. I was really thirsty, though, and the ale was pretty good, I decided. I was having a second glass when my mom came over.

"Take it easy, sweetheart," she whispered in my ear. "I'm heading up to read for a bit before I turn in. Not too late, okay?" I assured her I would be fine, and after I'd showed her that I did indeed have my room key, she followed Elaine through the bar, turning to give a little wave as she disappeared out the door.

Minutes later, I was up and dancing again. There was a whole group of us, and I just happened to accidentally on purpose bump into Sean. Then we were dancing together. When the band took a short break, it felt only natural to slide into the seat next to him. I grabbed my half-empty glass of beer and drank some of it.

"Hey, are you sure you're not overdoing it there, Becca?" Sean looked concerned.

"Nah, I'm good. And anyway, I'm not driving," I said with a grin. Then I burped. *Classy.*

"Okay, just watch out, okay? I do not want to face your ma if I bring you home all rat-arsed."

I just giggled. Gotta love those Irish expressions.

"Don't you worry about me, Sean Donovan." *Hmmm,* I thought. *Sean.* Ollie was Oliver, Carrie was Carolyn, my mom was Jacqueline, and I was Rebecca. "Hey, why don't you have a nickname?"

He grinned back at me. "Who says I don't?" he teased and pulled me up on my feet and back out onto the dance floor.

A few beers and several dances later, the place started to clear out. Ollie, Geoff, Sean, and I were the only ones left at our table, and I learned a lot about my traveling companions. It was like true confessions.

Ollie confided he had almost dropped out of school at the age of sixteen, but that Carrie had convinced him to stick it out. Geoff had tried out for a Chippendales-type dance troupe in his early twenties but hadn't made the final cut, so he applied for a temp job at Richard's company. The rest is history. He got kind of choked up, telling us about how he had fallen in love with his boss.

And Sean? Apparently, his dad is a bit of a Beatles fanatic, and all three of his sons were proof: Declan John is the oldest, Sean Paul is next, and Liam George is the youngest. And Sean's unfortunate nickname? Paulie Boy. What a hoot!

I tried to think of something to confess, but came up empty. I was just about to blurt out that I hadn't actually graduated last month, when the burly lead singer announced they were going to "slow things down a bit." At that, Ollie and Geoff decided to pack it in, and Sean appeared ready to depart as well.

"How about one more dance? Last one," I pleaded.

He was about to say no, I just know it. But he looked at me kind of strangely before he agreed and let me lead him back to the dance floor. Then I was in his arms, and we made our way slowly around the floor. I didn't recognize the song we were dancing to, but I could have stayed there, in that pub and in those arms, forever. The cologne Sean wore was spicy and outdoorsy, and his arms just felt so right, looped around me. He was humming along to the music. I tripped suddenly over my own two big-ass feet, and he steadied me. I looked up at him, and he smiled slowly.

"Yeah, you're a fine thing," he murmured and pulled me in closer. I could feel his chest pressing hard against mine and the strength of his arms encircling me.

My hands slid down his back and rested on his belt. I used the opportunity to pull him even closer and quickly realized that he was as excited as I was. *Oh God, wait till I tell Lily*. He didn't pull away from me, so we just stayed like that for a precious few minutes.

The band closed out their set with an old hit from the '70s, "American Woman." I know this is a song that the Guess Who made popular long before Lenny Kravitz was even in grade school. My parents and Uncle Coop are rock-and-roll aficionados. I grew up listening to the Beatles, the Stones, the Eagles—I know them all.

We continued to slow dance, despite the song's faster tempo. "American Woman," he sang softly in my ear. "Stay away from me-e-e."

I am pretty certain, if it weren't for Sean holding me tight and upright, I would have collapsed. I wanted to whisper in his ear, "Don't stay away from me. Please don't." But I kept quiet and let him lead me around the empty dance floor.

Next thing I knew, the house lights were going on and the music had ended. Sean started to pull away from me, but I knew I needed to kiss him. To have him kiss me back. I decided to make the first move. I tilted my head back, so I had a clear shot at that oh-so-kissable mouth. And I went for it.

His lips were warm and soft and just drew me in. I nibbled gently on his lower lip. He tasted like beer and something minty. So I kissed him, and, after just a moment's hesitation, he kissed me back. I parted my lips slightly, hoping he would take the hint, when suddenly he pushed away from me, gasping for breath.

"Becca, what are you doing to me?" he groaned. "We can't." He looked around anxiously. "If anyone saw us. Shite. C'mon, I need to get you back to your room. Your ma will have my ass." *Crap.*

I tried to re-assure him. "Don't worry, Sean. It's fine. Just…"

"No," he growled. "I need to get you to your room. It's late." He propelled me out of the empty bar, where stools were being turned upside down and someone had started to mop the floor over in the corner. The blast of cool night air may not have sobered me up, but it did get my attention.

"But Sean," I protested, shivering.

"You're going to bed," he said sternly.

"With you…" I wanted to add. But the moment we'd shared was over. We were once again the responsible tour guide and the American idiot who wanted to jump his Irish bones. *Oh well.*

He dug into the back pocket of my snug jeans and pulled out my room key. He got the door open, handed me back my key, and, with a little shove, pushed me into the dark room.

"G'night, Becca. Lock the door after me, okay?" And, closing the door behind him, he was gone.

I collapsed onto the nearest bed, glad to no longer have to struggle to remain upright. And very glad that it wasn't the bed occupied by my mom. The room was spinning, and I closed my eyes to keep from getting even more disoriented.

I must have fallen asleep right away, because here I am, a few hours later, fully dressed, shoes and all.

I feel so lousy. Headache? Nausea? Dry mouth? Check, check, and check. All of the symptoms of a hangover that so many of my classmates have yacked on and on about for years. It is my turn to suffer. And I really need to pee.

I slither out of bed and lurch into the bathroom. Perched on the toilet seat, I empty my bursting bladder for what seems like forever. I lean forward and try to prop up my aching head on my hands. "I will never drink again," I tell myself....

In a few more hours, I will have puked, showered, and puked again. I will be ready for a breakfast of tea and toast at a table set for nine. I will have dry-swallowed three extra-strength Tylenol. I will have ignored the concerned glances thrown by my mother. I will have smiled at the others, avoiding eye contact with Sean and gladly giving up the opportunity to sit up front with him, as we take off for another day of fun and sightseeing.

But at the moment? I just want the earth to open up and swallow me whole. *Kill Me Now!*

CHAPTER EIGHT

JACKIE

I LEAN BACK in my seat and try to get comfortable. We have been driving all day and only made a few stops. I desperately need to stretch my legs and find a restroom. Sean promised us a chance to get some fresh air and a snack.

He has been pretty quiet all day, I realize. He continues to narrate and call our attention to points of interest, but his usual non-stop patter of jokes and stories has been absent. It must get awfully tiring, driving a bunch of tourists around, explaining everything and keeping us all entertained. Sean is entitled to an off day.

I suddenly flash back to a conversation I had with Rick, wow, twenty-three years ago. *Rick...* Before this Ireland trip, it has been a while since I've thought of him, and much longer since I've seen him. I smile, remembering how young and handsome he was when we first met.

Several years younger than me, he was a big, strapping guy with massive, tan forearms, a shock of sun-bleached hair, and abs that...whoa! Don't go there! Our hot romance did cool down pretty quickly, though. Long before Rob's first visit to Sedona, I knew that Rick and I weren't going to be "Rick and I."

Rick used to tell me the answers he always counted on to keep the conversation going, when he was just *not* feeling it. He could answer like he was on autopilot. "Just around the bend," "About ten minutes or so," and, "In about a mile" were the stock responses that answered so many of the questions that eager tourists continually asked. I smile, remembering that.

Good old Rick. God, when was the last time I saw him? Four or five years ago, maybe?

Coop and Edie were hosting a large holiday gathering, and I had turned and bumped into Rick as I was making my way to the bar. He grabbed my arm.

"Hey you."

I smiled up at him. "Hey, Rick. How're you doing?"

"Good, Jackie. Really good. God, it's been too long. What have you been up to?"

"Same old thing," I replied. "Becca just got her driver's license, so stay off the roads for a bit, huh? How's Chrissy?" Rick had started dating his co-worker Chrissy shortly after he and I stopped seeing each other. They had been on and off for years. "Hasn't she made an honest man of you yet?"

"Nah. Once burned, you know?" He quickly flashed his mega-watt grin at me. "Maybe if you had been available."

"Oh please, just what you would have wanted. An older…"

"Sexy…"

"Middle-aged…"

"Experienced…"

"Stalker tourist," I finished triumphantly. He still wore that grin, and his eyes were twinkling at me. Time to change the subject. "Anyhoo, do you still have the cabin?"

"Yeah, more or less. We spend most of our time in the condo in Uptown. Chrissy's been after me to sell it and buy something out in Cottonwood, but I just don't see that happening, you know?" I chuckled at that as Rick looked over my shoulder. "So, how's your other half? Is he here?"

"Yeah, he and Becca ran out to get more ice. Becca wanted to drive. Oh, here they come now." I waved at my family across the patio and wondered, was it my imagination, or did Rob pause just a second when he saw me talking to Rick?

Becca headed towards the kitchen with the ice, so Rob strolled over to us alone.

"Hey, sweetheart," Robbie greeted me. "Oh, hey, Rick. How's it going?" The two men faced each other and performed some half-hearted fist bump thing as they sized each other up.

Rob was almost entirely gray, and Rick had packed on some weight, but both men were still so good looking. Rob is usually pretty chatty, but he clams up around Rick. Even after all these years, he seems awkward around him.

I chuckle, remembering how crazy I had been about Rick at one point. Crazy enough to chuck everything and move to Sedona. But I never let go of Rob, not really. It just took us a little time and a second try to get it right. I know I have a decision to make and soon. I can't even imagine my future if it doesn't include Rob.

I stretch again and try in vain to get comfortable. Tracie has been upfront with Sean all day. I wonder if there is anything going on with them. She is several years older than Sean, but I've seen her flirting with him. To be honest, we all flirt with him. He just seems to draw women in, like moths to a flame.

Geoff and Richard commandeered the back row, so that leaves Becca, Elaine, Ollie, Carrie, and me in the middle two rows, facing each other. Ollie's long, lanky form stretches out the whole length of the seat; his head is in his wife's lap. Not much of a lap, I realize. We have only been on the road for four days, but I swear that her baby bump has gotten bigger. She is leaning back in her seat with her eyes closed, absentmindedly stroking Ollie's hair and smiling. What a great mom she will make. She's already had a ton of practice with her young-at-heart husband.

Becca is curled up in the corner directly opposite me. Her back is towards me, and her slow, steady breaths lead me to believe that she, too, is sleeping. I hope that a nap will refresh her. She has been quiet and withdrawn all day and resisted my efforts to have any sort of conversation. She joined us late for breakfast this morning and only nibbled at some toast and had a few sips of tea. I tried to get her to eat.

"They could probably whip you up an egg sandwich or something sweetie," I suggested before we left the B&B. "I bet Sean wouldn't mind if you ate it in the van, just this once." She looked a bit green around the gills when she brushed me off.

"I'm not hungry. Just give it a rest, will you?"

"Hey, Becca. Your mom's just looking out for you," Ollie teased.

"Butt out, Ollie. No one asked you," Becca snarled and stomped away.

"Sorry, Ollie," I apologized with a shrug. "I have no idea what's gotten into her today."

"You don't have to explain it to me. I live with a pregnant woman, remember?" Ollie grinned and ambled out to the lobby, and, a short while later, we were off. It has been a long day in the van, and everyone is beat.

Only Elaine and I are wide-awake and chattering when Sean's voice comes over the speaker system. We will be stopping in less than five minutes. I can hardly wait to hop out and make a mad dash for the bathroom.

Becca

The pub is buzzing with a mix of locals and tourists. Another tour group arrived while I was in the bathroom, and it's standing room only around the bar. Half of the patrons are focused on their pints, but others are opting for coffee or tea and a mid-afternoon snack. Carrie is making real progress, digging into a large portion of sticky toffee pudding. Mom is sharing a pot of tea with Elaine and Tracie, and the guys are waiting their turn at the bar.

The thought of food makes me queasy, so I consider lining up for a ginger ale. To be honest, the smells of tobacco, fried food, and stale beer are causing me some serious internal distress. I see there are five or six women at the door to the ladies room. If things don't settle down soon, I'll have to make a run for the exit. My mom is looking at me with a worried look on her face. *Oh no, here we go.*

"Are you sure you don't want some tea, Bex? Or maybe a scone? You've hardly eaten all day."

"I need some air," I tell my mom. "I'll see you on the van, okay?"

"Sweetheart, is everything all right? You seem kind of..."

"I'm fine. God. Stop worrying about me, okay? I just need..." I hurry towards the door. What exactly *do* I need? Fresh air? Some peace and quiet? A nonstop flight home? Or maybe... I push the door open and walk straight into Sean.

"Hey, Becca. Where are you rushing off to?"

"I just need some air, okay?" *What is everyone's problem anyway?* What does a girl have to do to get a little me-time? I turn left out of the pub, as I am pretty certain that the van is parked down the street in the other direction.

"Hold up, Becca. You've been dodging me all day." Sean hurries after me and grabs my arm. I spin around.

"What? What do you want, Sean?"

"We have to talk, Becca. C'mon."

"There's nothing to say. I get it, okay?"

"What do you get? Will you at least listen to me?"

"I'm too young. You already have a girlfriend. You're not attracted to me. Blah, blah, blah. Whatever. It doesn't matter. I won't bother you anymore."

"It's not like that, Becca. Nomad has real strict rules about this. You're my responsibility. I could lose my job."

I relent a bit at that. "Okay. I get it, I really do. I just thought you liked me and..."

"I *do* like you. But we can't date the guests. I know guys who have, and they're gone. Just like that. Called on the carpet. Sacked. No references. I can't take that chance."

Well, when you put it that way! I shrug my shoulders and start to walk away. "It's okay. Forget about it. It won't happen again."

"I've got some vacation days, Becca," he calls after me. "When we're back in Dublin, we could..." I rush back and throw myself into Sean's arms. "Whoa there, girl. We have three more days till then. We have to be careful. But when we get back, you and Jackie are going to be sticking around, right? Where's the harm in a chap like me just happening to drop by for a friendly pint with a couple of lovely ladies visiting my fair city from the States? There's no rules against that now," he finishes with a grin.

"But can you get the time? You're not taking off again on Sunday?"

"Nah, I already called in. Said something came up. Got another guy to take my tour. I'll have a whole week off."

"You already got the time off? What made you so sure I would want to go out with you?"

Sean pulls me closer.

"I had a hunch," he murmurs.

"Something came up, huh?" I tease.

I think he's about to kiss me when, "Hey you two." *Damn*. It's Ollie. "Are we taking off any time soon? The missus needs to hit the loo again. Don't leave without us, okay?"

Sean pulls away from me, and turns to face Ollie.

"No worries, old man. You tell your wife to take all the time she needs." Sean starts off towards the van. "Wheels up in five," he calls back over his shoulder. Ollie leans in and grins at me.

"Sean is sure a great guy, huh, Becca?"

Yeah, great. Really great.

CHAPTER NINE

JACKIE

I AM ALONE in the van for the first time. My efforts to be a good sport have vanished, just like the sun! It's been pouring rain for two days straight, and I'm down to my last pair of dry shoes. I want to get to the hotel, take a long hot shower, and shove all of my footwear under the radiator.

Maybe tonight I'll see about getting room service. It's been great travelling together all week, but I am craving a little solitude. I doubt Becca will mind if I bail. She and Carrie are always together, laughing about something or other. And Sean! Yeah, Becca is spending a lot of time with our tour guide. Most times, she sits up front with him and seems to hang on his every word.

I peer out through the foggy windows. It's hard to see, but I'm pretty sure that the two tall forms I can barely make out are Becca and Sean. We're in County Kerry at Inch Beach (where *Ryan's Daughter* was filmed), but I elected to stay in the van while the others explore. The surf is pounding the shoreline, and I can just make out Carrie's squeals of delight as she and Ollie run in and out, dodging the waves.

Sean promised us a visit to a nearby café after "hitting the beach." *Great, more coffee!*

What a crappy mood I'm in. I started out okay this morning. My "full Irish" breakfast was in the very modest range: a solitary egg, a couple of sausage links, a scoop of beans, and that freakin' black pudding. *Ugh,* don't get me started. It's nasty looking, and I've yet to meet a single person who loves the hard, little hockey pucks. Not even Sean, who raves about all the amazing Irish food and the gorgeous salmon and the lovely prawns. I've never seen *him* eat the daily dose of black pudding. But the coffee was good and I had a couple of bites of Elaine's yummy currant scone as well.

So what is the reason for my funk? The weather isn't helping much. I mean no one comes to Ireland expecting perfect beach weather (although Sean swears that the country's fastest growing sport, and his personal favorite, is surfing), but "damp" is a given most of the time. Everyone on the tour is great. The accommodations have been good, and the food and music top-notch. Beautiful scenery, lots to see and do… So why am I feeling so low?

I rack my brain. Something is off, but what?

I have no idea how Sean was able to see, in order to drive today, as the rain has been coming down in sheets at times. Becca was Sean's co-pilot again this morning. After a couple of days of shifting seats after most stops, we have fallen into a bit of a pattern. Richard and Geoff almost always claim the back row, leaving Carrie, Ollie, Elaine, Tracie, and me to face each other in the center.

Maybe I am just missing Rob? He'd have gotten a bit antsy during some of the longer stints in the van, but he would have really enjoyed the music and the pubs. And everyone would enjoy his company, as well. He's such an easy guy to spend time with. Less than a week from now, he will be arriving in Dublin. I smile, picturing his face when I tell him that I'm ready to hand over the reins at Encore and take an extended trip with him. I'll show him some of the RV websites that I've been checking out. If thinking about seeing him doesn't put me in a better mood, well, I don't know what will.

BECCA

I take the small towel that Elaine offers and wipe the cool damp mist off my face. My hair is dripping, and I know it has already started to frizz. I pat the ends with the damp towel before I realize how useless it is. I pull off my soaked-through windbreaker (water-resistant my ass!) and let it fall at my feet. The inside of Bertha is like a big, wet cocoon, steamy windows and all.

We are driving inland after leaving the beach, and Ollie is playing co-pilot, trying to wipe the windshield enough for Sean to see the road. Most of my fellow Nomads are also wet, but nothing like me. And Sean.

"Becca, you're soaking wet. What were you thinking, staying out so long in this weather?" My mom's voice is full of concern and maybe a little annoyance, as well. What *was* I thinking?

Living in the desert most of my life, I have never been a big fan of the whole "walking in the rain" thing, you know? I never saw the romance in it. But today, wandering around the nearly deserted beach with Sean, I could have handled a freakin' monsoon if need be.

I have no idea what will happen when we get back to Dublin in a couple of days. I plan to see Sean, go out with him. But who knows? Maybe there won't be any real chemistry. Maybe we'll just have a drink or grab some dinner, talk a bit, and find out there's nothing there…

Yeah, I don't believe that for a minute. I am pretty certain that the sexual tension that has been building between us for the past five days will explode into something amazing. I get chills just thinking about that kiss we just shared out there on the beach.

The whole lot of us had been happy to arrive at Inch Beach an hour ago. Well, except for my mom that is. She's trying to be a good sport and all, but her last pair of dry shoes got soaked in a puddle when she was climbing into the van earlier today, and that was it. She is not up for any more wet weather. In all honesty, if it hadn't been for Sean, I might have stayed in the van, myself. But Sean said "C'mon," so I went. I would follow him just about anywhere at this point.

The other Nomads stayed pretty close together and explored the windswept beach. The surf was wild, and Ollie was carrying Carrie around, running in and out of the waves. They are so cute together, it is almost sickening. Elaine was looking for sea glass, and Tracie and Geoff were half-heartedly helping her. Richard was pacing back and forth, puffing away on a cigarette, desperate to satisfy his nicotine cravings before we boarded Bertha again.

That left Sean and me. We were casually strolling along, moving steadily out of view of the others. At one point, he almost grabbed my hand but quickly moved a few steps away. Was he being a tad over-cautious? Maybe so, although I can't really blame him. But when we passed a weather-beaten structure, probably used to rent beach umbrellas in season, he dragged me in behind him and kissed me like he did… Well, who can blame him for that, either?

So I totally gave myself up to the sheer joy of being soundly and thoroughly kissed. When he let me go, I couldn't catch my breath at first. The walls of the tiny structure seemed to close in around me, and I actually felt like I could faint, right there and then. I'm usually quite a hardy sort of girl, so being kissed into a near-fainting state was certainly new to me.

"Sean, I need…"

"Yeah, love, I need you, too," he moaned and pulled me back into his arms. He was about to start kissing me again, but I pushed him away, gasping for breath.

"No, not that. I can't breathe," I cried, and that finally got his full attention. "I need air," I added weakly. He pushed me back out onto the beach but held on, to keep me from falling.

"Take slow breaths, Becca. Nice and easy," he advised. "Yeah, that's it. Nice and slow."

I did as he ordered and quickly felt like I was safe from fainting. A bit light-headed perhaps, but I must have started to look a little better, because the look of concern on Sean's face was replaced with one of, *hmmm,* amusement? Was he smirking at me?

"Well, that's a first," he commented drily. "I don't think I've ever kissed a girl into unconsciousness. Rapture, sure. Deliriousness, always. But not full on passing out. No, that's definitely a first." I punched him in the arm, probably harder than I intended.

"I'm so glad that I could entertain you. If I had known just how much you enjoyed watching girls fainting at your feet, well, I would have tried harder. Wait, maybe I can still swoon a little more. Yeah, no. Sorry. Show's over for today." I tried to extricate myself from his strong grasp.

"At least I know I can get you weak in the knees lass," he teased before adopting a more serious tone. "But Becca, seriously. Are you okay? Can you make it to the van? We should probably be getting back there, you know?" Fun and games were over. He was once again the conscientious professional.

"Don't flatter yourself." I couldn't stay mad at him. I assured him that I was fine. He really did get me weak in the knees, and he is truly the best kisser I have ever, well, kissed. I leaned in and gave him a final quick nuzzle, before pushing him away, and we started back towards the others. The mist had turned into a fairly steady rain by this point, so, pulling our jackets up over our heads, we made a run for it.

"Did we just have our first fight?" Sean asked with a grin. I couldn't do much more than shake my head at his silliness, winded as I was, slogging through the wet sand, battered by rain and the persistent sea breeze. If the impact of this make-out session is any indication of what's to follow later this week, I had better pace myself...

So yeah, *that's* what I was thinking. I shake my head to clear away the sexy thoughts I am having, but I can't quite meet my mom's gaze.

"I'm fine, Mom. Nothing that a big dry towel and a hot cup of tea won't fix," I assure her.

Sean is listening, I realize, intent as he is on maneuvering Bertha through the increasingly foul weather.

"Coming right up, Becca," he calls out. "We'll stop up here and get you that tea right away."

Elaine and my mom exchange a smile. Is it the idea of a hot beverage that delights them? Or the fact that Sean is so eagerly doting on me? Well, I certainly am not about to ask them. I have two more days to go before we go public.

After a quick stop, we climb back into Bertha for the last leg of our journey for the day. Despite my preoccupation with the man sitting just a few feet away from me, I am totally enthralled with the amazing sights that greet us as we head towards the Dingle Peninsula. The Conor Pass is just spectacular, and, according to Sean, it's the highest mountain pass in Ireland. After countless miles of rolling patchwork hills, we begin to spot the coastal town of Dingle and smell the tang of heavily salted air.

"Perhaps we'll get a warm welcome from Fungie the dolphin," Sean predicts. But there is no sign of the city's official mascot as we drive past the harbor and through town. The sun starts to peek through the heavy cloud cover as we arrive in Dingle, our home base for the next two days.

CHAPTER TEN

JACKIE

BECCA LEFT THE ROOM a short while ago, after telling me she would catch up with me later, and Elaine begged off with a headache, so I slip on a pair of still-wet running shoes and take off on foot, intent on purchasing at least one pair of shoes, if not more. Fashion be damned, I am looking for sturdy and waterproof footwear, and I have the rest of the afternoon to accomplish my goal. I turn right out of the door, heading towards a couple of shops that look promising, when I hear my name being called. I turn back and see Carrie rushing towards me.

"I'm just off to look for some shoes," I tell her. She smiles and shows me the credit card she is holding in her hand.

"I love to shop," she assures me. "Do you mind if I come with? Maybe we'll find Edie's teapot."

What could I say? I was actually looking forward to a little alone time, but why not?

"Sure. C'mon along then."

Together, we set off. By the time we reach the first shop, she admits that I was *not* her first choice for company this afternoon.

"Ollie's lying down. Says he needs a nap, that big baby. I looked all over for Becca but couldn't find her anywhere. I thought of Tracie, but, *ugh,* she's a little too high-end for me. I'd be digging through the clearance racks, and she'd be all... Oh wait, I mean, I'm glad to have caught up with you, Jackie," she adds quickly. I assure her that no offense was taken and make my way over to investigate the rather limited shoe selection. With a wave, Carrie goes to check out the sales in the back of the store. I find a couple of possibilities, but when I tell the salesclerk my size, she shakes her head.

"No miss, sorry. We're almost sold out on those. We only have a few pairs in, *em*, smaller sizes.

"What do you carry for those of us requiring larger sizes then?" I ask, and soon I'm trying on a selection of large, totally unattractive shoes. But they are dry, and if I want to enjoy the rest of the tour, I need to buy something. I pick the two pairs that are the least hideous and pay with my credit card, just as Carrie wanders over.

"So, what did you find? You got some shoes, heh?" She insists on seeing them, so I dig them out of my bag and show them to her.

Crestfallen, she remarks, "Well, at least they'll keep your feet dry."

I laugh at that and assure her that I am quite satisfied with my purchases.

"Well, c'mon back here with me, Jackie. I want to get your opinion on something." So I follow her to the back of the store, and we spend most of the next half hour debating the merits of a pair of tea towels for her mother-in-law, a variety of T-shirts for her brother and dad, and a pretty china mug with a floral design for her mom. No sign of anything even remotely resembling Edie's teapot. Carrie wears me out, racing from one display to the next, holding up T-shirts to compare sizes and keeping up a steady stream of chatter the whole time.

"Do you always have this much energy?" I ask with a smile when she takes a breath.

"Who me? Oh yeah, keep moving, right? Lots to see, lots to do." She's about to say more when she suddenly crouches down, holding her stomach and moaning. I panic but help her to a nearby bench and squat down next to her.

"Carrie? Honey, are you okay? Tell me what's wrong," I ask as calmly as I can. I hold her small, clammy hands in mine and advise her to control her breathing, which is coming in short, ragged bursts. She's unnaturally pale and despite the blasting air conditioning, her forehead is dotted with sweat. I let go of her hands long enough to reach into my pocket for a tissue and use it to pat her face dry. Her eyes are closed, but she attempts to smile and lets out a sigh. Her breathing slows down, and I take it as an opportunity to get help.

"Carrie. I'm going to go up front. We need to get you looked at."

Her eyes open wide as she grasps my hands again. "Don't leave me, Jackie. Please," she begs.

I brush her bangs off her forehead and look at her closely. The eyes looking back at me are wide and frightened. This girl has to see a doctor, of that I am certain. I tell her I will be back in a flash and rush towards the front, looking for the young woman who had just rung me up.

"Miss, miss. We need help back here. You need to call 911, *um,* an ambulance. My friend almost fainted. And she's pregnant," I add.

That does the trick. She picks up the phone, and within minutes, the EMTs arrive. I hover over Carrie while we wait and use her phone to call Ollie. The EMTs have her lying on a stretcher and are checking her pulse and other vital signs when he bursts in.

"Carrie. Care-Bear. What happened? Are you okay?" The poor guy is completely beside himself. I pull him aside as soon as Carrie gives him a weak thumbs up. "Jackie, what the hell? Is she gonna make it? And the baby?"

Wow, what do I know?

"Ollie, Carrie's gonna be fine," I assure him, and I really want to believe me. "She got a little dizzy is all. Has she been drinking enough water? They're just checking her over, but you'll see. She'll be okay. Has anything like this happened at home?"

"No, never. Christ, her mom was right. I should have listened to her. She told us we were crazy to take a trip right now. Crap, I will never hear the end of this," he moans. "I just wanted one last hurrah, you know? I thought Carrie would be fine. She's always been healthy as a horse. I just wanted us to, you know… Before the baby comes, take a trip and make some memories, just the two of us." He starts pacing nervously. I want to calm him down, since Carrie can see him from where she lies on the stretcher. She needs to focus on herself and not be worrying about her husband.

"Ollie, listen to me. Sit down next to me, okay? Carrie can see you. She'll know you're worried, and that's not going to help the situation any. Pretend I just said something funny. Laugh," I command.

Ollie must be used to taking orders. He looks confused but throws his head back and lets out a kind of strangled laugh.

"Good," I assure him. "Now smile. Think of something nice. Something you love about Carrie."

He must pick something really good, because he's grinning ear to ear when one of the EMTs approaches him. The two of them move out of earshot, and suddenly Ollie is smiling for real this time and shaking the guy's hand, so the news must be good. When Ollie gives me a big thumbs up, I let go of the breath I didn't even realize I was holding.

I wave to Ollie and blow a kiss to Carrie as I prepare to leave and go back to find Becca. My work here is done.

Becca

"It's nothing. Just something I have to do, okay? I'll catch up with you after a bit. Maybe I'll even break my own rule and eat dinner with you lot." Sean seems impatient to take off after he and I spend an hour together strolling around town.

"Wow, what parallel universe have we entered? The day that Sean Donovan actually deigns to break bread with us common Nomads? Forget pigs flying or hell freezing over. This is bigger…"

"Okay, that's enough out of you, lassie." He leans towards me, after looking around. The coast is clear. He pulls me in his arms, and his muscular chest crushes against me. A light kiss quickly escalates into something more, and, seconds later, he pulls away from me, groaning. "Jaysus, what you do to me, Becca." He shakes his head in mock despair. "What is it about you American tourists?"

Oh yeah?

"You guessed it, Paulie Boy. Us 'tourists' come all the way to Ireland just to have our way with you ginger-haired, freckle-faced lads. And now you're onto us." I giggle.

Sean starts to walk away but turns suddenly.

"I'll see you after a bit, okay? Save me a seat," he adds with a wink. I watch him hustle down the street from the doorway where we huddled. He certainly is in a hurry. He has been in a kind of antsy mood all day, and I wonder where he is rushing off to. But I'm not a clingy sort of girl. If he has something to do, well, then that's fine. I have plenty of things to keep me busy.

An hour later, I have investigated many of the quaint shops on the main street that runs through Dingle, which is as picturesque and lovely as Sean and all of the tour books promised. There is still no sign of Edie's teapot. I begin to wonder if it will ever be found. I head out towards the harbor and watch the colorful sailboats dancing over the waves for a while. What would it be like to get on one of those boats with Sean and just sail away? I see signs advertising a new sports center opening soon. There's mention of surf lessons in Brandon Bay, and I wonder if that is where Sean likes to go surfing. There are so many things I want to know, so many questions I want to ask him.

I decide to grab a coffee and enjoy the last of the late-afternoon sunshine. I spotted a café on the corner directly across the street from where we checked in, a couple hours earlier, so I head over there. I order my latte and, while I wait for it, watch Tracie ambling along towards me. She sees me, and, when I wave, she crosses the street. It's funny how, after hours together crammed in the van, we all still choose to seek each other out.

Tracie is flushed and seems really excited as she greets me with an uncharacteristic hug.

"Hey, Becca. How're you doing?"

You mean since I saw you an hour ago?

"Good, Tracie. Really good. I ordered a latte. Want to join me?"

She scrunches up her face as she considers her response.

"What do you think the odds are that they can slip a little something in mine? It's five o'clock somewhere, right? I'll go check it out." She strides up to the counter to place her order. My name is called, so I retrieve my drink and find us a sunny table. I plop down into the chair and groan in relief. We have been walking and hiking all day, and my feet are killing me. *Can I slip off my hikers here, or should I wait till I'm back in the room?*

Tracie comes bopping over to me. *Her* feet seem to be working just fine.

"They're making me a *special* latte," she admits with a wicked grin then leans towards me. "So, it looks like our boy Sean has made another conquest," she teases. *Oh crap*. I thought we had been doing such a good job keeping our budding relationship under wraps.

Is it time to come clean? Just what does she actually know? I'm trying to decide if I should admit that I have actual feelings for Sean when she continues on. "But from what I can tell, looks like the feelings might be one-sided." *Huh?* "Oh, terrific. Thank you sooo much," she drawls as a large, steaming drink is placed in front of her. I can smell the whiskey or whatever has been liberally added to it from across the table. "You're an angel," she trills, pressing a ten-euro note into the server's hand. Tracie takes a large sip and smiles happily. "Wow, that's just what the doctor ordered. Anyway, where were we?" She smiles expectantly at me.

I am hesitant to hear what she has to say about Sean and me, but I figure I might as well get it over with. Nothing has really happened between us. At least, not yet. Just some serious kissing and a couple of quick butt grabs. Oh yeah, and a few X-rated comments about what might conceivably take place between us when the tour ends. But still. I clear my throat. Just get it over with.

"Well, with Sean, it's really just…"

"Just nothing, Becca. I knew that guy was a player. I pegged him right from the start. Guys like him, seem to get a real charge of roping in some unsuspecting girl, and then, when they get what they want, finito." She mimes wiping her hands. "Poor kid. She probably never saw it coming."

What the fuck is this chick talking about? I have to know.

"What do you mean? What girl?"

Tracie leans forward again. In a conspiratorial tone, she continues. "I was walking down by the docks a little while ago. I am so sick of shopping. I never in a million years thought that I would ever say those words. I swear to you, if I have to step foot in one more of those little lace shops, I will scream. How many freaking doilies does anyone really need, anyway?" At my impatient expression, she gets back on track. "Anyway, I am walking along, minding my own business, and who do I see but our trusty tour guide, snogging some girl on a bench. Holier than thou Sean Donovan, getting busy with some little chickie right in broad daylight."

My heart sinks, and I think I might lose my lunch. I have no claim on Sean. I get that. But to be kissing me and, minutes later, kissing some Dingle girl? That just doesn't seem like Sean. Not the Sean I know. *Oh, just what the fuck do I really know?* But maybe Tracie saw a guy who just *looked* like Sean. That has to be it.

"Are you sure it was Sean? I mean lots of guys around here are tall and look like him." And are gorgeous with flirty green eyes and a muscular build. And very kissable lips.

"Oh, it was him all right," Tracie tells me confidently. "Yeah, our Sean sure gets around." She chuckles. "And here I thought *you* were going to be his next conquest, Becca."

Oh crap. I sip the dregs of my latte and take an extra few seconds to collect myself.

"Oh, like that would ever happen," I tell her coolly. "Just what I need in my life right now, a fling with an Irish van driver. I'm heading off to grad school when we get back to the States. I have a life, you know. A holiday hookup? Ain't nobody got time for that." I conclude with swagger. My hands are shaking, but I have pulled it off. Maybe.

"I'm not saying you *should* get involved with him, Becca. But he's single, and so are you. And Christ, he's hot. You don't have to marry him, you goose. But just a little fun? Where's the harm in that?" she asks innocently.

Well, okay. I've had just about enough of this conversation. I hop up and leave a couple of euros next to my empty cup.

"Hey, Tracie, this has been great. Really. But I promised my mom that I would help with her, *um*, packing. You know, how to fit all she's been buying in her suitcase." Yeah, that's it. "So, hey, I'll see you at dinner then." I give a quick wave and rush out of the café.

Tears are already streaming down my face as I race across the street and pull open the door leading into the lobby. *Ack*! Three Nomads are playing cribbage over in the corner. Knowing I am just seconds away from a total meltdown, I scurry through the lobby, ignoring Elaine, Richard, and Geoff.

I take the back stairs two at a time and burst into the room I share with my mom. There is no sign of her, and I'm glad of the reprieve. I'm not quite ready to talk about Sean's betrayal. I haven't told my mom about my plans to spend time with off-duty Sean when we get back to Dublin.

Hah! As if! I don't need to get involved with someone like him. Maybe Mom and I can head up to Belfast a few days early. I wouldn't want to run into Sean and his parade of girlfriends in Dublin. This is getting awfully fucking complicated awfully fast.

I stretch out on my bed and pull the blanket over me. I keep seeing Sean leaning in to kiss me, and then I picture him kissing some nameless, faceless local girl, then another. *Grrrrr*. I have never been particularly jealous, but… Oh, who am I kidding? I'm jealous all right. I pound the pillow in frustration and let the tears come.

CHAPTER ELEVEN

JACKIE

THINGS HAVE GOTTEN awfully weird in the last twenty-four hours, as if the drama with Carrie and the close call yesterday wasn't upsetting enough. After the EMTs diagnosed her as dehydrated but fit to be released from their care, Ollie carried his wife in his arms and got her settled in for the night. He made her some tea and, as soon as the pub next door started serving dinner, raced over to place an order. A short while later, he breezed through the lobby, carrying a huge tray loaded with food and several bottles of water, and made his way back to his wife.

"Don't save a place for me tonight," he called out to me and Elaine. "I'm staying in with Carrie." I wouldn't have expected anything less from him.

When Elaine and I walked over to the pub a little bit later, only Geoff and Richard were waiting for us. We grabbed a table for six, figuring Tracie and Becca would join us shortly, but, after waiting for a half hour, we gave up and ordered. I finally texted Becca, but all I got was a quick TTYL in response. No one was really in a talkative mood. I pushed my food around the plate and finally gave up.

When I got back to our room, Becca was in bed and appeared to be sleeping. I slipped into the bathroom and pulled on a nightshirt after brushing my teeth. Makeup removal could wait, I decided, so I crawled into bed and, for once, fell asleep rather quickly.

This morning, I feel well rested but kind of uneasy. I have this prickly sense of dread. *What is happening?*

Maybe it's a good thing that we will be back in Dublin tomorrow. I mean take nine strangers and throw them in a van named Bertha, drive them all over the country for days on end and fill them full of caffeine and alcohol. It's potentially a recipe for disaster. Only Elaine and I seem to be immune. The old broads. Tracie seems unnaturally hostile this morning. She's always a bit edgy, if you ask me, but today she seems particularly bitchy. She snapped at our waiter and sent back her breakfast after deciding her eggs were overcooked. Then she complained the coffee wasn't hot enough after pouring half the pitcher of cream into her cup. Everyone seemed relieved when she finally threw her napkin down and left the dining room.

Becca has been so withdrawn today. Last night, she skipped dinner, and this morning, she grabbed a coffee and sat outside drinking it instead of joining us for breakfast. I've asked her what is wrong a couple of times, but whatever it is, she's not talking. Not to me. Not to anyone, and that includes Sean, who has been wandering around with a dazed look on his face. He's been completely out of sorts and actually got us lost on our way out of town this morning.

To make matters worse, Richard and Geoff have been sniping at each other all day. It began innocently enough this morning at breakfast, when a fresh-faced young waiter flirted just a bit with Geoff, who flirted right back. Well, Richard took great offense at this.

"Right under my nose," he kept hissing at Geoff. "Right under my very nose."

Geoff was nonplussed, giving me the feeling that this scene had already been played out more than a few times back home. Geoff is extremely good looking and can grab attention whenever he feels like it. He tends to get uber-flamboyant at times, if you know what I mean. Richard is many years older than his young and sexy mate and rather drab, not the type that *anyone* would flirt with, gay or straight.

"You're overreacting Richard. Nothing was going on," Geoff insisted with a shrug of his shoulders. The calmer he remained, the more annoyed Richard became. So those two had been at it on and off all day, witnessed by their fellow Nomads. It is getting kind of old.

There's trouble in paradise with our other married couple, as well. They have been arguing a lot, and it's really hard to ignore. Carrie blames her growing baby bump for thwarting her goal of a solid ten hours of sleep each night. Her constant tossing and turning is preventing her hubby from getting much sleep either, even in his separate twin bed. Ollie is probably drinking more on this trip than he does at home and is frequently hung over in the morning.

Watching them fight is like witnessing two kittens going at it. Neither is particularly mean or vicious, so they just kept taking ineffectual jabs at each other. And, according to Ollie, there isn't even a chance for makeup sex. I hope for both their sakes that Carrie will relax the no-sex rule and soon. Just ten minutes ago, they were arguing again. Carrie wanted her husband to help her pick out the perfect Irish souvenir for her sister back home. The normally agreeable Ollie refused. I would have thought that, after yesterday's health scare, he'd be falling all over himself, doing whatever it takes to please her. But that was then and this is now, and now they are hissing and snapping at each other. Most of the time, the disagreements between the two couples seem to come to a head at meals or during our frequent stops. While riding in the van, it's mainly a strained silence and awkward gaps in the conversation. And we were getting along really well up until this point.

Watching the two couples makes me miss my husband. Aside from our current conflict about how to spend the rest of our lives, Rob and I are usually not much for arguing. We fight, sure. Every once in a while, we have a total blow out, complete with yelling (mostly him) and tears (mostly me). Afterwards, we can rarely remember what caused the disagreement in the first place. Usually it is something small, like the cap on the toothpaste tube or running out of coffee filters. It doesn't really matter what lights the fuse. It is just that something throws one of us off kilter, and, rather than ignore it or give the other person the benefit of the doubt, the fight begins. A good fight every so often is healthy. It clears the air.

Meanwhile, the rest of us tiptoe around, and even Sean seems to be at a loss for words. He tries to tell us a story about leprechauns this morning, but I don't think any of us are really in the mood. Poor guy, he's just trying to keep us entertained, but after his opener, about how the leprechaun is the most widely known type of fairy in Ireland, gets only a snicker from Geoff, he plods on. According to Sean, leprechauns often appear to humans as old men.

Another snicker from Geoff, who pokes his partner in the ribs and affectionately calls him, "My old man."

Silence. Wow, we're a tough crowd. Yesterday, Sean could have read from the phone directory and we would have been thrilled, but that was then and this is now. Time to step up, I decide.

"What's the connection with leprechauns and gold?" I ask with interest. Sean glances back at me and smiles gratefully.

"Good question, Jackie. Legend holds that the wee ones love to collect gold, which they store in a pot and hide at the end of a rainbow. And if a human is lucky enough to catch a leprechaun, they must be granted three wishes."

"Maybe that's where Edie's frigging teapot is, huh, Jackie?" Tracie drawls. "Have you looked at the end of a rainbow yet?"

Way to kill the mood, Tracie. I glare at her, and she rolls her eyes. Sean shuts down again, and Bertha's occupants are silent once more. The tension is so thick at times, you can cut it with a knife. I know all the arguing really bothers Elaine. After all, she was in a tumultuous relationship with her husband for decades. It is probably dredging up some painful memories.

Late afternoon, when we meet up in the lobby, she opens up a bit after I ask her how she is doing.

"You've been so quiet, Elaine. Is everything okay?"

She smiles at me, but it is a sad sort of smile and doesn't quite reach her eyes.

"Oh me? I'm okay, I guess. I just, *um*, well, I just hate this, don't you Jackie? All the arguing?"

I have to agree with her.

"I know what you mean. It really gets on my nerves after a while. I want to say to them, 'Just stop. Let these petty differences go. You love each other. That's what matters.'" I really want to say that both couples could probably benefit from a little time together between the sheets. Trust me, I speak from experience. But there is something so buttoned up about Elaine, such a prim and proper vibe, I usually refrain from speaking frankly around her.

So I'm shocked when she leans over to me and whispers in my ear, "I think they could all stand to get laid, don't you?" She sits back with a twinkle in her eye.

Well, I'll be.

"I think you're right, Elaine. We probably all could." That sets us both off, and we laugh together as Sean comes over.

"What are you two laughing about, and can you spread some of this good cheer around, do ya think?" He has a puzzled look on his face. "Most groups get this way at some point," he admits. "But you lot, well, you seemed different. I thought that you'd be immune to it."

"Well, that shows what you know, Sean Donovan," Tracie calls out as she joins us. I hadn't seen her, but if she heard Sean's last comment, she must have been close by. I hope she didn't hear me and Elaine gossiping about our fellow traveler's sex lives. "Maybe you should take a look in the mirror, before you start judging anyone else."

Wow, where had that come from? Sean looks surprised, but, ever the professional, he refuses to take the bait.

"Hey now, Tracie. I've never meant to imply that I have all the answers, okay? I'm just saying that this is a really great group and everyone's been getting along so well. It's just a shame."

Suddenly Becca is in the middle of our rapidly growing circle.

"Yeah, just a shame, huh, Sean? It's a shame you've got all of us pesky tourists to deal with. Wouldn't it be 'just grand' to walk away from it all?" she says, mocking him.

What the hell has gotten into everyone? First Tracie, then Becca? Why are they so pissed at Sean? Becca's outburst seems to shake him out of his rather dazed and confused state.

"Well now, ladies. At long last we hear from the college girl. The expert on relationships, *huh*, Rebecca? Is there a psychiatric term you learned in your studies to describe all this? Well, is there?" he goads her.

Becca is furious. I have never seen this side of her before. Her eyes are like lasers and her tone is pure ice, as she stands toe to toe with Sean.

"First off, it's psychology, not psychiatry, you dumbass. And as far as all 'this' goes, yeah, the term? It's bullshit. Just like everything that comes out of your mouth. Bullshit. Go to hell," she lashes out and races off.

WTF? Becca is taking all this way too personally. I watch in amazement as Sean rushes out of the lobby after her. And why is Tracie standing there, suddenly grinning like a fool?

"I knew it," she exclaims triumphantly. When no one responds to her attempt at a high five, she turns it into a fist pump. "I called it, Jackie. Sean and Becca, that's the missing piece of the puzzle."

I can't believe what I am hearing. "Tracie, no. I think you've got it all wrong," I protest feebly. Buy why else would Becca be so angry? Was it a lover's quarrel after all?

"Trust me," Tracie continues gleefully. "I have a sixth sense when it come to this sort of thing. It's like radar. I've been feeling it for days. Maybe his other girl back in Dingle found out. Maybe that's what she was crying about?"

I can feel a tension headache coming on.

"Who was crying? Was it Becca?" If that little bastard hurts my daughter, I will be all over him. There would be no tip for him, I promise myself.

"No, Jackie. It was some little Dingle chickie. But I think Mr. Charm may have overextended himself just a bit this week. He's travelling the country, leaving a trail of broken hearts along the way. And his latest victim? It's Becca!" she exclaims triumphantly.

I want to slap her smug face or pull that orange scarf she is wearing around her neck so tight, her eyes will bug right out of her head.

"You should mind your own business, Tracie. It's none of your concern, anyway." I end with a mumbled "bitch" in her general direction and, after patting the arm of a shell-shocked Elaine, stride purposefully out of the lobby and head up the stairs to our room. I let myself in and collapse on the nearest twin bed.

Images of Becca and Sean swirl in my head. *Could they have…?* No, no way. She and I have been sharing a room all week and practically joined at the hip, when we weren't riding around in the van. But those two had gotten to be thick as thieves over the last few days. Until last night. *What happened last night?*

I sit up on the bed. I need to talk to my daughter and find out just what is going on. It is probably some silly misunderstanding. But Becca is really angry with Sean. And who is this girl that Sean made cry? Oh crap, time to call in the big guns.

I dig out my phone and, after punching in the wrong country code three times, finally place my call to Robbie. My voice of reason. He answers on the second ring.

"Hey babe. I was hoping you would call." At the sound of his voice, I lose it. I burst into tears.

Becca

"Becca, what the fuck? Talk to me. What did I do?" I am moving pretty quickly, but, as his legs are even longer than mine, he is right behind me by the time I make it to the corner. "Yesterday, everything seemed so great. We were gonna meet up, grab some dinner. What the hell happened?" I turn to face him so fast, he would have knocked me down, if I were a tiny bit of a thing. Well, I'm not.

"What did you do? Are you serious right now? What did you do, Sean? Really? Is that how you're gonna play this? Oh, look at me. I'm poor Sean, no one understands me." I am done. I turn and start to storm away, but he grabs my arm to stop me. "Ow, you're hurting me. First you cheat, and then you get all up in my face? Bugger off, you lousy fucker. I never want to see you again." I wriggle away from him, which is actually pretty easy as he's just standing there with this stupid look on his face, his arms slack at his sides. *Oh, give me a break.* "Well, what do you have to say for yourself?"

Sean looks really confused, as he tries to collect his thoughts.

"Cheat? Cheat on you? Becca, what the fuck? I haven't even looked at another girl since I laid eyes on you six days ago. Where did you…?"

"That girl in the alley yesterday. She was crying, and you were making out with her. Is that how you get off then? Get 'em all teary-eyed and then jump their bones? Classy, Donovan. Really classy."

Sean turns away from me, and, for a second, I think he is crying. His shoulders are shaking, and the sound coming out of him is like muffled… *laughter*? He is laughing at me! I really have had enough of this guy.

"You're an even bigger jerk than I thought. What the hell is wrong with you?" Now I am really pissed. "Stop fucking laughing at me, you asshole."

Once again I turn to go and am about to cross the street when I hear him.

He's not laughing anymore, and he sounds sad. "Becca, that was Fiona. My little sister. That was Fi that you saw crying."

What?

"You never said anything about a sister, Sean *Paul*. Christ, I've heard all about Declan *John* and Liam *George*. Are you sure her name's not *Ringo*?" He shakes his head, and a grin once again stretches across his face.

"No, it's Fiona. Fiona Rose. My mum actually had a say in it, seeing as how me da got to name us lot." He shakes his head. "Poor girl, growing up in that house after Mum passed. All us guys and little Fi." I am still confused.

"But how come you never mentioned her, Sean? Does she live here in Dingle? And why was she crying anyway?"

"That's quite a story, lass. Maybe we can get some liquid refreshments and I can tell you. I'll tell you everything."

I am game, so he takes my arm and leads me down the road to the nearest pub, finds us an empty booth, and goes to fetch a couple of drinks. I text my mom as I know she will worry.

Be back soon. Taking a walk.

By the time he returns, he's already downed almost half of his beer. Christ, this must be some story. He plunks our mugs down and slides into the booth across from me. He looks nervous, and I reach across and place a hand over his to slow the nervous drumming of his fingers.

"It's okay, Sean," I say in a half-whisper. "You can tell me anything."

He smiles at that and, after a small sip of his beer, starts to talk.

"You have to understand, Becca. Before I tell you, you have to know this, okay? Me da, Billy, he's a good man. He tries to be, at least. This whole thing is killing him, you know?" I don't, but I nod as if I do, just so that he will continue. I have no idea what he is talking about. "And the Irish? Well, we're still old-fashioned, and certain things just don't sit well with us." The suspense is killing me.

"Tell me what you're talking about. What happened to Fi?"

His eyes fill with tears, and he grabs both my hands and holds them in his.

"She got knocked up. Only seventeen and keeping time with this fecker from the neighborhood. A real jerk. We tried to warn her about him, but she wouldn't listen. Dec even went over to this guy's flat. Told him straight out to leave Fi alone. Threatened to kick his ass. He's way too old for Fi. He's twenty, went to school with Liam. They even hung together for a while, till Li realized what a punk he is. But this arsehole, Brian," he virtually spits out his name like it is physically causing him pain, "he remembered our little sister. Little Fi."

"About a year after he stopped comin' around, he met up with Fi. She was walking home with a few of her mates, and, suddenly, there was Brian. Plenty of cash to spend, had a car and knew all the right moves. So, they start spending time together. A lot of time. No one really was watching, at first. Billy never knew what to do with a daughter, you know? When Dec was fifteen, he gave him a box of rubbers. 'Use these. Suit up, Dec. Don't be bringin' home any little tossers.' A couple years later, he did the same for me, and then Li. But with Fiona, he didn't know what to do. So he did nothing. Li tried to help, told her what a fecker Brian is, begged her to stay away from him. Dec and I couldn't do too much. I was on the road with the tours, and Dec, well, he was nearly eleven when Fi was born. They've never been close. He threatened to beat up the bastard. That was about it."

He wipes his eyes with a bar napkin, then takes another sip of his beer.

"So Fi gets pregnant. She's scared. Scared that Brian will leave her, that our da will kill her or kill Brian. Doesn't want to disappoint her family. So she hides it as long as she can. Doesn't even go to a doctor. She was so ashamed. Finally, Li caught on. Heard her being sick in the loo. He asked her point blank, and she told him. She begged him not to tell anyone, especially Dec or Billy. He convinced her to come clean with Brian. Give him a chance to be a man. To stand up." At my blank look, he adds, "To marry her."

Oh my God, that poor, scared girl. I have to speak up.

"But Sean, why would you want such a loser to marry your sister? He sounds horrible. I don't get it."

It's Sean's turn to give me a blank look.

"Why? Are you serious? We're not some posh family, Becca. None of us got to go to *university*, okay? Single girls from working-class families are a dime a dozen." At my look of horror, he recants. "Okay, not really, but all I'm saying is that guys in my neighborhood? They won't even consider marrying some girl who's got a baby. Unless it's theirs, of course. But not some other bloke's. No way."

I ponder this for a minute. There is a lot more than an ocean separating our two countries, it seems.

"And abortion?" I venture meekly.

Sean just shakes his head at that.

"No way. They're near impossible to get here, and me da would kill her if she did that."

Christ, what a hypocritical son of a bitch that Billy Donovan must be.

"So, tossing your daughter out on the street, that's okay. But allowing her to make a decision about her own body? Standing up and supporting her? That's horrible, Sean. Surely you see that."

Sean smiles for probably the first time all day. It's not much of a smile, kind of sad, but still.

"Tell me how you really feel, Becca. C'mon. Don't hold back."

I'm confused again.

"Where's the baby? Did she already have it?"

Sean shakes his head sadly.

"She lost the baby. I guess she was about five months gone. Doctor says she'll be fine and no reason to think that the next one won't be okay. But she's taking it pretty hard, you know? Cries a lot. Poor kid."

Now I am *really* confused.

"So, if she's not pregnant, what's the problem? Why can't she go back to Dublin?"

Sean shakes his head again. "You don't understand. A guy like Billy? He wouldn't be able to show his face at the pub. He's...."

Now I'm furious again.

"He's more concerned with his stupid pride than taking care of his only daughter? God, that sucks. I can't believe you're okay with that."

Sean's eyes are like steel and cut right through me.

"I'm not *okay*, Rebecca. I hate that my little sister's not welcome at my father's house. But I see her every time I come to Dingle. Every couple of weeks. I got her a job at one of the B&Bs that Nomad sometime uses. She's a chambermaid, changing dirty sheets and cleaning up other people's shite. They let her stay there even. She shares a small room with a girl who works in the kitchen. The pay's not much, but I slip her some cash whenever I can. Enough to buy a latte or a pack of smokes. Maybe a new dress or whatever."

Okay, well at least he's not a total dick.

"What about Declan? And Liam? What's their story? How are they handling 'the situation'?" I ask, using air quotes.

Sean looks at his empty beer mug for a couple of seconds before he answers me.

"They're, well, they're with Billy on this. Dec is so mad at her, he can't even say her name. He tried to talk some sense into Brian, like I said, and Liam's got nothing to do with him anymore, either. But neither of them is very happy about the whole thing."

"Well, it sounds like poor Fiona isn't all that happy, either, Sean. I can't believe that her own family can't find it in their hearts to support her. It's just so sad."

"So, you're an only child, right?" At my nod, he says, "Sometimes, relationships in a family don't make much sense to someone on the outside looking in." Sensing I am about to explode, he hurries on. "Yeah, I get it. It's fucked, okay? I've tried talking to me da. I let him know how she's doing. I think he's maybe starting to come around."

I shake my head in disbelief.

"There is nothing in the world that I could ever do to cause my dad to stop talking to me. To totally shut me out. My mom, either," I say confidently. The sun will come up tomorrow, Sylvester Stallone will make yet another Rocky movie, and my parents will always love me. Not a doubt in my mind.

"Wow, lucky you," Sean fires back bitterly. "Unconditional love, huh? I've heard of it. Never experienced it myself. At least not any more. Mum was... Well, let's just say things would be different if she were still with us."

He looks lost, and I feel badly about our fight. He's probably doing the best he can under difficult circumstances. I slip over to his side of the booth.

"Hey, you. C'mere," I whisper and pull him into my arms. "Maybe you're not such a bad sort after all." He remains stiff and doesn't make it very easy for me to comfort him. I pat his back awkwardly. Poor guy.

Finally, he relents and hugs me back. We stay like that for a while, just holding each other, not speaking and doing our best to ignore the other patrons. A few of them suggest, "Get a room, would ya?"

Finally, I pull away just enough to plant a kiss on him. Smack dab on the lips. It is heaven, I tell you. Nothing short of magical. I could seriously get real used to kissing those lips. After some more kissing, we walk back to the inn, hand in hand. He tells me that he will join us for dinner tonight. Our last night together as tour guide and tourist.

I just about fly up the stairs to get ready. I am falling for this guy. I know I am.

CHAPTER TWELVE

JACKIE

SO, IT'S OUR LAST day in good old Bertha. We are heading back to Dublin, and whatever dark cloud was hanging over us yesterday seems to have magically lifted. Everyone seems happier, lighter somehow.

Carrie and Ollie are holding hands and grinning when they walk into the dining room this morning. I have no clue if either of them got any sleep or if they had sex, but the tension between them is gone. Ollie's back to waiting hand and foot on his "Care-Bear," and Carrie is positively glowing. Richard and Geoff seem to be in good spirits, too, and Richard is not sniping this morning. Geoff sat with his arm around his husband throughout the meal, and the older waitress who took care of our table didn't flirt with either of them. Tracie is her usual aloof self, but I witness her smile at Ollie's antics a couple of times; she seems to have ceased all of her signature smirking and eye-rolling.

Elaine and I beam at each other as we watch our little group in such good spirits. It is going to be a great last day! And, most important to me, whatever was bugging Becca seems to have vanished. Last night, she swore that the altercation I had witnessed was nothing more than a simple misunderstanding and then clammed up on the subject. She attacks her full Irish breakfast with gusto this morning and beams at Sean when he comes striding into the room.

He joins us for a final cup of coffee before heading out to "check on a few things." Soon after, Becca and I go back up to our room. We've been here for two nights, and I've grown rather fond of the shabby furnishings and friendly staff.

She bustles around our room, packing all of her clothes and makeup, reminding me in a joking manner to check the hook on the back of the bathroom door. I have lost more lingerie, robes, and swimsuits over the years than I care to recall.

"Sleep well?" I ask lightly. God, I love this girl. I hated to see her down in the dumps.

"Yeah, really well." She grins at me. "So, we need to talk, okay?"

"What's up, Bex?" She has suddenly turned very serious.

"It's Sean. You know, Sean Donovan?"

What is up? "Yes, Rebecca, I certainly *do* know Sean Donovan. What's this about?"

"I really like him. A lot. And he likes me, too."

"You mean *like* like?" Is he really the player that Tracie made him out to be? Who was that girl she saw him with and why was she crying?

"Yes, Mom. Like that. He wants, I mean *we* want to spend some time together. You know? When we get back to Dublin."

"Well, Becca, what about…?"

"I know what you're going to say. There's no conflict, because I won't be a Nomad anymore after today."

"But Becca..."

"I know. He's older than me. Five years, okay? But seriously? You've been telling me forever just how mature I am. I heard you tell Aunt Edie that I was an 'old soul,' whatever that means. And you know that most guys my age just want to party, right? That's not for me."

"No, but Bec—"

"And you know you can trust him, right? I mean we've been together just about 24/7 for a whole week. He's responsible. He won't—"

"Rebecca, listen to me. Let me speak, okay? Any fool can see that you and Sean are attracted to each other. Everyone knows that you two are going to end up going on a date or whatever. What I've been trying to ask you about is our plan to head north. To Belfast. Will spending time with Sean change that?"

Becca looks surprised, her brows knit in confusion.

"What, you mean all of you knew that we were talking, me and Sean? I didn't think..."

"Oh, sweetheart, trust me on this. Everyone knows. That lover's quarrel yesterday left us wondering if you two would have a chance to fix things. And I guess you did." I smile broadly. I may have been slow to see the developing attraction between them, but it all makes sense to me now, and, for the most part, I'm pretty much okay with it.

Becca jumps in to clarify her position. She should have been on a debate team.

"It wasn't exactly a quarrel. More of a misunderstanding. You see, Tracie saw Sean with another girl. And she told me. She was all, 'That guy is a player, can't trust him,' and I was like, 'Yeah, well, whatever. Not my business.' And she was like, 'Well, don't say I didn't warn you.' But Sean told me it was his little sister. Fiona Rose. Isn't that sooo pretty? She lives here in Dingle, Mom. He wants me to meet her, if we get to come back here, *um*, next week," she finishes weakly.

"Next week? Back here to Dingle? Well, it sounds like you *have* made other plans then." I am a little hurt, and I don't particularly mind that my daughter knows it.

"It's just a maybe. We haven't made any definite plans. I wanted to talk to you first. I told Sean I've got to talk to you about this. And besides, Daddy is flying over soon. Don't you want a little alone time with your husband? Huh? Don't you?" She bats her eyes at me and presses her hands together as if in prayer. "Please. This is important to me."

Christ, this is a lot to ponder and all before 9 a.m. Stalling tactics are in order.

"Don't turn this back on me. If you and your boyfriend want to take a trip, that's on you, okay? And I *would* like you to hold off a few days. Let's get to Dublin and take a breath, huh? Give your dad a chance to meet him first, before you go traipsing across the country. And besides," I say with a mischievous grin, "maybe if you two actually spend some real time together, you'll find that sneaking around is half the fun."

I duck just in time to miss getting hit with the rolled-up pair of socks lobbed by my daughter. Crisis averted for now. But hold on here, I *am* her mother and have to weigh in.

"All kidding aside, sweetie. I get the attraction, okay? He's adorable and I think you two will have a great time together, but let's not forget that we barely know him. No, Bex, let me speak my piece," I warn, as I see her start to protest. "I just want you to remember that he's older than you and Dublin is a big city. You have to be careful, okay? Don't give me that look. You know exactly what I mean, Becca. A fling on vacation is romantic and exciting. I get it. And you know I know what I'm talking about. But just watch yourself, please."

Becca rolls her eyes at me, but she's smiling as she heads into the bathroom. I hope she heard me. We'll have a few days in Dublin to work things out, then, after Rob joins us, well, who knows? Maybe the four of us will head north together. Well, maybe we'll have dinner first. No need to rush things.

Becca

So, my mom and I checked back into our Dublin hotel. The same one we stayed in the night before we became Nomads. It's in a great location and only a few blocks away from Sean's flat. How convenient! Hard to believe that it's only been a week ago since we stayed here. So much has happened since then.

Well, really, just one thing. I have fallen in love with a sexy, Irish tour guide. I know, if you don't believe in love at first sight, it's a bit of a stretch. And it wasn't first sight, not really. I thought he was a bit of a tool, when I first laid eyes on him. A handsome tool, that's for sure, but he just seemed kind of arrogant.

I tend to wait in the wings most of the time. I don't like being the center of attention, so please don't take me out on my birthday and have the wait staff sing and bring some lame-o cake. Please don't. I guess, because I'm not comfortable with standing out, I'm kind of suspicious of people who do. *What are you really hiding, that you have to make it look like you're putting it all out there?*

Hey, I've taken a lot of psych classes in the last few years, so it's entirely possible that I'm over-thinking this here. But I learned something this week. Something no classroom or textbook could ever teach me. I learned there's a lot more than meets the eye when it comes to Sean Donovan. Sure, he is probably a bit *too* good looking. A lot of folks probably underestimate him and his abilities, writing him off as a pretty boy or something. He's glib and funny, but he's wicked smart and has more people sense than anyone I've ever known.

It's called social intelligence. He can read a room like no one I know. Possibly even more than my dad. Even when Sean was upset about Fiona and our misunderstanding, he mostly stayed positive and professional. Okay, so maybe making out with me every chance we get isn't exactly part of the definition of being professional, but, in his defense, we've had a lot of catching up to do these last three days. And, until today, we've been able to keep it pretty well hidden.

I thought my mom might have been exaggerating this morning when she said that our mutual attraction is common knowledge among the Nomads. This morning, as we were loading up the van, I might have just wandered off for a second and happened to run into Sean in the alley… It was just for a minute or two, but kissing that boy? Oh my, what a great way to start the day. I could easily make it a habit. Well, not really *easily,* as it would involve one of us moving to another country, so there's that. But back to kissing.

After we disentangled ourselves, he gave me a quick peck on the cheek and took off towards the van and waiting Nomads. So I held back a couple of minutes, to give him a head start, then walked in the opposite direction towards the street. The problem was we both ended up back at the van at the exact same moment. As I rounded the corner towards Bertha, Sean was coming around the other way. Everyone saw us at the exact same time. We got a rousing cheer and a standing ovation. Actually, the van was locked, so everyone was standing around waiting. Then clapping.

Sean later told me that he had taken an extra moment to, *um,* adjust himself and wait for all the excitement to die down, if you catch my drift, before turning onto the street. So we got cheers and applause, and all of our sneaking around for the last few days was kind of pointless, after all. Even Tracie is supportive. She muttered something like, "Well, it's about time," which isn't exactly a ringing endorsement, but you take what you can get where Tracie's concerned.

Everyone seems really happy for us. I sat next to Sean in the van all day, and we sat together at lunch and even held hands as we hiked up our last hill as official Nomads.

So, all in all, it's been a wonderful day but bittersweet. Even though I think that all of us know, in our hearts, that it is unlikely we will ever see each other again, we exchanged email addresses and Twitter handles and made plans to friend each other on Facebook.

Carrie and Ollie promised to let us know when their baby arrives in a few months. We encouraged Elaine to give her kids another chance to connect with her, as she continues to rebuild her life. Everyone told my mom to have a great time when my dad shows up, and they wished me well in grad school.

We got back to the Dublin terminal mid-afternoon, and Sean raced inside to do a bit of paperwork. We stood around with our luggage, which was kind of awkward. Just like that first day. No one wanted to be the first to leave, so my mom took the bull by the horns. She clasped hands and pecked cheeks and wished everyone well. But Elaine, she hugged.

I heard Mom whisper in her ear, "You're stronger than you think."

"So are you, Jackie."

I won't be surprised if those two keep things going, even if it is only a holiday card.

Then Sean came strolling out, and he hugged everyone and encouraged us to tell our friends about the whole experience and be sure to post comments on the company's website. He saved hugging me till last. What he whispered in my ear wasn't as inspirational as what my mom told Elaine, but it was pretty special in its own way. I won't bother you with all of the details, but it involved tonight and my being ready and his picking me up at the hotel at eight. *Squeeee*!

So here I am, sitting in the hotel lobby, and it's only half seven. (I love Irish expressions and will gladly use them whenever I can.) When we got to our room a few hours ago, I half unpacked and picked out an outfit for tonight: a cute sundress, sandals, and a lightweight cardigan. I read for a while, showered, and grabbed a bite with my mom. Do tonight's plans include a meal? If not, I decided to have a little something first and keep my mom company, too. If dinner *is* on tonight's agenda, well, I can nibble on a salad or something.

Honestly, my tummy is doing flip-flops right now, and I'm already regretting the shrimp scampi I just ate. I'm going out with Sean tonight! We can hold hands and kiss all we want and even… Well, *that*, too. If it feels right. I mean, it's not actually a first date. Not really. And time is definitely *not* on our side. I don't even want to estimate just how much alone time we will actually be able to spend together before he goes back to work and I fly home.

I planned to have Sean pick me up in our room, but Mom wanted to relax in the tub, so I came down to the lobby to wait for him.

I'm really excited. It's only been a few hours, but I miss him already. God, what a hopeless cliché. But, honestly? I can't wait to see him. I keep wondering what the sex will be like. Will he be all kinds of masterful? Will he hurry me along, like a tour guide sometimes needs to do? *Now, over here. Okay, we're moving, we're moving.*

The first boy I had sex with was equally as inexperienced as I was. Josh was so gentle and so apologetic the whole time, which lasted all of about five minutes, I guess. The one time I let out an involuntary moan, he got all scared and asked if he was hurting me. *Um,* no. We lost touch after that summer between high school and college.

I had a few flings in Boston. One with Alex, a family friend from Sedona. Too much alcohol on his part contributed to a less-than-stellar hookup. I dated Kevin for a year or so. He was a lot of fun, but it was more of a friendship than some red-hot romance. He even brought me home to meet his parents. Mainline Philadelphia family with a big estate and full-time domestic help.

His dad was pretty cool, but his mom? Well, she disapproved of me, I could tell that. Every time I answered one of her questions, she repeated my answers with a questioning inflection in her tone. Sedona? Colby? Irish? Oh, advertising? I am wicked proud of my family and how hard my parents work. She was just too much of a tight-ass to appreciate us, and she definitely has considerable influence over her son. A week after we got back from our weekend away, he broke things off with me. Spineless little prick. Couldn't even make eye contact with me. He suddenly realized that he needed to spend more time on his studies, raise that GPA, and start thinking about his future. My roommate took me out that night, and I got totally shitfaced on Jäger and ended my evening puking my guts out.

So, yeah, you can say I am a little nervous, in addition to being real excited. Sean is a man. I am fairly certain that it would take a lot more than a disapproving parent to cause him to break things off with a woman he loves. *Loves*? Oh crap, I am getting way too ahead of myself. We are just going out for a drink or something. He is excited to show me his hometown. Nothing more.

Ooh, a text from Sean.

On my way.

I feel a tingle all the way down to my toes. Yeah, who am I kidding? I am prepared to jump his bones or let him jump mine or whatever. Tonight. Yes.

While my body focuses on the evening ahead, my mind fast-forwards. We have already decided to do some sightseeing around Dublin tomorrow. The three of us. Sean insists that he wants to take us on an insider's tour of his city. The plans include dinner, as well.

I wonder just how early we could eat, so he and I can have more alone time, after we drop Mom off. I'm sure it sounds horrible to put it like that, but I know her well enough to know that a day of sightseeing and an early dinner will be just fine with her.

The next day is still up in the air. We may do some exploring, and he wants me to meet up with some of his mates, maybe get together with his brother Declan and his girlfriend, Sarah, later in the day. A trip back to Dingle is in the works, as well. I hope that we can do it. I would love to meet Fiona and am thrilled that Sean wants me to.

I don't know where we would stay out there. Maybe where Fiona works? We have to plan it around her day off, which I guess changes every week. I don't want it to be awkward, taking off with Sean I mean, especially if my dad gets here before we leave.

Mom and Dad talked earlier today and it turns out that his partner Joe developed a few complications from his recent surgery. He'll be fine, though, and I think Dad will try to be here by midweek, even if it means leaving the agency to run without a partner-in-residence. There are at least a couple dozen people on the agency's payroll, so I hope that he can.

Maybe Sean and I can get in a trip to Dingle and be back in Dublin when Dad arrives. But that will leave Mom all alone here. That doesn't seem very nice.

I am so caught up in the logistics of the week ahead, it's not until Sean is just a few feet away that I notice him strolling towards me. I stand up just in time for him to sweep me in his arms.

"Hey, gorgeous," he growls in my ear between kisses. "Come here often?"

CHAPTER THIRTEEN

JACKIE

I TRIED TO WAIT up for her, but my book just didn't hold my interest and my eyes kept closing. I swear I read the same page five times in a row. I finally decided to call it a night and turned off my bedside lamp just before midnight.

I am not a very sound sleeper, so I fully expected to be awakened when Becca came in. I knew she would want to tell me all about her night and where they went, so I was kind of surprised when I woke suddenly, hours later. Squinting at my little travel alarm clock, I saw it was just after four in the morning. Becca had made it home and was sleeping soundly in the bed next to mine. Home from her big date.

My little girl is not so little anymore. I wonder if Sean took her dancing or if she met any of his friends. I fell back asleep after a while and didn't wake up again until a few minutes ago. After a quick trip to the bathroom, I find Becca is awake as well, and greet her with a smile.

"Hey, sunshine. How'd you sleep?"

"Oh, good, Mom. You?" Before I have a chance to answer, she hurries on. "Can I hop into the shower? Then we can grab a bite, okay?" She hustles into the bathroom. Seconds later, I hear the sound of running water.

I am dying to hear about Becca's night. Her first date with Sean. I get busy picking out what to wear and find myself waiting to hear the shower stop running, so I can pounce on Becca. I want details!

Becca

I lean back in the shower stall and let the water cascade over me. Is there anything more satisfying than a steaming hot shower?

I grin as images flash though my brain. Images of a certain smoking-hot, naked Irishman. Okay, yeah. *Way* more satisfying. That guy has some serious moves.

I pour a generous amount of peach-scented body wash across my shoulders and lather myself up as I reflect on a few of his most memorable ones. Last night was our first time. First, second, and third, I recall and feel my knees go weak.

I lean against the cold tile and take a long, deep breath. My mom is waiting for me to go down to breakfast. A play-by-play of last night's shenanigans is definitely *not* in order. I have to keep focused on the day ahead and would really love to spend another couple of hours in bed right now. I came creeping in just after two, smelling like, well, sex, I guess. Here I am, just six hours later, trying to erase the scent of Sean from my body and the thoughts of our night together from my mind.

I promised to have breakfast with Mom and hang out for a while this morning. Sean is picking us up for lunch at a café that he likes, followed by an afternoon of sightseeing. I know exactly what sights I wouldn't mind seeing, but I will have to wait.

God, one night with Sean and I am turning into a sex-crazed maniac! But, man, never have I ever been with anyone like him. We started off kissing in the hotel lobby when he came to pick me up. I knew right there and then that I was in for it. Or down for it. Whatever.

We strolled around for a little while, just taking in the sights. Dublin is such a lovely city at night. We walked towards the River Liffey, and Sean pointed out his apartment building, while we stood on the bridge. He asked if I was hungry, then if I wanted to get a drink or a coffee. I turned them all down. Honestly? I was getting so turned on just walking around, holding this guy's hand, that I had no interest in eating or drinking anything.

I shivered at the thought of getting naked with him, and he asked if I wanted his sweater. "No," I told him. "All I want is you."

I think that was what he was waiting to hear, because we race-walked the two blocks to his apartment and made it up two flights of stairs before starting to make out like a couple of horny teenagers. Sean fumbled with the key to his front door.

"Dec's not home," he mumbled as the door finally opened and we launched ourselves into his apartment.

We must have passed through a living room and made it down the hall, because suddenly we were sprawled on his bed, and his hands were all over me, and I was unbuckling his belt, and he was kissing me. He kept saying my name, whispering all kinds of things in my ear. I lost the ability to speak after the first few minutes, but I heard it all.

Now, I am standing in a shower that is quickly growing cold, blushing like a schoolgirl and hoping to Christ that my mother won't be able to look at me and know just how spectacular my night was. A cold shower is probably just what I need.

I turn the faucets off and reaching for a towel, I hear my mom's knock on the door.

"Becca," she calls out. "Are you coming or what?"

Wait. Is that a trick question?

CHAPTER FOURTEEN

JACKIE

"PENNY FOR YOUR THOUGHTS," I tease Becca, as she stares into her coffee cup. She blushes and takes a long sip before putting the cup back down.

"Huh? *Um,* what?" she asks.

"Did you two have fun last night? I didn't hear you come in, so it must have been late."

"Oh yeah, fun. Late. Uh-huh."

Alrighty then. I let it slide, and we eat our breakfast in silence and then make ourselves comfortable in the lobby with our books. I figure that if Becca wants to talk to me, she will when she is good and ready. Problem is, I'm good and ready now!

After a lazy morning, Sean shows up for our lunch date. He greets me with a hug and gives Becca a chaste peck on the cheek. I go back up to the room to drop off my book and grab a sweater, and when I come back down, I find the two of them sitting close to each other, deep in conversation. They jump apart as they see me crossing the lobby. Just who do they think they are kidding?

"You two ready?" I call out, and off we go. The food at the café is just as yummy as Sean promised. We sit outside on the patio overlooking the river, and I order some sort of tilefish, the house special and they share a giant broiled seafood platter. We chatter on about our plans for the next couple of days. Well, at least Sean and I do. Unusually silent, Becca pushes the food around her plate and lets Sean devour at least two-thirds of the huge portion. He insists on picking up the tab and won't hear of me leaving the tip. He's a good tipper, I realize happily as I notice the number of euros he leaves for the waiter. I can't tolerate cheapskates. We spend the afternoon strolling around several art galleries that Sean thought we might enjoy. I purchase a print that Rob will love for his office. It is large and brightly colored, featuring a number of sailboats in what Sean assures me is Dingle Bay. I make arrangements to have the print framed, and am promised that it will be delivered to our hotel before we are scheduled to depart next week. We move on to another design studio next door. Sean is on a first name basis with the owner and he introduces us to him. I am delighted by Sean's apparent interest in art.

"So, you're a real fan, huh?" I ask him as we browse the large selection of oil paintings. Sean grins, but shakes his head.

"Nah, Jackie. I'd like to say I'm some kind of expert, but I just know what I like, you know?" He pulls Becca into a casual one-armed hug as he continues. "And I like what I see," he teases.

Becca blushes, but makes no effort to pull away from him. They really are adorable, but maybe three *is* a crowd. After a few more minutes of aimless browsing, I admit that I am a little tired from all the walking and the fresh air. And the glass of wine I had at lunch.

After promising to join them for dinner in a few hours, I wave goodbye and make my way back to the hotel. All I want is an opportunity to put my feet up and close my eyes, but once I get back into the room and kick off my shoes, I find that I can't relax. Becca is wandering around a strange city with a man we hardly know, but I'm not worried that anything bad will happen to her. I am concerned that she is falling in love and won't want to leave.

Becca

"Don't look at me like that," I warn him. Sean is all wide-eyed innocence as he stirs more sugar into his coffee.

"Like what, exactly?"

Yeah, sure.

"You know like what. Like the cat that just ate the canary or something," I grumble and get a huge grin in return.

"A canary, huh? Is that what you think I'm imagining when I look at you? Like you're some tasty morsel that I just want to devour?"

His green eyes are sparkling, and I feel a shiver run right through me. *Oh, what is this man doing to me?*

"Just behave yourself is all. Don't get ahead of yourself, mister." He moves closer to me and murmurs in my ear. I can feel his warm breath on my neck.

"Oh, I'll behave myself, love. You can count on me," he promises. "We'll take the check please," he calls out to our waiter.

Another shiver. We are about to leave the coffee shop that we stopped into shortly after my mom returned to the hotel. Giving up the pretense that either of us is the least bit interested in the cappuccinos we ordered, Sean stands up and, after dropping several euros on the table, reaches for my hand. "C'mon, Bec. Let's get outta here. What do you say?"

What do I say? Yeah, let's get out of here. It's about time. We've got more important things to do. Like shagging each other senseless. I flush at the thought of Sean's naked body pressing against me. I brush my bangs off my forehead and take a breath. He is waiting for my response. It's sweet that he's not taking for granted that I automatically want to go back to his flat with him and continue where we left off just twelve hours earlier. But I do. I nod in agreement.

"Lead the way, lover-boy," I tease and follow him out to the street.

We hold hands as we head back to his place, and I can feel my excitement building as we make our way up the three flights of stairs. Or maybe it *is* the stairs. Something is making my heart beat just a little faster. We have the place to ourselves again today, at least for the next hour or two. I laughingly refuse Sean's offer of tea. Tea is *not* what I need right now. He seems, well, nervous, I guess, pacing around his tiny living room.

"You okay?" I ask him gently. Maybe this is going just a bit too fast. "We don't have to, *um*, you know." I swallow. At his look of concern, I hurry on. "Not that I don't want to, cuz I do. I really do."

He plops down into a tattered armchair and pulls me on to his lap.

"I want to. You know I do. I just don't want to, I don't know, give you the wrong impression, you know?" He is watching me closely now.

Impression of what? A relationship? Something more than just a quick hook-up? I take another deep breath.

"Do you like me, Sean?" He nods, still waiting. "Do you want to be with me, to make love with me?" He nods again and pulls me in closer.

"More than anything, love. I do like you, and I am dying to make love with you. You're not some fling, okay? You're… special. I have no idea what's going to happen next, but right now, the only thing I can think about is how much I want to be holding you, kissing you, loving you."

I smile happily and swing my leg around, so that I am facing him, straddling him. I slowly plant kisses across his jaw and down his neck as I hitch my thumbs under his belt and pull him in even closer. He groans and, somehow, stands up with me wrapped around him, and then carries me effortlessly down the hall to his room. Christ, he must be even stronger than he looks, because I am *not* some delicate little thing. He lays me down gently on his unmade bed and grins at me.

"Now what was that I said about you being devoured, huh, lass?" he asks as he pulls his shirt over his head.

CHAPTER FIFTEEN

JACKIE

WALKS AROUND WITH a goofy smile on her face? Check.

Frequently appears to be on another planet? Check.

Disappears for hours at a time and can't or won't provide details as to where she's been? Check.

Yes, it is official. My daughter is in love.

Becca's never been one of those boy-crazy girls, you know? She had plenty of boys as friends all through high school, mostly due to her involvement in sports, especially field hockey. Some of her friends had official boyfriends, starting from the age of thirteen, but Becca seemed to prefer group dating or hanging out or whatever.

When she was a junior in high school, she started seeing a senior, the captain of the boys' soccer team. I liked Tyler just fine, but Robbie was *not* a fan. He told me privately that he thought this kid was just a bit too cocky. "He's a smug little bastard," were his exact words. Of course, he didn't share his feelings with Becca, as we both know there is no more sure-fire way to push our daughter further into a relationship with Mr. Wrong than by declaring the object of her affections off-limits. After a while, Tyler stopped coming around, and Becca was back into the group-dating thing.

A U of Arizona student who was interning with Rob's agency during the summer before Becca's senior year caught her eye, and this time I was the one who was not supportive. But Kyle left just before Labor Day and that was that. She ended up dating a few guys and, just in time for prom, started seeing Josh. Nice kid, very polite, but I never got the sense that he had that much going on upstairs, if you know what I mean.

Then Becca left for four years of college in Boston. On breaks and over the summers, she would hang out with local friends and seemed to be very happy with her single status. Guess I'm taking a long way of saying that I haven't seen Becca so into any young man, ever. I think she's really fallen hard for Sean. It's only been three days since we got back to Dublin, and those two are positively inseparable.

Sean certainly seems to be crazy about Becca, too. He doesn't miss an opportunity to hug her or stroke her arm, if she's sitting next to him. I'm certain that they've slept together, as evidenced by the long absences and the subtle intimacies that I've witnessed. Becca's been on the pill since she was seventeen, and I really hope that all our family discussions about STDs have been taken to heart.

My bigger fear right now is that Becca is not prepared for the fact that, like it or not, we are returning to the States in just eight days. Part of that time is meant to be spent up in Belfast and the Northern Coast. Rob is due to arrive soon, and I imagine that we'll have to face the inevitable impact that will have on their plans and private time.

They do spend just about every waking moment together, although I have insisted that Becca wake up in her own bed every morning. Probably a bit hypocritical of me, as anything they are choosing to do can be done at any time of the day, and it's certainly not that I give a damn about what anyone else thinks, either. I just think that spending the night and waking up together adds a dangerous degree of added intimacy to a new relationship, and I don't feel like Becca is really ready for that.

We've talked, the three of us, and they both know how I feel and have, so far, respected my wishes. I never hear Becca come in, as I've all but abandoned the practice of remaining awake until she is safely home. All I know is that, when I open my eyes every morning, she is sleeping soundly in the bed next to mine.

We plan to get a second room when Rob arrives, but now I wonder if that's just silly. Would Becca prefer to stay at Sean's? Would she do it anyway? How would Rob react? She's always been her dad's little girl, but maybe if he meets Sean, he'll be okay with her staying with him.

I hope Rob will get to know Sean first, before he judges him to be a "smug little bastard." Sean is really sweet and sincere and treats Becca like she deserves to be treated. I think Rob will be able to see that.

Or do we just continue the charade and insist that Becca be back in her own room in time for breakfast with her family? Oh Christ, this is getting complicated. Maybe I should just wait and see how things work out, but I've never really been much of a wait-and-see kind of person. I really prefer to have a plan, even if it's subject to change. I *do* try to be flexible, in spite of what Rob and Becca seem to think.

They make a really cute couple, Becca and Sean do. I see heads turn as we make our way down the street or when we're walking through a crowded restaurant or pub. And I'm certain that no one is looking at me. They are both quite tall and slim, with similar coloring: pale skin, reddish-brown hair, and green eyes. They could be mistaken for siblings, even twins, if not for the fact that they are usually arm in arm or hugging or making out.

I've never been a big one for public displays of affection, and, as I said, I haven't really seen Becca with that many guys. So it was a bit odd at first to watch them greet each other or hug and kiss, as we travel around Dublin. She's twenty-one and very mature, but she's still my baby. And I really do like Sean quite a bit, but the bottom line is that he lives here and she doesn't.

Also, I'm enough of a snob to admit that I would prefer someone more educated for my daughter. Now, my own husband doesn't have a degree, and he's done fabulously well for himself with just over three years of college. But not everyone is Rob, and I see how hard it is to make your way in the world without an education.

It's my business to help people switch careers, and Sean and I have had several conversations related to that over the last ten days. He frankly seems more interested in helping his younger sister explore her career options than anything for himself, but he has expressed some job dissatisfaction to me, along with his desire to move away from Dublin.

Will he consider moving to Boston to be with Becca? I know it's way too soon in their relationship to be in favor of such a move, and I hope it doesn't come to that. But a strong attraction to someone can cause even the most levelheaded among us to do something impulsive. I speak from experience, you know. Been there, done that. This morning, when Becca and I were having breakfast, I brought up the subject of what will happen in a week, when it's time for us to leave. Her sunny smile disappears, and she shakes her head at me.

"I dunno, Mom," she says soberly. "I guess we'll just have to see, won't we?"

I wonder if they have talked much about all that. Probably not, and that's probably good. What is there to say, really?

I decide to strike while the proverbial iron is hot and try to get some more info from my unusually tight-lipped daughter.

"So, have you given any more thought about going to Dingle? Didn't you say you want to meet his sister?"

Another shake of the head.

"Fiona's still not sure which day she will have off this week. I guess we could go and just see her at night, when she gets out of work, but she puts in a long day, so she's pretty beat at the end of it. Plus, I want to wait until Dad gets here. Didn't you say you want him to meet Sean first?"

I vaguely remember saying something of the sort, but these days I barely recall what I ate for lunch, so it's kind of fuzzy.

"Oh, sure, honey. Maybe we should play this one by ear, you know?"

My daughter looks astonished.

"Wow, Mom, you need to leave the country more often," she teases. "Look at you, all playing it by ear and everything." She gets a broad smile from me in return.

"Let's just say that life's too short to spend too much time worrying and planning everything, okay?"

"Now you sound just like Aunt Edie. And you know that's a good thing, right?"

I do know. But I also know that, despite all of my easy, breezy talk, deep down, I am still worried. I know putting any extra pressure on Becca right now isn't a smart thing to do. We will just have to give it more time.

I spend the afternoon in Dublin shopping on my own, which is glorious. Although I have shopped quite a bit since arriving here in Ireland, today is different. The Nomad tour promised to take us on the back roads of Ireland, and they delivered on that promise in spades. We were off the beaten track for most of the past week. The majority of the small shops we frequented catered mainly to tourists looking for souvenirs made from Irish lace, Waterford crystal, or anything Guinness. Edie's teapot continues to elude us, however, despite scouring all those shops.

Dublin is another story. It is quite cosmopolitan, and the shopping is amazing. It even has trendy Sedona beat by a mile. Sean recommended that I start out on Grafton Street, on the south side of the River Liffey. It is a bustling area, teeming with upscale department stores and funky boutiques. I am in my glory.

I decide to stop and take a break when I come across a particularly sunny outdoor café. A quick look at my watch convinces me that it is too late in the afternoon for anything caffeinated. So I order an iced decaf latte, and, while I wait for it, I engage in more people watching. There is a young couple sitting nearby. Drinks forgotten, they hold hands and gaze into each other's eyes. Ah, young love!

Speaking of which, I wonder what my daughter and her young lover are up to. I can only imagine. The mom in me hopes that they are being safe. And that Becca isn't getting in too deep. I see the way she looks at Sean. And the way he looks at her. They are both head-over-heels in love, I am pretty certain.

But it can't last. We are going to be leaving town in a few days, and, soon after that, we are traveling home. Becca has plans to spend the summer in Arizona before going back to Boston right before Labor Day. And Sean is due back at work soon, leading another group of Nomads across Ireland. They will both need to get back on with their respective lives.

But the romantic in me? Yeah, she is still there, hiding in plain sight. My hair is starting to go gray, and I have finally conceded defeat to the crisscross of crow's feet that have taken up permanent residence around my eyes. But the young woman who truly believes that love conquers all and that fate can bring two people together in the most unlikely of scenarios? Yeah, I still feel like that. Maybe Becca and Sean are meant to be together. Becca has this glow about her, and Sean never stops smiling, not for a second.

Maybe their instant attraction that grew into friendship and possibly even love is destiny. What do I know? But as I sip my drink and bask in the late afternoon sunshine, I shiver just a bit. What will Robbie think? He can be as romantic as the next guy, but when it comes to his only daughter?

I am getting used to the casual intimacy that the two of them exhibit. I will have to prepare Rob, so that he doesn't freak out the first time he sees that rangy Irishman hugging and kissing his little girl.

BECCA

It was one of those days, you know? Perfect, just about. Sean came to pick us up shortly after my mom and I had breakfast. He joined us in the sunny hotel dining room for a cup of coffee, and the three of us sat and chatted for an hour before heading out. I think my mom really likes him. Likes him for me, I mean.

There are still plenty of places we want to see in Dublin, but we had a hard time deciding which ones to go to before my dad shows up the day after tomorrow. We are definitely holding off on the Guinness Storehouse. My dad will just love that place and the 360-degree views from the Gravity Bar. I was in favor of a trip to the Dublin Zoo, and Mom really wanted to check out the Book of Kells over at Trinity College. We started out by walking towards the park we visited on our first morning in Dublin, just twelve short days ago. Time sure flies when you're having fun.

"So, that's my church," Sean told us with a hint of pride as he pointed to a huge building made of gray stones. "That's where me da married mum, and where all four of us kids got baptized and made our first communion." We stopped and looked at the huge pillars and colorful stained glass windows. It must be 500 years old. Nothing in Arizona comes even close to being that old, except for the red rocks, of course.

"So, you grew up around here then?" Mom asked him.

"Yeah, right down the next block there." He pointed in the general direction of some large multi-family houses. "I grew up playing in this very park." He indicated the grassy area just past the church.

"Does your dad still live there?" I asked tentatively. I know the subject of Billy Donovan can be a touchy one for Sean, but he shakes his head vigorously.

"Nah, not any more. After my ma passed and Dec and I moved out, it was just Liam and Fi home with him. Then he got, *um*, sick and lost his job, so they moved to a smaller place. Cheaper. That's when Liam started hanging around with that fucker Brian. Oh, sorry Jackie. And then Fi started keeping company with him and got knocked— Well, you know the rest." He started walking faster, and Mom and I hurried to keep up with him as he turned into the park. He wiped at his eyes with balled up fists. "Ah Christ, I'm sorry, ladies. You don't need me sobbing like a tosser, huh?"

We spotted the same bench Mom and I hung out on last week, and the three of us sat in silence for a moment.

"How's your dad doing, Sean? You said he'd been sick?" Mom asked gently.

"Yeah, he's okay now, I guess. Still drinks too much, but Liam says he's eating better, and he gets up every day and goes to work, so that's good."

My mom smiled at him. "What kind of work does he do?"

"Well, he was a mechanic, you know? A skilled tradesman at a factory. Pretty good job, considering he left school at thirteen. But then he got sick, and now he's a janitor. Works at the school that we all went to, cleaning everyone's shite, washing the blackboards." He shook his head in amazement. "When I was little, I thought he could do anything, you know? That he was the biggest, strongest guy in the world. But now, he's just this little old man. I went to see him a few weeks ago, and he was walking down the street just a few feet ahead of me. I followed him for a couple of blocks and didn't even recognize…." His voice caught and for a second, I thought he might break down again. But he didn't. My mom, who always seems to know what to do, reached for Sean's hand and squeezed it tightly.

"We always think our parents are larger than life when we're younger, Sean," she told him gently. "But your dad is just a man. And I'm sure he's really proud of you." He nodded at that, and we continued to sit for a while in the park where Sean used to play, in the shadow of the church that had been a big part of his Catholic upbringing.

I consider myself a spiritual person, but my folks aren't big on organized religion. The only times I've been in a church were for weddings and once for a baptism. I find the whole thing kind of confusing, and, in my limited experience, I haven't found those who identify with a specific faith any nicer or kinder than those of us who don't.

I was kind of relieved when Sean suggested going for ice cream and happily followed him and Mom out of the park and down the street to a place he said we would love. And we did. Shortly after that, Mom excused herself, saying that she wanted to reach Dad before he leaves for work. A quick glance at my watch confirmed that it is still early morning in Sedona. Have I gotten used to the time change yet?

"You two go somewhere fun," she suggested with a smile, and, with a wave, she was gone.

"Fun? How about the zoo? Or, I know! Let's go to your place"

Sean grinned in response. Such an agreeable boyfriend I have. A while later, we were lying together in his bed, spent and very happy. I was half asleep when I felt him stir.

"I'm half Yank, ya know?"

"What?" I rolled over to face Sean. This guy is full of surprises.

"Billy was born in the States. Came here when he was just a little guy, maybe three or four. He's from New Jersey, like on *The Jersey Shore*?"

"You're kidding. I figured you were one hundred percent Irish."

"Well, I am. Just half Irish-American. It's no big deal. Just that the company, you know, they want us to really lay on the whole *Oirish* experience as thick as possible. You tourists just eat it up." He smirked and I swatted him playfully.

"Have you been there? To New Jersey, I mean."

"Just the one time."

"Yeah, when?"

"It was years ago. I was a little kid. Mum was still healthy, and Fi was in diapers. Me da's sister, my aunt Leah, hit it rich, and she paid to have all of us come visit. She footed the whole bill, and we had the first and last ever Donovan family reunion. I met cousins and family that I had never even heard of."

"What did she do? Your aunt? Win the lottery or something?"

"No, even better. She sued a former boyfriend for the writing credit on one of his songs, and they settled out of court. Even after all the lawyers and their fees, she walked away with like five million dollars."

"Yikes, that's cool. What is the song? Would I know it?"

"Maybe. Her ex was Jamie Sheridan. He was really big in the 90s. Aunt Leah proved she wrote half of his first hit, 'Over You.'"

Jamie Sheridan. I vaguely recalled a tall, dark-haired singer with a really deep voice. Dead or alive? Dead, I think. My folks are always listening to music. They are like little kids, getting all excited about some song and then playing it for each other, sharing a pair of ear buds. I smiled at the image.

"Wow. So what does she do now? Leah, I mean. Is she still making music?"

"Not any more. Between you and me, I don't think she was ever really that into it. The music, that is. Billy says she was just looking for an excuse to sleep with rock stars and smoke weed."

"Well, I guess, if you're gonna sleep around, you might as well sleep with someone famous, right? Any more secrets you wanna share?"

"Nah, I'm good. How 'bout you? Any skeletons in your closet?"

"Me? No way. Pure as the driven snow." I leaned into him and peppered his broad chest with kisses. I knew it was getting close to the time I need to get back by.

Mom has been pretty cool about me and Sean taking off, but I feel kind of bad leaving her alone too long. I hate thinking of her eating by herself in our room. Plus, I do not need her getting curious about how Sean and I are spending all our time. As long as she doesn't ask, I won't have to tell.

I lay back in his arms. Just a little while more, I promised myself.

I felt Sean move, and he propped himself up on one elbow to face me. "Hey, Becca?"

"Hmmm?" I kept my eyes closed and tried to pretend we have all the time in the world.

"We should be getting back, huh? Your ma will be worryin'."

Ugh.

"I know. We really should. It's just so nice here, and it feels good to just be *with* you, ya know?" I opened my eyes to see him grinning at me.

"Yeah, I know."

He lay back on the pillow and pulled me over to him. As he ran his fingers through my hair, I felt his warm breath against my ear. Never have I ever felt so comfortable with another human being. I love this man. This tall, broad-shouldered, almost-ginger tour guide leaves me breathless. But, just this morning, I had to admit to my mom that I had no clue what would happen when we flew home.

I wished I could just stay here with Sean, in his double bed with the rumpled sheets or sitting on his couch with him, eating Chinese takeaway and watching TV.

"You hungry, Becca? I could make us some eggs or find you a snack to tide you over." I had seen the contents of the Donovan brothers' fridge. They take bachelorhood to a whole new low, so I couldn't imagine finding anything in there worth eating.

"No I'm good," I told him. His eyes sparkled, and he smiled at me with that sexy grin of his.

"Yeah, you are," he told me.

Christ, everything that comes out of this guy's mouth sounds sexy, I thought. *Oh God, that mouth of his!*

"C'mon, we better get moving. I'm gonna grab a quick shower first, okay?"

I managed what I hoped was my own kind of sexy grin, and he responded with a growl.

"Woman, you're killing me, I swear. I can't hardly keep up with you." He gave me a playful swat on the behind then strolled, bare-assed, out of his room towards the hall bathroom. The brightly colored Celtic cross tattoo was in sharp contrast to his pale skin. As if he knew I was still watching, he turned to me and winked. "See anything you like?" With a grin, he disappeared into the bathroom.

Seconds later, I heard the shower start up and I lay back in bed with a smile on my face. I could just picture him in there, all steamy, soaping up his…

"Hey, Sean, where're you at?"

Oh, crap, I thought with a start. *It's Declan, and, from the sound of his voice, he is coming down the hall.* I had just started to pull the sheets up to cover myself when he stuck his head into the room.

"Oh hey, Becca. Sorry, didn't mean to startle you." He made a point of averting his eyes while I tried to pull the rumpled sheets over all of my exposed lady parts, but the grin he wore left me no doubt that he saw way more of me than I would choose to show him. "So, my brother is in the shower, eh?"

Yes, genius. You guessed it. I nodded.

"And you're having a bit of a lie-in then?"

"Well, yeah, just for a second. We're meeting my mom for dinner soon, you know?" Why was I sounding all apologetic? He chuckled at that.

"So, just working up a bit of an appetite, I guess, heh? So how's my little brother treating you? Is he showing you everything our fair city has to offer?"

Yuck! This guy tries to make everything sound sexy, but it comes across more pervy than anything. I gave another tug on the sheets and tried to sit up, growing increasingly uncomfortable sprawled in Sean's bed with his older brother standing over me. Looking down on me.

"Sean's an amazing tour guide, Declan. He's been showing me everything." I tried to put a bit more emphasis on the "everything." Two can play at this sexual innuendo game. He started to answer me back but then Sean came striding in.

He looked a bit apprehensive at first, but when he saw that I was sitting up and, more importantly, covered up, he relaxed. At least as much as a naked fellow could relax, dripping wet and wrapped in a skimpy towel, while talking to his fully clothed older brother.

"So, Dec. You're home early."

His brother turned to face him, and I took the opportunity to reach down and grab my sweatshirt off the floor. I needed Sean to keep his brother talking long enough to pull it over my head, and I *really* needed to locate my panties.

Sean looked over at me as his brother told him how the pub was pretty dead and that his girl Sarah was paying a visit to her mom. I gave him a look to communicate my need to get dressed, and it worked.

"So come on, let's give Becca some privacy then," he said and, with a final glance at me, led Declan out, closing the door behind them.

I immediately sprang into action, hopping up and pulling on my sweatshirt, and then located not only my panties but my jeans, as well. Both had been discarded in our hasty rush to hop into bed a couple of hours earlier. I opened the door to look out into the hall and, finding the coast clear, hurried into the bathroom.

A few minutes later, I was freshened up and fully clothed. I grabbed Sean's jeans and boxers from the floor and trotted back down the hall towards the kitchen. Declan was pouring a cup of tea for himself and asked me if I wanted a cuppa.

"No, I'm good, but thank you," I told him as I tossed Sean his clothes.

Not wanting to leave me alone again, Sean finished drying off and pulled on his pants.

Declan shook his head and smirked at me. "You'll have to excuse my little brother. Becca. I've tried to teach him some manners, but I see I've failed." He crossed the room and grabbed Sean's discarded damp towel off the floor. "How many times must I tell you—," he began in a mocking tone.

Sean didn't let him finish. "So, I'm gonna grab a clean shirt, and we'll be off then." He nodded at me and started to leave the room.

"So, where are you taking the lovely ladies tonight?" Declan asked and actually seemed interested. They discussed the merits of a few restaurants. Declan favored a place that sounded really great and I knew my mom would love.

"Why don't you join us, Dec?" I surprised myself by asking. I got a quizzical look from Sean that turned into a smile as Declan enthusiastically agreed.

Sean's bro is joining us. C u soon, I managed to text my mom, as both brothers went in search of clean shirts.

Minutes later, the three of us were heading over to the hotel to pick up Mom.

I looked back and forth at their handsome faces as we made our way through rush-hour crowds of pedestrians. I was going out on the town with the two best-looking guys in Dublin, I marveled. Amazing how your whole life can be turned upside down by a chance meeting with the right guy.

Life in Boston as a grad student on a tight budget will be a sharp contrast to the high life I am currently living. And Sean won't be a part of it, I realized with a lump in my throat.

CHAPTER SIXTEEN

JACKIE

AS I GET READY for bed later that night, I brush my teeth and apply a nighttime moisturizer guaranteed to take years off my appearance. At least it smells nice. I pour my mostly untouched tea down the drain and get comfortable under the down comforter.

I enjoyed the evening, for the most part. Sean and his older brother Declan joined me and Becca for dinner. The restaurant was just a short walk from the hotel. Becca and I had decided earlier that we would dress up a bit, but she got back from Sean's so late, with the brothers in tow, there was no time for her to change clothes.

We needn't have hurried. It wasn't until we were finishing our main course that the place started to really fill in. Sean bought us a round of drinks before we were seated, which was really sweet of him. I was trying to be subtle about it, but I wanted Sean to know that dinner was on me tonight. He has been treating us to lunches and coffees all over town for days. I told Becca on the way over, and she must have told Sean, because, right after we opened our menus, he looked up worriedly at me. I smiled and nodded, and he looked really relieved. The prices were much higher than any of the restaurants we had been going to for the last couple of weeks. But it was one of our last nights in town, and I wanted the evening to be special.

We were enjoying our starters (I vow to start calling appetizers "starters" from now on; it sounds like more fun) and chatting. It was interesting watching Sean and his older brother together. Declan is a little huskier than Sean, not quite as tall, and he wears his dark hair fairly long, but there is no mistaking that they are brothers. I am an only child, and so is Rob, and, of course, Becca is too. Maybe that's why sibling dynamics are always fascinating to me. The normally self-assured Sean seems to defer to his older brother's opinions on local politics and the economy. Declan seems quite knowledgeable on these subjects and spoke confidently as we enjoyed our entrees.

These were not topics that I had much to add to, so I kept busy with my black sole. Becca was attacking her prawns with great relish and hogged the dish of chili sauce meant for the whole table. Sean grinned at her and nodded along with his brother, not speaking much as we ate.

After stacking and removing our plates, our server encouraged us to give the brownie sundae, topped with their house-made ice cream, a try. I groaned. *Did I have room for dessert?* What a silly question.

"What do you think, Bex? What to share a sundae with your mom?" I asked with a grin. When she agreed, I told our server, "One sundae, two spoons please. Unless you gentlemen want to join us?" I added mischievously.

"You can share mine, Sean," Becca assured him with a giggle. Declan asked for a cappuccino, and we all settled back in our seats, stuffed and contented. I admitted to having a sweet tooth and that ice cream is a real weakness of mine.

"So, where have you had ice cream since you've been in town?" Declan asked in a conversational tone.

Several places, I recalled, but I looked to Sean to supply the names. He rattled off a few to his brother, who shook his head in amazement.

"So, you haven't been to Smythe's then?" he asked incredulously. "Seriously," he assured us, "the best ice cream in town is at Smythe's. All the other places are shite. I'm disappointed in you, Paulie Boy."

Sean flushed at that but was quick to respond. "Declan here, he has an opinion about everything, ladies. As you probably already have seen. The problem is that he doesn't like it when anyone disagrees with him."

Uh-oh. Declan started to glare at him but ended up in an awkward grimace. He looked like he wanted to say something and then seemed to decide against it.

"Hey, it's just ice cream, huh?" Becca interjected nervously. "Right, Mom? But maybe tomorrow we can check it out. Or when Dad comes. He's not a big ice cream fan, but maybe they have Italian ice? *Oooh,* will you look at that sundae?"

As our server approached, Sean assured us that Smythe's would be added to the growing list of "places we still had to see while we were in Dublin," while Declan smirked and sipped his steaming drink. Sean, Becca, and I dove into the sundae, and it was just about as good as promised. After a few minutes, I realized I was done. Time to throw in the towel, which, in this case, was a big, white linen napkin.

"You lightweight," Sean teased me just before Becca spoon-fed him another drippy mouthful.

God, they are a seriously cute couple. I chuckled and turned my attention back to Declan, who had been silent as he watched the sundae disappear.

"So, your other brother is Liam, is it?" When he nodded, I continued, not realizing that I was skating on some pretty thin ice. "And Fiona? She's your sister?"

Sean flushed, looking down at his plate. Becca suddenly looked tense, but it was Declan about whom I was most concerned. He glared at Sean, his handsome face darkened, and he swore softly under his breath. He was gripping the napkin on his lap, and I thought that he might rip the damn thing in two, but then he took a deep breath and seemed to calm down. Becca did tell me that Fiona was somewhat estranged from her family and lived apart from them, but I didn't realize just how off limits the subject of the youngest Donovan was.

Not sure if I should just let it drop or try to diffuse the situation, I said, "I'm sorry. I didn't mean to touch on a sore subject. I mean every family has their issues, right?"

Becca leaned over and squeezed Sean's arm, and he seemed to relax. Declan recovered nicely, as well.

"Yes, Jackie. The subject of our sister is quite a bone of

contention, you might say," he said genially. "Some of us have forgotten how she's carried on and what she's done, but it's hard, you know?" Sean pushed back from the table and glared at his brother.

"Forget? You're the one who's forgotten, Declan. Forgotten that you even have a little sister, haven't you?"

Declan refused to take the bait and sat calmly, seemingly waiting for Sean to cause a scene. Once he realized that he wasn't going to get a response, Sean backed down, shaking his head and mumbling something about "family" under his breath.

As luck would have it, our server happened by with the check, and by the time I had signed the credit card receipt, the tension at our table had dissipated. Sean led the way single-file out of the restaurant, and we faced each other again when we reached the sidewalk. Declan spoke up first.

"Well, this has been grand, Jackie. I can't thank you enough for a wonderful evening. It was good to meet you." He drew me in for a hug. I assured him that it had been my pleasure and that I hoped to see him again before we left next week. He was noncommittal as he hugged Becca quickly and then punched his brother's arm. "I'm off to meet Sarah then, but don't forget what I said. Make my eejit brother take you ladies for a proper ice cream, won't you?" With a wave, he was off. We watched silently as he disappeared into the throngs of people entering and exiting the nearby clubs and cafés.

"Jackie, I'm so sorry," Sean said softly. "I feel horrible that you had to witness all that."

Becca hugged him gently, and he relaxed against her, letting out the breath he had been holding. I assured him that it was okay and that these things happened.

"It's been a long day, my dears," I told them with a smile. "I am going to take a cab back to the hotel. No, seriously," I responded to Sean, who looked like he was going to insist on seeing me to my door. I was certain that the two of them would enjoy a little time to themselves, and honestly? I was looking forward to time alone myself. Emotional situations always wear me out, even if I am just a spectator.

I strode towards the street and held up my hand to hail an approaching taxi. I let Sean give the driver my destination and hugged Becca then Sean in turn. "Not too late Bex," I advised with a look that I hoped was firm yet understanding.

Sean assured me that Becca would get back to the hotel safely, and they stood and waved to me as the taxi took off down the block. I leaned back against the seat in relief. A hot mug of tea sounded like just the ticket, I decided, and closed my eyes for the duration of the short ride.

Becca

So my mom hopped into a cab, and Sean and I are walking back to his apartment. I am feeling kind of guilty that I'm leaving my mother alone again, but the thought of an hour with my boyfriend is just too good to resist.

Mom insisted on picking up the tab for what had turned out to be an amazing and very expensive meal. I hope Sean didn't feel awkward about her paying, but he has been spending a lot of money, taking us all over town, and I imagine that paying the tab for tonight's meal would put a serious dent into his finances.

Halfway through the evening, I decided that when Declan isn't showing off, he is actually quite charming and agreeable. He turned out to be as verbally gifted as his brother and had us laughing at his tales and stories. I just wish that he could show more compassion to Fiona.

I squeeze Sean's hand as we turn the corner right before his apartment building.

"He's something, you know? Declan. He's a really good guy." Sean grins and then turns thoughtful.

"He hasn't always had an easy go of it, Becca. My dad rode him pretty hard." I shudder at that. Sean confided that his dad could get physical when he had been drinking and that the target of his anger was frequently Declan. "After Mum passed, Billy took to drinking every day. Dec is the oldest, so he was left in charge of us lot. He kept us fed and made sure we had clothes and school supplies and all. I owe him, Becca. A lot. I know he can get pretty carried away with the whole big-brother act, but he's starting to mellow out. Sarah's been good for him. And we've all turned out okay, you know?"

I nod, thinking how Sean's upbringing couldn't be any more different from mine. My parents have a rock-solid marriage, and both found careers that they love. And, of course, I am an amazingly awesome child. I grin at Sean as he unlocks the door of his apartment building.

"I can't stay long tonight, lover boy. And don't look at me like that," I chide as he does that puppy-dog face thing. "I can stay for a cup of tea, but that's it," I tell him firmly. But before the kettle even starts whistling, we are making out and grabbing at each other, so he turns off the stove and follows me into his bedroom. Next thing I know…

"Shite. Becca. C'mon, girl. Wake up! We fell asleep. For fuck's sake, c'mon. Your ma'll tear me a new one, fer sure." Sean is dashing around, gathering up clothes, and appears to be looking for something. *His keys?*

I am waking up slowly and roll over on my side. *Uh oh.* This isn't good. The sunshine pouring in through the partially closed blinds is a sure sign. My plan to slip back into the hotel had fallen through. It's morning, and I have stayed out all night.

My phone starts buzzing, and I glance at it quickly. *Oh crap, my mom.* I have twelve missed calls and three new voicemails, and now Mom is calling again. I decide to ignore the call until we have a plan.

I hop up and race towards the bathroom, as I really have to pee, and call over my shoulder to Sean, who is still freaking out. "It'll be okay. Stop worrying. My mom is cool." *Cool*? Cool about her only daughter shacking up? I don't think she is all *that* cool. But it's too late to worry about that now. I wash my hands and splash water on my face. *Okay, time to deal with this.*

"I'm going to call her. Tell her that it got too late and that we'd had some drinks. Maybe she'll think I slept on the couch." My phone buzzes with an incoming call. Who else? "Hi, Mom."

"Becca. Is that you? Where are you?" She sounds pretty hysterical. *Not* cool.

"I'm fine. We're fine. It got late and…"

"Late? No, Becca, it's way beyond late. It's almost eight a.m. I've been calling and calling. Why didn't you answer your phone?"

"I'm sorry, Mom. Really. My phone is on vibrate. I couldn't hear it. I'm with Sean," I finish lamely.

"Well, I figured as much. You should have called me to let me know. Or at least answered your phone."

"Sorry, Mom. My phone was about to die. I forgot my charger."

"Which is it, Becca? You couldn't *hear* your phone, or you couldn't *use* your phone?" Her voice is like ice.

"Look, I'm sorry, okay? What do you want me to say? It got late. We fell asleep. I'll be back soon."

There is silence on the other end. Then I hear my mom let out a huge sigh.

"When, Becca? When will you be back?"

"Very soon, Mom. I promise." She hangs up, so I turn to face Sean. "I'd better be getting back," I tell him sadly, as I make my way down the hall to the bathroom. Looking at my reflection in the tiny mirror, I groan and then try unsuccessfully to get rid of the black mascara rings under my eyes using a square of toilet paper. I pull on last night's top and jeans, which are in a crumpled heap on the floor. I stuff my bra into my jeans pocket but give up looking for my underwear. I approach Sean, who got dressed with lightning speed.

"C'mon, love. I'll take you," he assures me.

"No, I should do this alone." I square my shoulders and let out the breath I had been holding. "I'll call you later, okay? Don't worry, Sean. We'll work this out." I want to kiss him until I get a smile, but I turn away and make my way out.

Sean's apartment is only a short distance from our hotel. A brisk fifteen-minute walk or a short five-minute cab ride? I decide to walk. It will give me a few extra minutes to work out my story.

But why do I need one? I am twenty-one, dammit. I am old enough to make my own decisions, aren't I? Sean is, well, important to me. Really important. But the only thing my mom asked is that I be back in time to sleep in my own bed and then join her for breakfast. It wasn't much to ask, and we did promise. *Crap*. And after she treated us all to a really swanky dinner last night, too. It had been a pretty great evening overall, despite the argument between Sean and his brother.

I hurry along towards the hotel. The first thing I will do, I decide—after groveling, that is—is take a shower and put on a pair of panties. My jeans are definitely rubbing me the wrong way. Maybe I should leave a spare pair at Sean's, for times like these. But that's just silly. There will only be a few more "times like these," and that's if we're lucky. My dad is due tomorrow, and we're supposed to be heading to Belfast.

Unless I can stay here, with Sean, and let my folks travel on their own. I picture spending hours in bed and waking up together, and I smile happily at the thought. *Maybe*? Cripes, we only have a little time before I am scheduled to fly home. First things first, I remind myself. Time to face my mom: apologize, grovel, cry, or all of the above.

CHAPTER SEVENTEEN

Jackie

I WISH I COULD take it back. Not *all* back, maybe. Just the mean parts. Pointing out how naïve it is to believe in a romance built on a few days of shared jokes and warm smiles, the unlikely chance that this is anything more than a passing fling.

I blew it, I guess. It just came out of nowhere. Becca stayed out all night. I was so worked up by the time she walked in, I just started yelling. After I hugged her, that is. She's never done that before. She's twenty-one, a legal adult. I get that. But we are in a big city in a foreign country, and she's only known Sean for a few days, if you don't count the week we spent together touring the Irish countryside.

They've gone out together every day since we arrived in Dublin six days ago. I have hung out with them a number of times. Yesterday, we had a great morning exploring the National Botanic Gardens and walking the Ha' Penny Bridge over the River Liffey. Sean and Becca are an adorable couple, and I'm happy to see my daughter so happy. After a busy day, I almost begged off on dinner last night. I would have been happy to put my feet up and order a salad and a split of white wine from room service. But we had agreed to go out for a nice dinner, and then Sean's brother joined us.

I returned to the hotel alone at about ten and read for a while. My eyes kept closing, so I decided not to wait up for Becca and turned in just after eleven, thinking that Becca would be home within an hour or so. Around 3 a.m., I woke out of a sound sleep, and the first thing I noticed was that Becca was not in her bed. *WTF?*

I hopped up and checked the bathroom and our postage-stamp-sized balcony, just in case. Still no Becca. Dammit. This isn't like my girl, not at all. I called her cell, but it went straight to her voice mail. Her phone is like an extra appendage, so it's unlikely that she didn't have it with her. I tried again, and this time I left a message. Trying to keep the anger and fear that I was experiencing out of my voice, I kept it short.

"Becca, it's three in the morning. Where are you? Call me please."

I wasn't going back to sleep, not until I heard her voice, saw her face. I knew Sean lived with his brother, in an apartment not that far from the hotel. I had never put his cell phone number in my phone and figured there were more than a few Donovans in Dublin.

Where's my daughter?

I called her cell, and again it went straight to voice mail. I clicked off without leaving a message. Surely she would notice the missed calls and call me back.

Should I call Rob? Tell him that his little girl is missing? That she's shacking up with a local guy? Sean seems great and all, but he's a bit old for my daughter, and he lives in a different country. That's two strikes against him.

I had my share of flings when I was younger, and I certainly can't say anything against falling for a charming tour guide—I'm not that much of a hypocrite. But I was an adult when I met Rick and convinced myself that moving cross-country made sense. Becca's only twenty-one! She's been on her own, and God knows how often she stayed out all night in Boston. But she should have at least called me. It isn't like her to be so thoughtless.

I called again, and this time my message was less friendly. "Rebecca. You need to call me right away. I am going to start calling police stations and hospitals. Where are you? *Call me*!" I wished that I could slam down my phone, but all I could do was click off.

I stayed like that for hours, sitting up in bed, propped against the pillows. Making deals with myself. If she's not home in fifteen minutes, I'll call her again. If she doesn't call me by 5 a.m., I'm going to call the front desk. Ask for help. How do you report someone missing? It's 999, not 911, I think.

Okay, 6 a.m. More unanswered calls, and then it was 7 a.m. By that point, I was beyond frantic. Unable to sit still, I paced back and forth and jumped when the room phone rang at 7:30. It wasn't Becca. I had left a wakeup call last night, because we had planned to go to the National Gallery this morning to check out their collection of Western European art and wanted to get an early start. I automatically thanked the robo-caller and placed the receiver back down.

I decided to give her one more try. And she answered the phone. Our conversation was brief. I really wasn't all that interested in how her phone had died or how she couldn't hear it. After she promised that she would see me shortly, I hung up. She was okay. Alive and well. Until I kill her, that is.

A short while later, she let herself into the room. I had ordered coffee and showered and was sitting calmly at the little table by the window, swathed in terrycloth and drinking my second cup. She quickly crossed the room to me and leaned down to hug me.

"I'm so sorry, Mommy. Really. We didn't mean for it to happen," she said tearfully. I half-heartedly hugged her back and asked her to sit down with me. She poured herself a cup of coffee and then sat back and waited.

She didn't have to wait long. I squared my shoulders and faced her, right before I let her have it. I told her she was thoughtless and careless. Lacking in good judgment. Irresponsible. Foolish. I told her I had pictured her lying in a hospital or, worse, in a morgue. Not calling, not answering her phone? Cruel and, again, irresponsible. That I hadn't raised her like that and that Sean should have known better.

Becca cried and tried to defend him. Told me that he had wanted to come this morning. To explain things to me. To apologize.

"Sean feels terrible, Mom. Please don't blame him. We would never do anything to hurt you, not on purpose. Sean is very important to me. I kind of, *um*, love him," she added in a whisper.

That's when I told her that this whole mess wasn't love. That it was a foolish fling. That Sean will have moved on before our flight even takes off next week. Becca went from being sad and weepy to totally pissed off.

"You don't get it. You have no idea what it's like. Sean and I are in love, okay? I don't care what you say. I love him, and I'm not going to listen to you anymore." And with that, she raced out of the room, and the door closed behind her. My daughter was gone.

BECCA

"You don't understand Sean. You weren't there. She said some horrible things to me. Called me stupid and irresponsible. Told me that you were just using me."

Sean flinches at that but continues holding me in his arms like I am a child. One who needs to be comforted.

"Hold yer whist now, Becca. You gotta see things from her point of view. She's worried sick about you. She's been up for hours, totally knackered. You've got to give her a chance."

I pull away and glare at him.

"You didn't hear her. She was mean and hateful. She's just jealous that I—"

"Listen to me. I'll not be the cause of this kind of rift with yer ma. I'm going to call her. No, Becca, I'm going to call her and let her know that you're safe. We'll give her a bit to collect herself, and then I'll bring you back to the hotel. Maybe we can have a coffee, talk things through, and have a proper catch-up. Now, where's your phone? We'll sort it out, you'll see!" Then seconds later, "Hey Jackie? So it's Sean. I'm here with Becca. We really want to talk to you. To explain. How'd it be if we were to nip over to see you in a bit?" I can't hear my mother's response, but he nods at whatever she says. "I'm really sorry, Jackie. It was thoughtless and irresponsible. We should have reached out to you sooner. We didn't mean… Okay then, what if we all get a bit of rest and come to you about half one? Okay, we'll see you soon then. Right ye be." He disconnects the call and grins at me. "That's sorted out then. How about we grab a few hours of sleep, so we're fresh to see her?" He pulls me back towards his tiny bedroom. "I'll set the alarm, okay? We can't take any chances."

I must have fallen asleep pretty quickly. When I wake up a couple of hours later, I am alone in the rumpled double bed. It is just before noon, so I have time to grab a quick shower before we head over to see my mom. Together.

Where is Sean? I get up and cover myself with the Oxford button-down he wore last night and head for the door. *Still no panties, damn.* I am about to make my way towards the kitchen when I hear voices. Sean's and Declan's. Sean sounds upset.

"It's not like that."

"Hey, I'm not sayin' she's not a fine bit of stuff. She is. But Jaysus, lad, what're you thinking and with which head? She's a posh kid, and she's American. How thick're you?"

"Go and shite, Declan. It's just fun and games. Becca knows that. She's not looking for anything serious. She'll be leaving next week, and that'll be that."

"Famous last words, boyo. Are you thinking she's not looking for a commitment, heh?"

"Ask me arse, fecker. I think I know what she…"

"I'm just sayin'. You need to be careful. Maybe let her down easy, huh? Tell her you'll keep in touch."

"I will in me hole, Declan. I just want..."

I didn't hear the rest of it, and now I'll never know what that bastard wants. The whole time the two brothers are arguing, I'm getting dressed. Once I heard Sean tell his brother that I am just a quick lay, I knew I had to get out of there.

Mom was right. I don't mean a thing to him. I am a fool for thinking that I matter to him. That he cares for me.

I tiptoe out to the hall and make my way to the front door. I can see them standing in the kitchen. Sean has his back to me, and Declan is giving a steaming mug of tea all of his attention. I slip out the door and, for the second time this morning, rush down the stairs and through the old fashioned vestibule. Seconds later, I am running down the now familiar street towards the hotel. Tears streaming down my face and heart pounding, I ignore the looks I get. I want to go home. I need my mom.

CHAPTER EIGHTEEN

JACKIE

WELL, I KNOW something's up right away, even in my sleep-deprived state. Becca bursts into the room a full hour before the time Sean and I agreed to. And she is alone, no Sean.

After his call, I went down for breakfast and a brisk walk around the neighborhood. I wanted to clear my head. So many thoughts swirling around. Now that the initial shock has worn off, there are a lot of things to consider. Would we still head up to Belfast and explore Northern Ireland in a few days? What if she wants to stay here? Would we fly home early?

Rob is due to arrive in less than twenty-four hours. I had been looking forward to telling him that I was ready to take the plunge and plan our future. But first things first. If we do stay in Dublin, do I look the other way or put my foot down and forbid future sleepovers? *Damn. I should ask Rob.* Despite the fact that he's totally besotted with his daughter, he is probably the most logical and reasonable person I know. Rob will know what to do. I try to figure out what time it is back in Arizona. No, calling him will have to wait.

I have just finished up in the bathroom after admitting defeat at minimizing the dark circles that ring my eyes. Lack of sleep and retaining fluids like a champ. I vow to wear my dark glasses and search out a new concealer. I hear the door open and then slam shut. *What the…?*

"Becca, is that you?" I peer out the door just in time to see my daughter collapse in a heap on her bed. *Now what?* I cross the room and plop down on the bed. Oh *no, she's crying. Sobbing.* I haven't seen her this upset since, well, ever. "Bex, what is it? Talk to me."

With difficulty, she rolls over on her side, facing me. Her eyes are red, and her cheeks are streaked with tears. Plus, her nose is running. I never go anywhere without a tissue in my pocket, so I whip one out and try to blot her tears.

"Honey, what is it?"

Still shaking, Becca attempts to talk to me. "Oh, Mommy, you were right. He's a jerk. Just out for a fast fuck with a dumb tourist. I hate him."

A new round of tears temporarily leaves her speechless again, giving me time to reflect on what she said. *A jerk? A fast fuck?* Had I actually used those words? Either way, what had that bastard done? The mother lioness protecting her cub, I lean down and try to gather her up in my arms. She is getting more hysterical, not less. I have to act fast.

"Becca." My tone is sharp. "What happened? Where's Sean?"

It seems to work. She raises herself up on her elbow and peers at me through a thick tangle of reddish-brown hair.

"You were right about Sean, Mom. I heard him telling his brother that I was just an easy piece of ass. That I'd be leaving soon and he would forget all about me-e-e." That last bit does her in, and she's once again shaking with anger and grief.

An easy piece of ass? That little bastard. I would kick his skinny Irish butt. Who does he think he is?

"Oh, sweetheart, I'm sure that's not how he really feels. Maybe he was just…"

Becca rolls over and glares at me. "I can't believe this. You're defending him? Seriously?" She throws herself facedown in her pillow once more. "I hate him, okay? I just want to go home."

I rub her back, and, little by little, the shudders stop and the sobs subside. *Home? Is that what I should be thinking about? Call the airlines, then grab a cab and kick some ass on the way to the airport? Or head north?*

"What if we check out of here and head up to Belfast like we planned? Go and see the Giant's Causeway, and visit the Northern coast. It would be fun, huh?" And a welcome change of pace, I realize. In the last twelve hours, I have seen just about enough of this room. I could ask Rob to fly into Belfast instead of Dublin. "Bex, what do you think?"

Becca gazes at me sadly. "What, you mean today? Leave here?"

I stop myself from rolling my eyes. I am exhausted, sure, but affairs of the heart are more familiar to me. This is pretty much uncharted territory for Becca, and I need to be patient.

"Well, maybe we could rest up a bit. Get on the computer and double check the hotels and train schedule. Leave tomorrow?" We could pick up Rob at the airport and hop on a train. Easy peasy.

Becca groans. "God, Mom. I don't know. Just let me sleep, okay? And eat. I'm starving. Can we order in?"

"Sure, sweetheart. Let me grab the room service menu." I cross the room and unearth the laminated menu. "It's too late for breakfast, but maybe sandwiches? Or soup? Bex, what do you think?"

But my darling girl doesn't answer me. She has fallen asleep, so I pull the covers over her and retreat to the table by the window. The coffee is now tepid, but I swallow some down and decide to try to read for a bit, watching my daughter sleep.

Becca

The last twenty-four hours have done me in.

After a long nap yesterday afternoon, I woke up to a veritable room service feast. Pepperoni pizza, a turkey club, a mound of fries, diet Cokes, and a yummy chocolate shake. We attacked the food and made a serious dent in it. After slurping down the last of my shake, I turned to my mom and burped. I am a really classy girl, if you haven't already figured that out.

"So good. Thanks, Mom." She beamed at me.

"Glad you enjoyed it, Bex. Thought an all-American feast was in order. So, *um,* Bex, what do you think about heading out tomorrow? Dad will be here late morning. Should we make some plans?"

"*Ugh,* Mom. You and your plans. Let's just see what we feel like in the morning, okay?"

She started to turn away and I knew she was getting impatient with me. I was fully prepared for her to launch into a whole "you don't know how hard it is, how complicated things are" type of speech. She often seems convinced that my dad and I just roll along without a care in the world, while she does all of the planning and heavy lifting. But she appeared to stop herself and just shrugged her shoulders.

"Okay, Bex, I don't want to argue with you. How about a pay-per-view movie? Or is that too much of a chore, to pick one?" I grinned at her and leaned over to grab the remote.

"No problem, Mom. Let's see what we've got here."

I scrolled through until we found a title that appealed to both of us, a rom-com that we had missed when it played in the theaters last year. We settled in on our beds and gave full attention to the film, which, while predictable, managed to hold my attention.

I only checked my phone a few times. Still no call from Sean. It was like he had written me off. I wasn't sure if what I was feeling was truly heartbreak, but it felt pretty horrible, let me tell you. Even if he doesn't care as much as I do, I kept thinking, wouldn't he still want to know what happened? Did he realize that I overheard him talking to Declan? That I knew how little he thought of me?

His behavior was so puzzling. He never said the words per se, but he certainly acted like he cared about me. He was always grabbing me and kissing me. He held my hand as we walked on the street. He was thoughtful and tender and very passionate. Oh my God, so very passionate. He was an amazing lover, but I, apparently, was just another piece of ass to him. Some American skank to fuck and forget.

Well, fuck that! I deserve better. But why hadn't he even called just to say, "Hey, did you make it back to the hotel okay? What are your plans for the week?"

When my mom started to talk to me, I turned and looked at her. "Huh, what?"

"Sweetheart, the movie's over. Do you want to turn in? Should I make some tea?"

More decisions. *Ugh.*

"No, Mom, I'm good. I'm going to try to sleep." It's pretty late, and I was thoroughly exhausted. Despite my long nap earlier, I felt like I could sleep for a week straight.

My mom got up slowly and headed for the bathroom.

"Okay then. I'm going to brush my teeth. Can I get you anything?"

Yeah, how about a sweater or a bowl of ice cream?

"No, Mom, I'm good. See you in the morning."

She walked back over to me and sat down on the edge of the bed. Her right hand stroked my shoulder and, with her left hand, she cupped my chin. Looking into her green eyes was almost like looking into a mirror. Her tone was gentle but firm when she spoke to me.

"You'll get through this, Bex. You have to trust me. You will. I know it hurts. But you will be okay."

I whimpered in response. "I just thought Sean was different. I thought he really cared about me."

"Maybe you should try to talk to him, sweetie. Give him a chance to..."

I groaned and pulled away. "No way. You didn't hear him. I can't face him after this. I just want to go home, okay? Please. I can't talk about this anymore." I slumped back down and pulled the covers up to my chin. After giving my shoulder a final squeeze, she padded back to the bathroom.

"Okay. Nite-nite. I love you," she whispered.

"G'night, Mom," I managed. "Love you, too." Then the bathroom door closed, and I was alone in the dark.

CHAPTER NINETEEN

JACKIE

AFTER A SECOND long and mostly sleepless night, I lie in bed and watch my daughter. I marvel at how soundly she is sleeping. The first couple of hours were tough for her, complete with restless thrashing and a few moans. But, close to dawn, she appeared to relax and settle into a deep sleep. Just what she needs.

My anger has disappeared, and I know that she is in for a couple of difficult days. Sean is going to be hard for Becca to get over.

What happened? I consider myself a good judge of character and thought the world of Sean. Certainly he wasn't one to take advantage of my naïve daughter. Maybe I should call him.

"No, no. Danger, don't do that," a little voice warns me, but a louder more forceful voice intervenes. "Give him a chance," it says. "Hear him out."

I'm up before any more voices can weigh in. I grab Becca's phone and, heading to the bathroom, flip on the overhead light after carefully closing the door. Becca does not have to hear this. She needs her sleep, and, besides, she would probably try to stop me. But Sean is my friend, too, and I want to give him a chance to explain.

I easily find Sean's number and, resisting the urge to read what appears to be dozens of texts from him, the last few unread, hit send. Seconds later, Sean answers. It's obvious that I woke him up.

"Becca, where are you? Are you okay?" His voice is thick with sleep.

"Sean, it's me. Jackie." My tone is frosty, a bit hostile. Too bad, this isn't a social call.

"Jackie. Is everything okay? Where's Becca?" He sounds confused but definitely concerned.

"She's here at the hotel, Sean. With me. She's sleeping." No thanks to you, I want to add.

Sean lets out a groan, which turns into a loud yawn.

"Gee, sorry, did I wake you?" I ask, my voice dripping with sarcasm.

"*Aaah*, Jackie. I'm sorry. I really fucked this up. I never meant..."

"You never meant what, Sean? To use my daughter and toss her away when you were done? To tell your brother that she is just some American ho-bag? What didn't you mean, exactly?"

"Ah shite. Becca wasn't supposed to hear that. I didn't mean it, and I never called her a, what, a ho-bag? She misunderstood me, I swear."

"I don't get it, Sean. She likes you. She really likes you." Crap, she said she loves you. "Why would you say anything even remotely like that?"

Sean's voice is hoarse as he tries to explain. "You don't know my brother. You just met him the one time. If he knew how much I care about Becca, he'd be all over me. I would never hear the end of it."

Now, I'm really getting steamed.

"So, to keep from getting teased, you break my daughter's heart? She thinks, well, I already told you what she thinks. And why haven't you called her? Or come over to see her?"

"I'm a total wanker, Jackie. That's on me. When I came back into the bedroom yesterday, I panicked. Becca was gone, and I figured she heard me. What I said about her. I didn't know what to do. I was going to go after her, but Dec convinced me to let her cool down first. We went for a couple of beers, and, shit, I just kept thinking about how Becca must have felt, and I had another beer and then another, and then it was too late to call her. I sent her a couple of texts a few hours ago, before I passed out. I was gonna come over there as soon as I was sober," he ends sadly.

"You should have led with that, Sean. She cried herself to sleep, and I... Oh, hi, sweetie. Guess who I'm talking to? It's Sean, honey.

He was just saying that he wants to come over here and see you in a bit."

"Why're you on my phone? I told you I didn't want to talk to him. Why did you answer my phone?" Becca is furious and getting all worked up again. I have to come clean.

"I, *um,* called him, Bex. I didn't have his number, so I…"

"I can't believe this. Why did you call him? Hang up, Mom. Hang up now!"

She grabs the phone from my hand, and I can hear Sean pleading with her to talk to him just as she ends the call. I've seen her sad, and I've seen her scared, but I have never seen Rebecca Sullivan Colby this furious. Her eyes are cold and her breathing is labored as she tells me to butt out and mind my own business.

"I can't be here with you right now. I've got to get out of here." I want to tell her that she needs to change out of her flimsy nightshirt first but decide to keep silent, until she calms down a little. She pulls on a pair of jeans and slips her feet into a pair of sandals before heading into the bathroom. Over the sound of running water, I can hear her brushing her teeth. Seconds later, she emerges, and, in a voice like ice, she tells me that she's heading to the airport.

"I'm gonna call Daddy from the cab. I'll meet him at the airport, and he'll sort out my flight for me. I want to go to Boston. I can get a job there and find a place to stay for cheap until I can move back into the dorm. Daddy can ship all my stuff to me. I'm leaving my clothes here. I can't deal with this right now. Burn them, leave them, I don't care."

I try to protest. To tell her I want her to stay. To beg her to at least talk to Sean, to listen to what he has to say. But one look at my daughter's tear-stained face tells me all I need to know. I manage to mumble, "I love you Becca".

Right before she storms out, she turns to me.

"Oh yeah, Mom? Don't hold your breath waiting for my diploma to arrive. I didn't graduate."

Becca

So there. I guess I told her. I can't believe her. Siding with Sean? Seriously?

I race through the hotel lobby and push my way through the huge double doors, out into the bright sunshine. It should be raining to match my lousy mood. I pace back and forth on the sidewalk. Where is a cab when you need one? At this rate, I won't make it to the airport in time to catch my dad.

I grab my phone and send him a quick text.

Don't leave airport. On my way to meet you.

I hope he remembers to turn his phone on before he gets in a cab. He will know what to do. Maybe we can have lunch or something before I catch a flight to Boston.

I am so done with this goddamn place. Where the hell are all the cabs? Finally, I see one pull up, and I wait until the elderly couple gets out and pays the driver. As soon as they collect their luggage, I approach the cab and start to get into the back seat.

"I need to get to the airport," I mumble.

"Sorry, love. I'm waiting on a fare wanting to get to the train station. Did you check with the desk?"

Say what?

"Huh? No. You can't take me?" My words catch in my throat, and, for a second, I think I'm going to cry. The driver looks at me and apparently recognizes that I am in some kind of a crisis. He speaks slowly, as if I'm not capable of understanding much of anything.

"The hotel's pretty strict about the traffic out in front here. We're not allowed to loiter or pick up the guests. You need to arrange for all pickups through reception." I continue to stare at him blankly, so he points towards the lobby. "Go on now. Tell 'em you need to get to the airport. This looks like my fare now." He indicates the two women bustling towards us. " And girly?" he asks in a hushed tone.

"Yeah?"

"You might want to find a jumper or something before you head out to the airport," he tells me almost apologetically.

I look down. *Crap.* I left our room so quickly, it hadn't occurred to me how sheer my nightshirt is. The driver is right. I need a sweater or hoodie or something. My cheeks burn with embarrassment. I must look like a crazy person.

"*Um,* thanks. I will," I mumble as he winks at me, not in a pervy way. "Excuse me," I finish weakly and exit the cab so that the women who rightfully reserved it could get in.

I glance around. I know there's a souvenir shop a few doors down where I can find some crappy sweatshirt to cover up with. *Christ, you can see right through this damn top.* I cross my arms over my chest and, holding my handbag in front of me, rush down to the store before I get arrested for indecent exposure.

A few minutes later, I find an XL gray hoodie proclaiming *Slainte* across the front in bright green lettering. *Yeah, "Cheers" indeed.* "No bag," I tell the clerk. "I'll wear it now," and I pull it over my head.

The young woman nods at me. "Rough night, huh?" she asks half-heartedly.

"You have no idea," I respond, tearing the sales tag off. I leave the store without grabbing my receipt or the change she offers me. Time to get back to the hotel and arrange for the cab.

My phone pings as I rush out of the store. A text from my dad.

I'm already on my way to the hotel. See you in 15.

Crap. Now I will have to wait here for him. I can't leave without seeing him, and he is way better at changing airline tickets than I am. But he will want to get my mom involved in the whole thing, and I'll have to see her again after all. And on top of everything else, she'll want to know what I meant about not graduating. This is the worst day ever.

I decide to go back into the lobby and wait for my dad. I settle in on one of the couches facing the front, the exact same place I waited for Sean only a week ago. So much has happened since then. We spent probably a hundred hours together, many in his bed. My face burns as I think of all those kisses, all that amazing sex. The way his stupid Celtic cross tattoo covers most of his broad, pale back. The way that the reddish hair on his forearms glints in the late afternoon sunlight. The way his tongue... I shiver.

"Don't," I tell myself. "He is dead to you."

I close my eyes and lean back on the couch. I will talk to my dad and explain things to him. Give him the G-rated version. He'll help me to get out of Dublin and head home today. Maybe I can just see my mom for a minute. I hate to leave without at least saying goodbye. I'll tell her that I'll finish up that last paper and get a final grade for the course. I owe her that. She and Dad can still have a nice trip for themselves. Maybe stop in Boston on their way back to Arizona next week, and we can spend a little time together. I am still furious with her for interfering, but I know she acted out of love and concern for me. I just wish she hadn't called him. *Fuck him, anyway.*

"Bexie."

"Becca."

What the…? I open my eyes in time to see Sean and my dad, both walking towards me and calling my name. My dad strolls over and looks surprised when Sean hurries past him and calls my name again. I stand up just as Sean reaches me. He tries to pull me into his arms, but I push away from him.

"What do you want? I don't want to see you," I tell him between clenched teeth, just as my dad joins us.

He looks confused at first, and then really mad.

"Bex, what's going on? Is this guy bothering you?" He glares at Sean, who must realize that it was my father, since he steps back and holds up his hands in surrender.

"No, sir, Mr. Colby. It's not like that. I'm Sean. I'm Becca's, *um,* friend."

My dad starts to smile as he recognizes the name and the face from all the photos I'd been posting but then frowns at how I just reacted.

"Well, Sean. It looks like my daughter isn't feeling very friendly towards you right now, so maybe you should just back off, *huh*?" He turns to me. "Bex, are you okay?" His voice is full of concern, and I am so glad to see him.

I throw myself in his arms.

"I'm okay, Daddy. I'm just so glad you're here." I snuffle into his chest, trying to hold back my tears. I need to talk to him and fast, before…

"Rob—you made it! Becca, you didn't leave. Oh honey, I've been so…" My mom is crying and trying to hug my dad and me, as I struggle to regain my composure. Dad lets me go just long enough to focus for a second on my mom, and I take the opportunity to face Sean directly. He's standing there with this sheepish expression, and I just want to slap him.

"What do you want?" I snarl. "Haven't you done enough damage for one day?"

Sean looks at me sadly. My folks stop hugging long enough to focus their attention on the drama unfolding right before their eyes. My mom speaks up first.

"Becca, why don't you at least listen to what Sean has to say? He came here to talk to you, honey."

My dad watches us through narrowed eyes, studying Sean. He must decide that Sean is worthy, because he sticks out his hand. Clearly my mom's opinion of Sean counts more than mine.

"Rob Colby. I've been hearing a lot about you."

Sean grabs on like he is a drowning man and my dad's outstretched hand is a lifeline.

"I'm glad to meet you, sir. I've heard a lot about you, as well. Your wife and your daughter have been looking forward to your arrival. And, hey, welcome to Dublin."

I snort in derision. *What a two-faced jerk. Welcome, indeed. I've been fucking your daughter, but don't worry. It's all in great fun*. I hug my dad again.

"Daddy, I'm sorry. It's just a little disagreement. He is just leaving," I say sweetly. Ignoring Sean completely, I take my father's arm to lead him away. "Okay, then. Bye, Sean. Dad, c'mon, let's get you up to the room. You must be completely knackered, er, exhausted from that long flight. Maybe, after you rest up a bit, we can grab a bite, and I can talk to you about…"

But Sean is not going to let us go without a fight.

"Becca, wait. You misunderstood me. I never called you a ho-bag. Being with you, sleeping with you..."

Fuck, now my dad is on protective-father overload. He barrels back over to where Sean is standing. My mom mutters, "Oh shit," just as my dad explodes.

"Listen to me, Donovan. That's my daughter you're talking about, and if you think for one minute I'm going to stand here and let you..."

My mom attempts to take his arm.

"Rob, maybe we should just let them..."

My dad pulls away and faces her angrily.

"Let them what, Jackie? What the hell's been going on here, anyway? This clown is talking about our girl, ferchrissakes." He stops long enough to take a deep breath and notices that our little family drama has drawn a small but interested crowd of onlookers. "Okay, folks," he calls out. "Show's over. Nothing to see here." He turns to look at my mom then me, then back at my mom. He speaks in measured tones. "Ladies, let's go. C'mon. We need to continue this discussion in private." He glares again at Sean, who seems to have lost the gift of gab for once. "I think we're done here, Donovan. You should probably take off. This is a family matter." He grabs his carryon and starts to wheel his suitcase behind him. "C'mon, Jackie. Becca. Let's go."

But Sean still isn't ready to concede.

"Mr. Colby? Begging your pardon, sir, but I came here to speak with your daughter. She misunderstood something she overheard, and I need to set things right between us. Please just let me talk to her. Just for a moment, sir."

Wow, he has a pair of balls all right. For a second, I think my dad is going to haul off and punch him, but something about the way that Sean sounds or carries himself causes him to back down. My mom speaks up.

"Robbie, it's okay. He's just got to talk to Becca. C'mon sweetheart." He relents, after looking at me. I nod at him.

"It's okay, Dad. Why don't you head up? I'll be along in a minute, I swear." He looks again at my mom, and she leads him across the lobby as I turn to face Sean. I smile at him, for my dad's sake, but speak in a low voice. "You've got exactly sixty seconds. Go."

CHAPTER TWENTY

JACKIE

WE MAKE OUR WAY to the elevator, ride up seven flights, and walk down to our room at the end of the hall. I try to unlock the door. I hate these little magnetic key cards. They're always upside down. Rob hasn't said a single word, and his uncharacteristic silence is making me nervous.

"C'mon, Rob. Say what's on your mind."

He takes the card from my hand, inserts it smoothly, and the door unlocks. Pulling his suitcase behind him, he follows me into our room. "Okay, let me have it." He looks directly at me for the first time since we left Becca and Sean in the lobby. He shakes his head, starts to say something, and then stops.

"What? Are you upset with me?" Silence. "Christ, I hate when you do that. Just clam up and judge me. I know that look."

He gives me a half-smile in response.

"Is that what you think? That I'm judging you right now?"

"Yes, I do. You think I've let Becca run wild here in Dublin. But it's not true. Honest, it's not what it looks like."

"Which part? The part where some guy I've never seen before talks about sleeping with our daughter? Or the part where the two of you seem to know what Becca needs more than *she* does."

Oh crap, he has me there.

"I was going to tell you. I wanted to talk to you about it. But when Becca didn't come home that night, it would have been the middle of the night back home and I..." The shocked look on his face stops me cold. "What?"

"She stayed out all night? With that fucking tour guide? And this is the first I'm hearing about it? Christ, what else have I missed?"

Oh man, do I have some explaining to do. I lead him over to a comfortable chair.

"Take a load off, sweetheart. I've wanted to talk to you about all this, okay? Don't worry. She's doing fine. They had a misunderstanding, a lover's quarrel."

He winces at my choice of words but seems to be listening, so I go on. He already knows that his daughter had developed a crush on Sean and that it was clearly reciprocated. I reiterate how Sean has been spending a lot of time with us since we got back to Dublin and that the crush has escalated into something more serious. That, other than the one morning when I woke up alone, they have been very responsible and respectful of me. I end by telling him how much we have been looking forward to his arrival today and that we have lots of things planned.

"Sean is a lovely young man. You'll see that for yourself." Soon I hope.

I wonder what is going on down in the lobby. Have they made up? Or has Becca decided not to give Sean the benefit of the doubt?. He may have told Declan that he was only looking for a casual fling, but everything about Sean—the way he looks at Becca, the way he talks to her, the time he invested this week—all of that makes it clear to me that he is as crazy about her as she is about him.

"Give him a chance, Bexie," I silently message her. The more time they spend talking, the better the chance that they are likely to reconcile.

But to what end? And what the hell was that comment she made about not graduating? My daughter has some explaining to do of her own. Deep in thought, I hear my name being called.

"Earth to Jackie," Robbie teases. "C'mon. I'm beat." He does look exhausted. "Becca just texted me again. She's giving him another chance. We can meet them in the lobby later for a drink, and then we'll head out to eat. That gives us," he adds, with a quick look at his watch, "a few hours to catch up." He grins and pulls me closer to him.

Oh, that familiar Rob scent. God, I missed this man. Whatever happens with Becca and Sean, we will handle it together.

"Catch up, huh?" I chuckle. "Is that what the kids are calling it these days?"

A moan escapes my lips as my husband starts kissing my neck and then moves on to my lips. Kissing Rob is still the same thrill it has always been. But wait. I should tell him that I'm prepared to follow him anywhere. I should let him know about Becca and the whole "not graduating" thing. I should… Oh damn. Everything will just have to wait. I have a husband to get reacquainted with.

Becca

I tell Sean that I believe him, and I do. I tell him I understand he was not being truthful when he bragged to Declan that I was just a casual fling. Besides… He told me. He said it. Those three little words.

I don't know if he planned to. Probably not, because he looked as surprised as I felt when he told me that he loved me. But then he said it again. This time with an intensity that sent a chill down my spine.

He means it.

I had said something about how I understood, you know? How it was all fun and games. That it's all it can ever be between us. In just a few days, I am going home and he has to get back to work. But Sean was shaking his head at me.

"No, Becca. It's more than that for me. Way more." His eyes were kind of glassy, and, for a second, his voice cracked. Suddenly, I was looking at a young man who really wanted me. Who was worried that he wasn't going to have me. He reached for my hands and, grasping them in his, looked at me intently. "I love you," he stammered.

What?

He took a deep breath and seemed to get his second wind. He pulled me close. "Becca, I love you. I've never felt this way about anyone. You have to believe me," he murmured in my ear.

And I want to. I really want to. Because I am certain of just one thing right now. I love this man. This brash, gorgeous man with the pale skin, the broad shoulders, that crazy Celtic cross tattoo, and even that dumb cap he always wears. Who always has an answer for everything, always knows the right thing to say, and has the gift of making whomever he is talking to feel like they are the most important person in the world.

I have no idea what will happen between us. But right now, I don't much care. This will have to be enough, at least for now.

"I love you, too," I whisper. He pulls back and looks at me with so much surprise and so much joy, that I almost laugh.

Holding my face with his hands, he grins at me. I missed that sexy, mischievous grin of his.

"So what do we do now?" he asks.

I know what I want to do. Oh yeah. Drag his Irish ass off to the nearest bed and have some wild and crazy sex with him. I heard that makeup sex is pretty good, and I want to find out for myself.

Instead, I say, "You know my folks are upstairs waiting to hear from me, right? I'm sure they're worried sick about me."

"Yeah, and I didn't exactly get off on the right foot with your dad. I can't imagine what he must think of me." Sean shakes his head dejectedly. "I wish I could start over with the man. Show him that I love his daughter and respect her." I pull him to me and hug him tightly.

"He'll know. My dad isn't one to hold a grudge. We can all go grab some lunch, huh? You can charm him like you've charmed Mom and me. Go all full-scale Oirish on him, and he'll melt."

Sean chuckles at that and then whispers into my ear, "Then maybe, after lunch, you and I can head back to my place. Whattayathink?"

Oh, yeah.

"Sounds like a plan," I agree enthusiastically, as I extricate myself from his embrace. "Let me send them a quick text and ask them. Mom will want to know what's up."

The message goes through, but neither of my folks respond.

"That's weird. Usually my dad texts back right away. What could they…?"

Oh, wait a minute. My folks haven't seen each other in twelve days. Maybe they're... Oh, gross. They're like rabbits, I swear. They are always hugging each other and making out.

"Let's give them a little time to settle in first, okay? Maybe we can grab a coffee while we wait."

While I feel I can tell Sean just about anything, I can't imagine admitting to him that my parents are upstairs right at this moment, probably having sex. I shudder and push the image out of my mind.

But Sean is no fool. With a wink, he grabs my hand and leads me across the lobby to the small café near the main entrance.

"Let's let your folks get reacquainted. My Oirish charm is just going to have to wait."

CHAPTER TWENTY-ONE

JACKIE

I WRAP MYSELF up in a towel and attempt to wipe the steam off the bathroom mirror. I can barely make out my own reflection, but I know I'm smiling. A big shit-eating grin is most definitely plastered across my face. Rob always has that effect on me. Sex with Rob… Well, let's just say it doesn't get any better than that. Even after our marriage hit the skids and we were divorced, there was always that spark.

I wonder if he wants to grab a quick shower. Becca and Sean have made up, and I hope she isn't still upset with me. Maybe we shouldn't keep them waiting much longer. I call out to my husband.

"Sweetheart, are you going to hop in the shower? We should probably find the kids."

Silence. I open the door and walk back into the bedroom. Oh, so that's why he isn't answering me. My jetlagged mate is sound asleep, sprawled out on the bed, right where I left him not ten minutes ago. He is flat on his back and snoring ever so softly. My darling husband.

So, should I wake him? Let him sleep while I go meet Becca and Sean and then bring him back some food? Or join him in bed? My phone buzzes. A missed call from Becca. Okay, so that decides it for me. I'll leave a note for Rob and head down to the lobby. As I dig around on the nightstand for a scrap of paper, Rob stirs and then slowly opens his eyes.

"Where're you going?" he drawls. He pulls himself into a seated position and faces me. "Sneaking off without me, huh?"

I sit down on the bed next to him and kiss him lightly on the lips.

"No, sweetheart, I was thinking of waking you, but you looked so peaceful. Becca's been calling, so I'm going to head down to the lobby and check on things. Then I was going to come back up here and jump your bones again."

Rob stretches and groans softly.

"I need sustenance, woman. You can't expect me to perform without at least buying me a sandwich, now can you?"

I slip out of my towel and pretend to flick it at him.

"Then get your lazy ass out of bed," I tease as I try to grab his arms and pull him up. He is too quick for me. He pulls me down on top of him then rolls over, pinning me underneath him. I know where this might lead. "C'mon, sweetheart. Becca's waiting for us. With Sean," I add.

"Oh crap. Talk about a mood killer. Just what I need right now is an image of that jack-off tour guide and my daughter." He pushes himself off me and strides, bare-assed, into the shower. "Can you find me a shirt, babe? I just need a quick shower before I face Romeo again. Give me five minutes, okay?"

"He's a great guy. You'll see," I tell him confidently as the door closes behind him. If he gives him a chance, I know that Rob will come to like Sean. Once he gets over the fact that he is sleeping with his baby girl, that is.

An hour later, the four of us are sitting in a booth at a pub that Sean recommended. We split a pitcher of ale before switching to ice water as we enjoy our midafternoon pub grub. Rob takes over the storytelling role and has a captive audience in Sean, as he describes a recent meeting with a client that hadn't gone the way he planned.

"I kept trying to convince this guy that not all company founders make great company spokespersons. He wanted to star in his own commercials. 'Just like the Wendy's guy,' he keeps reminding me. How do you tell a guy that he's too old, too bald, and too out of shape to be the face of his upscale beauty salon? And he spoke with a lisp, too." Sean cracks up at that, and Robbie grins at him right before he turns serious.

"I'm going to miss it, you know?" *Oh crap, here we go.*

"Dad, what are you talking about?"

"I'm ready to sell my half of the business, Bex. Joe's son Max? He's expressed an interest in running the agency with his dad. He's got a few years of experience under his belt, and he wants to come back to Sedona." Rob shrugs his shoulders as if it's no big deal, but Becca isn't buying it.

"Mom, did you know about this?"

"Yes, Becca. Your dad and I have been talking about it for a couple of months. He wants me to turn Encore over to Amy and *um*, travel with him."

Becca is speechless, but Sean jumps in, all ready to congratulate us.

"That's a grand plan, Jackie. You two will have a ball." He stops when he sees me looking less than thrilled.

"Mom, what's up? Don't you want this? It sounds wonderful. What's the point of working so hard if you can't enjoy your success?"

I take a deep breath. I had wanted to tell Rob privately. Work out a few details first, like how I wanted to keep the house and start small. Baby steps. But everyone is waiting for me to say something.

It's time.

"Yes, Bex. I *do* want this. Rob, as soon as we get home, let's grab our calendars. We have a future to plan." Rob wraps me up in a hug, and Becca and Sean jump up to join him. We're all hugging and I'm crying and everything seems just about perfect, as my husband whispers in my ear.

"It'll be great sweetheart. We'll have a ball." I can only nod and squeeze his hand as everyone sits back down.

"Where will you head first, Rob?" Sean asks with interest and both men immediately begin plotting an itinerary. I shake my head as I hear exotic destinations like Machu Picchu, Bali, and Thailand being bandied about. I'm thinking more like the Pacific Northwest. Baby steps.

I look across the tabletop at my daughter.

"We okay, Bex?"

She smiles back at me.

"Yeah, Mom, we're fine. I just want you to be happy."

"I *am* happy, darling. I need some time on this, okay?"

"Okay. Whatever you want. Just look at them, will you?" She gazes affectionately at both guys. "I thought Dad would kill him for a second there. I guess I have you to thank for, *um,* calming him down, huh?"

I shrug nonchalantly.

"What can I say? I have mad skills, you know?" I decide it's time to change topics. "And you owe me an explanation, young lady. What was that crap about not graduating?"

Becca squirms in her seat and can't look me in the eye.

"It's just a silly thing, Mom. I'll work it out, okay? I'll tell you everything. Let's just not spoil this, huh?" she begs, indicating the men and their animated discussion.

I decide to let it go for the moment, after she promises to tell me everything tomorrow at breakfast. But I have one more question.

"So, how do you feel about dessert? All this excitement has got me craving something sweet."

"Let's get a couple of sticky toffee puddings for the table. Gee, I miss Carrie," Becca adds. "What a cutie."

I chuckle, remembering the little firecracker we spent the past week with. We will have to give her a call from home next week.

"She'll make a good mom, don't you think?"

My daughter leans over the table and plants a kiss on the top of my head.

"Takes one to know one. You *are* a good mom."

Awww. That's my girl!

Becca

I have said goodbye to my folks dozens of times in my life, but this goodbye has to be the toughest. Not that we are going to be separated for all that long or anything. It will just be a few days. And we aren't even going to be that far apart.

They are heading to Belfast and the Antrim Coast of Northern Ireland, and Sean and I are going to Dingle to see Fiona. Only a couple hundred miles apart, but it is already starting to feel like a million. We spent the last few days together, the four of us. My folks stayed at the hotel, and I was with Sean at his apartment. It was kind of weird the first night, saying goodnight in the lobby and then walking hand in hand back to my boyfriend's place.

That first evening, during dinner, my mom said something about me checking into my own room that she reserved earlier in the week. Awkward silence. Mom looked at me, and I looked at Sean, and he looked at Dad, and Dad just kind of smiled. Not a happy smile. More of an "oh shit, what can you do?" one.

My mom shrugged and said that I should stop by the desk after dinner and cancel the room. So that settled things. I am twenty-one years old and madly in love, and my folks are being pretty cool. After that, things got easier. At least they did, once I came clean about my disastrous last semester. I promised my folks that I would resolve things as soon as I got back to Sedona. Sean tried teasing me about being a college dropout, but I warned him that it was way too soon to make jokes.

We settled into a bit of a pattern over the next few days. Sean and I slept in and wandered over to the hotel after a couple of coffees and a pastry or breakfast sandwich. My folks waited for us in the lobby or came right down when we got there. Sean still has a bucket list of places to see in and around Dublin, so we didn't waste any time. The Guinness Storehouse was as big a hit with my dad as I'd predicted.

Yesterday, Sean borrowed a friend's car, and we drove out to Waterford for the day. It was cool, being back in a moving vehicle with Sean, cruising around the back roads. Dad rode shotgun and listened with great interest as Sean explained all of the intricacies of driving on the left. My folks plan to rent a car after taking the train to Belfast.

Now, I happen know that my dad has driven cars all over Europe and, after a couple of miles, will be perfectly acclimated to driving in Northern Ireland. But Sean didn't know that and seemed to take great pleasure in being able to teach him something. That is one of the loveliest things about Dad. He knew how important it was for Sean to impress him, to show him what a responsible and accomplished young man he is.

At one of our stops, I leaned in and gave him a hug.

"Thanks for that, Daddy," I whispered.

He pulled back and winked at me.

"Sean's a good teacher, Bex. I think I'm going to do just fine, driving around up there."

So here we are, saying goodbye to my folks at the train station. I feel like, somewhere along the way, we turned a corner, you know? Like I'm not their baby girl anymore. I finally told them about my disastrous last semester and my plan to make up the work over the summer, and it felt pretty good to finally talk about it. Neither of them was thrilled, obviously, but it's better to get things like that out in the open. I feel like such an adult as we wait for the train to arrive. That is, until the track is announced and it's time for them to go. My heart is pounding as I watch as my dad and Sean clasp hands, and then Dad pulls him in for a quick hug.

"Take care of my girl," he growls in my boyfriend's ear. Sean looks up to the challenge.

His response is quick and sincere. "No worries, Rob. I'll watch out for her. Now, you and Jackie go and have some fun."

My mom is busy hugging me, and, for a second, I think she is going to cry. Goodbyes are always tough for her, and we have spent so much time together on this trip, it will be weird not to be around her. She finally runs out of things I should be careful about and reminders to keep in touch with texts and calls.

"What am I gonna do without my Bex?" she whispers.

I hug her even tighter in response.

"I'm so happy, Mom. You can't even imagine."

She pulls back and looks at me closely. Her eyes are brimming with unshed tears, but her smile is genuine, even as her voice catches a bit. "Yeah, sweetheart, I think I can."

Then Dad is hugging me and my mom is hugging Sean, and, next thing you know, Sean and I are waving goodbye as my folks hustle off to board their train. Once they are out of sight, Sean turns to me, his voice all official.

"Well then, Miss Colby. I'll be on my way then. It's been grand," he adds, doffing an imaginary hat at me. The tears I have been holding back turn quickly to laughter. He can be such a clown sometimes. I pull him close to me.

"Oh no, you're not getting away from me that easily, boy-o," I threaten. "You promised me a holiday, and I'm holding you to it." I grab his hand. "C'mon then. Let's keep it moving now." Two can play at this bossy tour guide game.

CHAPTER TWENTY-TWO

JACKIE

NORTHERN IRELAND IS spectacular! Rob and I are having a really great time here. We spent the first night in Belfast. The Europa hotel is centrally located and notorious as the most-bombed hotel in all Great Britain. There are no longer any apparent signs of the turbulent not-so-distant past when you stroll through the lobby or explore the nearby city square.

Rob and I each have Irish ancestors, which makes the stories we hear and the sites we visit even more memorable. Sean told us that a Black Cab Tour through the "troubled" areas is a must, so the hotel concierge set it up for us. Our driver/tour guide is a lean, compact guy of about forty. He says his name is Jackie, but his accent is so strong, I think he says "Jaggy."

I say something like, "Oh, that's funny, Jaggy. My name is Jackie."

A look of confusion crosses his face, but, of course, Rob comes to the rescue. "Well, Sedona Jackie, meet Belfast Jackie," he quips smoothly and off we go.

I struggle to understand what Belfast Jackie is saying at first. Northern Irish have their own dialect, and it's sometimes hard to understand them until you get used to it. Rob has always had a way with languages. Give him a day in a different country and he could fill a guidebook with all of the necessary phrases. We went to France years ago, and I was disappointed that I had no opportunity to use the one phrase I could recall from high school French: *où est la piscine?* Turned out we had no need to locate a swimming pool the whole time we were there. It figures.

I sit in the back of the cab with my knees up around my ears while Rob and Belfast Jackie chatter on and on. Politics, history, world affairs—Rob is much better informed than I am. We always joke that, together, we are the perfect composite player and could win at *Jeopardy*. Rob would handle all of the science, geography, and history categories, and I would propel our team to victory with my knowledge of literature, film, and pop culture. Too bad that Team Jeopardy never got launched.

We are driving around the Shankill and Fall Road neighborhoods, long divided by religious differences. Belfast Jackie has a real workingman's practicality about him, as he shows us huge, colorful murals and shares stories of courage and oppression. You can tell that he is truly moved by the area's violent history, but he seems to be talking about events from centuries ago instead of during his own lifetime.

Our final stop is at one of the peace walls that separate the Protestant and Catholic communities. Signing my name to the wall actually brings me to tears. I wish that Becca were with us. She would have been moved, as well.

The next day, we rent a car and take off for the Antrim Coast. Sure enough, driving on the left is just another long-dormant but super-strong skill of Rob's. I always feel safe with my husband behind the wheel. Just keep him away from power tools (please!), and if the cause of a breakdown is anything other than a flat tire, we would be up shit's creek. He is not the handiest of guys. But driving is a pleasure for him. So here we are, speeding through the countryside on our way to the Giant's Causeway.

"How'm I doing?" Rob asks me, flashing a grin in my direction.

I have to tease him, just a little.

"Not bad," I tell him in what I hope is a bored tone. "You're no Sean, but you're not bad."

We enter a roundabout and he has to really concentrate but shakes his head at me, nonetheless.

"You're a riot, 'Jaggie.' Life with you? It's a laugh a freakin' minute."

I squeeze his left hand just before he pulls it away in order to shift.

"It's been a good life, huh? We have a good life, right?"

My voice catches, and I try to hold back a sudden bout of tears. I have been daydreaming about traipsing around Northern Ireland with my husband *and* my daughter for months, but now it's just the two of us. Becca is in love and off on her own adventure. My husband wants to travel around the world with me and have our own grand adventures, and I'm trying to damnedest to imagine a life like that. Things are changing just a little too fast for me. Rob notices the quaver in my voice and tear sliding down my cheek. He pulls off the road and kills the engine right before he reaches for me.

"It's okay. I'm not going to pressure you anymore. We'll plan a trip in the States, okay? We'll see the USA in an RV first. And we'll see Becca in a couple days. Then we'll have the rest of the summer at home. She's in a good place right now, and if that little bastard hurts her again, I'll kick his ass."

I have to smile at that image. Sean has a few inches on Rob and is roughly half his age. But we do what we have to do and we believe what we need to.

"But what if Becca wants to stay?"

"Stay? Stay here with him? No way." His tone is incredulous, but I can see doubt starting to take shape.

"I'm just saying it's a possibility, even a remote one." I keep my tone light. I don't want to freak him out and expose that protective-dad gene again. If I thought it would do some good, maybe. But I know our daughter. Once she makes up her mind, it is really hard to get her to change it.

"She's only twenty-one. She doesn't know what she wants. I was dropping out of college, getting stoned, and sleeping with every girl I… So, what were you doing when you were twenty-one?"

"I was burying my parents," I tell him somberly.

I can't help it. It is a true statement, and it just slips out. My parents had passed away within months of each other during my senior year in college. Rob's face turns an unhealthy shade of red. *Oooh,* I have touched a nerve.

"Wow. Are you really going there? You're a little old to play the poor little orphan girl, aren't you?"

"Hey, you asked. I'm just saying that Becca really seems to like this guy. I don't know. Maybe he's 'the one.'"

"Christ. She's only known the kid for a week. She can't possibly have feelings that strong that she'd give up everything and move across the ocean to be with him."

Oh yeah? Twenty-two years ago, I moved across the country in order to check out a hunky tour guide whom I had known for a single afternoon. Granted, I was older, more sure of myself, but was I really? Maybe my daughter and I aren't so different when it comes to affairs of the heart.

Can this be some wild, random case of history repeating itself? Is karma really that big of a bitch? I shake my head and clear my throat.

"How long after you met me? How long did it take before you knew you wanted to be with me?"

Rob lets out a chuckle. "Are you kidding? The minute I laid eyes on you at that stupid conference."

"Panel session."

"Whatever. You looked at me with such loathing. All prim and proper in your little suit."

"You were mocking me. You were telling my students that dropping out of school was the way to go. Instant success, my ass!" I glare at him, recalling how crazy he made me back then. And right now, too. "I thought you were an obnoxious jerk."

He refuses to take the bait and just grins at me. That wild, sexy grin that has led to all kinds of shenanigans when he uses it on me.

"All I knew was that I wanted to rip your clothes off and fuck you silly. You turned me on that day and every day since then, you wild woman, you." He tries to pull me in for a hug, maybe some kissing. But I still have things to say.

"You're making my point for me," I tell him gently. "Sometimes, love or lust or whatever it is makes us do crazy things. You might remember my little trek cross-country a few years back. What do you think that was all about?"

Rob starts to laugh at that. Apparently he's forgotten just how pissed off he was back then and how hurt, when he found out that my sudden decision to relocate was hatched only after I met sexy Rick.

"You were having a midlife crisis, just a few years early, sweetheart. You had an itch that needed to be scratched. I let the dust settle on that one and then came in to save the day. And here we are."

Oooh, that smug bastard.

"Listen, you. That was more than an itch, okay? And midlife or not, sexual attraction makes us do things. All kinds of things. Uprooting-your-life kind of things. Becca may want to stay here. Or Sean might want to come back with her. To Boston. It's a possibility, that's all I'm saying."

Robbie rubs his eyes with the palms of his hands. He suddenly looks much older than his years; dealing with his adult daughter's love life is clearly weighing on him. This is much harder for him than he lets on.

I pull him close to me. It's time for me to be the strong one.

"C'mon, sweetheart. We're still almost an hour away from the Causeway. Let's get going. You're right. Becca will figure things out. We can't solve everything today."

Rob brightens at that. He has accused me more than a few times over the last thirty years of wanting to talk things to death. It is a rare occasion for me to be the first one to encourage the tabling of a discussion. I get a grin in return. Not the sexy one. More of a relieved one.

I squeeze him tight one more time before we buckle our seatbelts. I push my too-long bangs out of my eyes and settle back in my seat as Robbie checks his mirrors and prepares to get us back on the road. But he isn't smiling, not really. A sense of dread still hangs over me like a dark cloud. We've come to an agreement about *our* future, but what about Becca's? What if she decides to stay here and not return to Sedona with us? Or what if Sean decides to come home with her?

I close my eyes and try to clear my head of such thoughts. *Don't go there,* I caution myself. The sun is shining, my family is safe and healthy, even if we are separated right now, and we are about to see some amazing sights. Life is good. Isn't it?

Becca

"Are we just about there?" I study the map I brought despite the protests of my tour guide boyfriend and then peer through the grimy windshield. I am just about bouncing out of my seat, quite excited to arrive in Dingle and meet Sean's sister, Fiona. "I wish you people had the sense to deal in miles and yards and all. This whole meters and kilometers crap is killing me here," I complain, only half joking.

"I'll thank you to fold that thing up and never speak of it again, Rebecca," Sean advises severely, gesturing at the map. "I'd probably lose my job or at least be the laughingstock of the shop, if anyone were to see me consulting a map made for tourists. And yes, in answer to your question, we *are* almost there. Another twenty minutes and we'll be parking the car. And if you ask me again in ten minutes, my response will be the same, minus ten minutes," he adds, a tad sarcastically.

"Geez, I think I liked you better when I was paying you to show me around," I complain, but I squeeze his arm as I say it. He *has* been a bit testy all morning, and I'm sure my childish behavior isn't helping matters any. I know that when it comes to his sister, he can be a little touchy.

He tried unsuccessfully to goad Declan into coming with us today. He pointed out that there was plenty of room in the borrowed car he had arranged, that the weather promised to be stellar (in Ireland, that means no monsoons, I think; their standards aren't very high when it comes to Mother Nature), and that it would be a grand opportunity to get to know me better, as well. I even batted my eyes, all cutesy- like.

Dec pretended to ponder the offer, but I could tell that his mind was made up.

"Give Fi my best, will ya?" he asked as we left the apartment this morning.

Sean barely spoke to me during the walk over to his mate Jimmy's flat to get the car keys. I wondered if he had told Fi that Declan might join us. I matched his silence as we loaded everything into the boot and maneuvered our way out of the city center, heading southwest. He perked up a little, the farther we got from Dublin, and has been downright chatty for the last couple of hours. But the closer we get to Dingle, the tenser and quieter he becomes.

I focus my attention on the beautiful countryside, the confusing map, and the tangy scent of the sea that is growing stronger. We are going to spend two nights at the inn where Fi works. Although she has only the one day off tomorrow, we are going to meet her at work then head out for a late lunch. Sean assures me that Fi is dying to meet me and will be joining us for dinner tonight, as well.

I look forward to checking into our own room with my sexy boyfriend. It seems like such a grown-up thing to do, to be off on holiday together. Also, it will be nice to have sex somewhere other than the messy apartment that Sean shares with Declan. We will have some privacy at last. Sweet!

A short while later, we park the car, and I follow Sean across a busy street. Our destination is a vine-covered white building with a big, welcoming front porch. It's lovely, and I smile as I picture myself sitting on one of the comfy-looking chairs and reading a book, maybe sipping some hot tea.

Apparently, Sean is picturing me sitting there, as well. He suggests that I wait out here, while he goes in and "sorts things out." He leaves without kissing me, and I watch him go through the door that leads into the lobby. I am really hoping that he finds Fi and maybe she can take a break to hang out with us for a bit.

I settle into the chair and decide to check my phone. There are several messages, all from my folks. Nothing urgent, just some photos and notes about what they have been seeing. It would have been nice to visit Belfast, but I am clearly where I need to be right now. I send a quick text telling them that we arrived in Dingle and include a selfie with the sign from the inn in the background. I hope my folks are having a ball, and, knowing them, I bet that they are. Although I can't quite imagine my mom the homebody traveling as extensively as Dad is picturing, the two of them are made for each other. I'm certain they'll figure something out.

I am lost in thought when Sean comes back out to the porch, followed by a small, dark-haired girl. She's pale and very slight, but, somehow, she looks pretty strong, almost tough. Sean puts a protective arm around her shoulders as he leads her over to me. I hop up and quickly split the distance between us. I hold out my hand and am ready to hug her, if it feels right.

It doesn't. She drops my hand almost immediately and begins to pull her long wavy hair out of her messy bun. She seems almost apologetic as she greets me.

"Well, Becca. Hallo. Good to meet you. I'm sorry, I haven't had a chance to clean myself up. It's been a busy morning and all." She trails off.

I don't want her to feel like she has to make excuses, not to me.

"It's nice to finally meet you, Fiona. Sean has told me so much about you," I tell her warmly.

She smiles at me and then at Sean, who is standing there with a big goofy grin on his face, silent for a change.

"Ah, the cheek of this one," she teases affectionately. "Now, don't go believing anything this fella has to say," she warns.

Sean beams and hugs his sister to him.

"I'm a happy man, I am. I've got a lunch date with the two prettiest girls in Dingle town."

Fi pulls away from him with a look of concern across her face.

"Just give me five minutes to wash up, huh? Do you want me to meet you down the street?"

Sean shakes his head as he glances at his watch.

"Nah, we'll wait for you right here then, won't we, Becca? You only get an hour, so we'll need to hustle, Fi."

She rolls her eyes at him and starts back into the lobby.

"Jaysus, Sean Paul, you're not on the job, all right? I'll be right back."

I ask, "Fi, can you point me towards the ladies room? This one wouldn't stop, and I've had to go since, like, forever." Over Sean's protests that he had stopped for me repeatedly since we left Dublin this morning, Fi grabs my hand and leads me through the door.

"He doesn't understand women, that one." She smirks. "C'mon then. I'll get you sorted, and then I'll be just a minute."

I turn back to look at Sean and blow him a kiss. I get a big smile in return. The lobby is plain and a bit shabby, I notice, as I hurry after Fi. For a tiny girl, she can move really fast!

A short while later, the three of us are settled in a cozy booth in a bustling pub next door. I watch Sean talking with his sister, and, although I am included in the conversation, I am content to sit and listen as I inhale the thick, creamy fish chowder.

Sean sounds more like her father than her brother, or at least what I imagine her father might sound like, if he actually spoke with his daughter. Fi is doing her best to convince him that she is a) eating enough, b) sleeping enough, and c) staying out of the pubs. Sean does not seem all that convinced, especially about the pubs.

"I know how things work, Fi. That's all I'm sayin'. A young girl like you, you've just got to be careful, okay?"

Fiona chooses that moment to dig into her steaming plate of bangers and mash. She manages to respond to his concerns through a mouthful of potatoes.

"Careful, yeah. It's a bit late for that now, isn't it? A girl could end up in the family way or worse," she adds dramatically.

Sean's face darkens as he watches his sister eat, his own meal untouched. I almost suggest that he dig in before everything gets cold because I am my mother's daughter, but I am too late.

"Don't go takin' the piss with me, young lady. You know as well as anyone that you need to be careful not to be making the same—"

Fi cuts him off. "Mistake? Yeah, sure. Here we go again. Sean the Perfect has spoken," she pronounces bitterly. "I have been judged, and I have been found wanting. Stupid Fi. Stupid slutty Fi," she finishes, wringing her hands for good measure. "Whatever will we do about that girl?"

I want to caution Sean to back off but decide to keep quiet. What do I know about their relationship? It is really none of my business.

Sean leans across the table and grabs his sister's tiny hands in his. He takes a deep breath and lets it out slowly. I can almost see him mentally counting to ten.

"It's not like that, okay? I just worry 'bout you. I don't want anything to happen to you. Christ, I'm trying to protect you. I do the same for any of my female Nomads. I want all of them to be careful at a bar. There's a lot of crazy feckers out there. Don't I say that to you a lot, Becca?"

I nod enthusiastically, despite the fact that he just referred to me as a Nomad. A customer instead of his girlfriend. I will cut him some slack, I decide. The last thing this table needs right now is more drama.

"He does, Fi. He's like an old mother hen." I chuckle. "Always going on and on. Don't forget your umbrella. Grab a sweater."

Fi joins in. "Yeah, and be sure to have some money on you for a cab or a phone call. And don't forget to take rubbers with you." I laugh at that last one, especially since Fiona snorted as she emphasized the word "rubbers." "I guess you could say I forgot my rubbers, heh, Sean?" She mimes having a big pregnant belly.

Wait, too soon? I watch with apprehension until Sean's look of shock morphs into a grin.

"See what I'm telling you? The world would be a better place if everyone would just ask themselves WWSD? What Would Sean Do?"

Fi lobs a piece of her roll at her brother, and he starts a dueling match with a French fry off his plate. The rest of our lunch passes quickly, and Fi rushes back to work right before the server drops off our check. Promising to phone as soon as she is done for the day, she is gone.

I reach for the check, but Sean pulls it out of my hand. "I've got this," he assures me.

Even though I realize that that he has probably been argued with enough for one meal, I decide to speak up.

"This is crazy. Please let me pay once in awhile, okay? You picked up checks all over Dublin for days. It's not right. Because of me, you're losing shifts. Let me just buy you lunch, okay? After all, I *am* the posh American, right?"

Sean blushes, perhaps recalling how I overheard his discussion with Dec last week. He drops the check on the table and throws up his hands in mock surrender.

"Fine. Have it your way. But if I had known you were buying,

I'd have ordered a starter and maybe a sweet. Or maybe I'd fancy a cappuccino."

I leave a few bills on the table and grab his arm as we prepare to depart.

"Don't worry, mate. I'll see that you get something sweet. Coming right up. And no worries, you'll earn that lunch. You'll work off every penny."

The gleam in his eyes tells me that he is willing to cooperate fully, so we hurry back towards the inn. Entering the lobby, we take a look around. Quiet, all clear. We race up the back stairs and find our room. Sean slips the keycard into the lock and, grabbing me in his arms, walks backward into our room, forgetting that our bags are lined up right inside the door. He starts to fall, and, despite the fact that I can clearly see what is happening, he's holding on to me so tightly that I have no choice but to crash down on top of him.

"Jaysus, lass, don't be rushing me now. I'll lie with ya, okay? No need to get rough," he warns me with a devilish grin.

I decide to let my actions speak louder than my words. After I push the door shut, I pin him down and wriggle out of my T-shirt as he lies sprawled out, flat on his back. I unhook my bra and hover over him, tempting him with my close proximity and the trail of kisses I am peppering his chest with. I sit back up and watch him struggle with his own shirt.

"Maybe I like it rough. Did you ever think of that, big boy?" I purr.

That does it. I am done for. Sean shifts his weight and, wrapping his arms around me, rolls me over on my back. His eyes are sparkling as he undoes his belt, right before he leans down to kiss me deeply.

Several hours later, we have dinner with Fi. She is flushed and quite animated, a far cry from the pale, rather sullen girl I met earlier in the day. She talks about the session she just left at the local community center. They offer a whole host of workshops and classes that she has been checking out lately.

Apparently, Fi is on a short list of teenagers being considered for a proposed mentoring program. If chosen, she will be partnered with a woman from the local business community, and they will be linked over the upcoming year, with the mentor helping Fi to develop life skills needed to become financially independent. I am glad to see her taking such an interest in her own future, especially since Sean led me to believe that she had been drifting rather aimlessly since suffering her miscarriage earlier in the year. This sounds great.

"It's really empowering to have the chance to connect with other women, and I bet the mentors love it, too, because they get to give back to the community. To pay it forward," I say excitedly.

"That's what she said, Becca," Fi assures me, as she digs into a huge platter of the catch of the day and a mountain of fries. "My mate Siobhan said the exact same thing." She looks at me in amazement.

I tell her I'm not surprised. "Programs like that can have a real impact on young women and their futures. I volunteered at a drop-in center for young women back home. Some are unwed mothers like you. I mean, you're not a mother, but still." *Oh crap, that's awkward.* "I'm sorry. I didn't mean…"

Fiona leans towards me and grabs my hands in her tiny ones.

"I know that. It's okay. It hurts like hell, but I've got to talk about it, you know? It happened. Pretending otherwise is just, well, foolish," she murmurs in Sean's general direction.

Her brother's ears burn bright red as we watch him squirm.

"Ah, shite. You know I'd do anything for ya. It's just hard, okay? I don't have a fecking clue how to talk to you about all, *um*, that."

I shake my head in amazement. Sean is the most sexually adventurous, sensual, and bold lover I could ever imagine. The man literally takes my breath away. He is creative and generous and was so fucking comfortable in his naked skin, strutting around our room this afternoon. To see him reduced to a stammering awkward ninny talking about his sister's sex life really gives me pause. I decide to jump in and try to smooth things over.

"All women, even those in university, can really benefit from learning basic life skills. Like how to balance a checkbook, how to write a cover letter and a résumé."

Sean flashes me a grateful smile in return.

"And don't forget birth control," Fi adds with a wicked grin, only partly obscured by a mouthful of fish. Sean flushes at that and suddenly decides that his own plate of food requires all of his attention. "C'mon, big brother, someone has to have 'the talk' with little Fi."

He grins slowly. "Well, if anyone has to have the talk with you, I can't imagine anyone better for the job than our Becca." He has what sounds like pride in his voice.

I blush at that, warmed by his vote of confidence. Fi is eager to turn the conversation back to the teen center.

"Becca, you have to meet Siobhan. She's brilliant. You'll love her, and she'll be blown away by you. Maybe, tomorrow afternoon, you can come to group with me, huh?"

Sean and I had planned on renting a sailboat and taking it out on Dingle Bay, but I am thrilled that Fi wants to spend more time with me. I look over at him. He is watching us as he finishes the last of his steak and kidney pie.

"What do you say? Surely we can move things around tomorrow, heh? I really want to check out this center, you know? Maybe I'll get some good ideas to bring back to Boston with me."

He chuckles as he folds his napkin and places it next to his nearly picked-clean plate.

"I bring my best girl on holiday and she wants to work," he complains good-naturedly. "But no worries. If I can drag your lazy arse outta bed in the morning, we'll have plenty of time to sail and get you back for your meeting."

I beam at him and decide to let the lazy arse comment die. I do love a good lay-in some mornings, especially if my sexy boyfriend is shagging me senseless into the wee hours of the morning.

Fi watches us with the most curious expression on her face.

"Well, enough 'bout me, then. I'm quite sorted out, heh? So what's going on with you two?" She favors us both with an inquisitive stare. "Are you two Facebook-official, or what?" she drawls in an "inquiring minds want to know" voice.

Uh oh. Just what are we anyway?

CHAPTER TWENTY-THREE

JACKIE

THERE ARE NO WORDS to describe The Giant's Causeway, but I'll try anyway. It is mystical, awe-inspiring, and amazing. I've never seen anyplace quite like it, and I've been to the Grand Canyon several times.

We walked over thousands of interlocking basalt columns clustered along the seacoast, the result of an ancient volcanic eruption. Just what is basalt anyway? I try to capture the whole thing for Becca and the mystery that it evokes, but I know that the camera on my cell phone won't do any justice to such a spectacular sight.

Then we drive to our next destination on the itinerary that Sean prepared for us. The Carrick a Rede Rope Bridge links the mainland to the tiny island of Carrickarede. The bridge is sixty-six feet long and is suspended almost one hundred feet above the rocks below. Sean warned me that, although no one has ever fallen off the bridge, there have been many instances where visitors, unable to face the walk back across, have had to be taken off the island by boat. I now fear that my husband will be joining their ranks.

"C'mon. You can do it," I call as I watch my husband, who is no longer moving, grip the ropes.

I walked across without incident, but we apparently underestimated Rob's fear of heights. It has him nearly paralyzed, at the moment. He made it halfway, trailing behind me, when he froze. I am almost all the way across before I notice he's stopped.

I situate myself on solid ground in order to better assess the situation. The bridge is swaying in the wind, and I watch silently as Rob tightens his grip and hangs on to the rope. His eyes are closed, and his face is screwed up in concentration. If I didn't know him as well as I do, I would think he is actually praying.

Three teenage girls hurry past him, giggling and laughing without a care in the world, barely acknowledging my poor husband. After they pass me, I call back to Rob. The wind has really picked up, and I have to yell in order for him to hear me.

"You're halfway there. Just take it nice and slow."

But even if, by some miracle, he is able to get to me, he still has to cross the bridge again for the return trip. Rob should not have to suffer the indignity of being taken off the island by boat. Time to cut our losses. I take a deep breath and make my way back across, heading slowly towards him. I call his name, and he finally opens his eyes. I warn him not to take his eyes off of me, not for a second. If he looks down at the waves crashing over the rocks below, well, I can only imagine that it won't help the situation any.

"We're heading back," I call to him. "C'mon, that's it. One step at a time."

And, miraculously, he slowly leads the way back over to the mainland. When we are once again on solid ground and his breathing returns to normal, he wants to take a picture of me with the bridge in the background.

"Why would you want a picture like that?" I ask in amazement.

He grins in response. "Next time I get to thinking that I'm all that and ready to hike Mt. Everest or some such shit, you can whip it out to remind me what a pussy I really am."

I laugh at that. Rob never had the need, like some guys, to prove how macho he is, but maybe just a little bit.

"Sean doesn't need to know about this," he whispers as we get in the car.

I agree, and we head back out to the main road en route to our hotel in the walled city of Derry. What happened on the Antrim Coast will stay on the Antrim Coast.

Becca

"You're awful quiet this morning, Bec. Everything okay?"

Sean's voice interrupts my reverie. I *have* been unusually quiet as we drive back to Dublin. There are so many thoughts swirling around in my brain. My sleep-deprived, alcohol-soaked brain.

We hit the pubs in Dingle pretty hard last night. Not to mention all of the things I am trying to keep straight. Returning to Dublin, getting ready to rejoin my folks, then turning around in a few days and saying goodbye to Sean. I groan at the thought.

"You hungry?" he asks gently. "You didn't eat much this morning."

I had barely been able to stomach any more than some tepid tea and a piece of toast earlier. But now? I can eat, I decide.

"Sure," I nod agreeably. "Do you mind stopping?"

He grins as he leans over to squeeze my hand.

"Whatever you wish, my fair lady. We'll pass a nice place in just a couple more kilometers. How does that sound?"

I squeeze back and close my eyes. A few more minutes before I need to address the elephant in the room, *er*, car. A great big one, unless I misunderstood somehow.

No, I heard it all right. Maybe it was the Guinness or maybe it was a heat of the moment thing, something that came on the heels of some very passionate lovemaking late last night. But Sean *did* say it. He asked me to stay, to never leave him, and I said I would. Stay, never leave. But how?

I decide to wait until I've had some coffee and something to eat. This is way too much to try to process on an empty stomach. Minutes later, we arrive at a little café. Sean assures me that he will order my coffee and a breakfast sandwich, while I rush off to use the restroom.

I splash cold water on my face and look at my haggard reflection in the small mirror. "You can do this," I tell myself. *Sure, I can.*

Determined to jump right in and discuss what might have been nothing more than a careless slip of the tongue, I walk back into the small dining area. But Sean isn't sitting alone. He is chatting up a short, bearded guy who is wearing what looks like… Oh yeah, it's the same green, long-sleeved, button-down that Sean wore the entire time we were touring the countryside last week. This must be a colleague of Sean's, I decide, as I notice a group of tourists circling about the room, crowding into the booths and chattering away.

As I approach the table, Sean jumps up and pulls out the remaining chair for me. I slip into it and wait for introductions to be made. Conor is indeed a fellow tour guide Sean trained with, when he first started, almost four years earlier. He is "a real great guy," and I am introduced as "my friend Becca."

Wow…, friend. This trip is getting weirder by the minute.

Conor shakes my hand but declines Sean's offer to join us for a coffee. With a wink in my general direction, he explains that he has a couple of calls to make, confirming his group's plans for later today.

"Besides," he adds with a twinkle in his eye, "the last thing a pair of lovebirds needs is some old codger like me playing the third wheel."

I smile and say something like, "Oh, it's fine," or whatever, and that does it.

Conor's ears perk up at the sound of my voice. My American voice.

"So, you're from the States then?" he asks with interest. "I'd have guessed you were one of Sean's regular girls, someone from town." Another wink.

Gross.

Sean winces at his co-worker's choice of words, but I am feeling pretty secure about our relationship this morning and decide to ignore the dig.

"I *am* American, Conor," I announce proudly. "But I do have a lot of Irish in me."

Conor laughs at that, and I cringe as I quickly realize how that sounded, especially to someone with his mind in the gutter.

"I mean I have ancestors who are Irish," I tell him in a prim voice.

Sean smiles at me and pulls me into a one armed hug, as he addresses Conor.

"So, what do you think I need to do to convince our Becca here to stick around for a while? To give up her plans to go back to the States in a few days."

What? I turn to Sean in amazement. Talk about addressing the issue head-on.

Conor takes it all in stride, as he shakes his head at his former protégé.

"Lad, I can't think of a single reason any lass in her right mind would stick around here with you," he declares. "You've got no money, no prospects, and I've seen you taking a leak, so I know it's not *that*." He laughs.

Sean blushes at that last comment, and I decide that I have heard quite enough from Conor.

"What about love?" I ask him. "Surely you've heard of it, huh? What if I love him?" I relax into Sean's arms and watch the guy's surprised reaction.

Then he grins, recovering quickly.

"Ah, sure, Rebecca. I'm familiar with love," he assures me in a genial tone. "Not firsthand, mind you, but for you two, yeah. Sure. Why not?" He shrugs and stands up, preparing to leave. "Well, look me up when you get back to work, Sean. After you finish enjoying your holiday, that is." He doffs an imaginary cap in my direction. "Whatever you decide, I wish you the best."

As he walks towards the exit, I watch him go and then quickly turn to Sean.

"I was beginning to think I'd imagined the whole thing," I admit. "What you said about me staying, I mean."

Sean regards me soberly as he shakes his head.

"I'm not ready to say goodbye to you. I don't know just what that means, but there's more here we have to figure out. I'm willing to try, if you are," he adds.

I stare into his red-rimmed green eyes. We are *having* this conversation.

CHAPTER TWENTY-FOUR

JACKIE

DERRY IS, I AM SURE, a beautiful and historic city. Yesterday, as we strolled along the walkway on top of the 500-year-old walls that completely surround it, I listened half-heartedly as Rob read aloud from the tour book. But I was getting anxious to return to Dublin, to Becca.

We have been texting each other several times a day. The only text of hers I ignored was the one asking what we thought of the rope bridge. I miss talking to my girl, but, even more, I need to lay my eyes on her. I know that she enjoyed Dingle and meeting Fiona, and it sounds like they have been having a great time since returning to Dublin a couple of days ago. Rob and I are going to drive back to Belfast this morning and then take the train to Dublin. We have plans to meet her and Sean this evening for dinner.

"Let's get going, huh?" I urge Rob.

He is enjoying his third cup of coffee and eyeing the basket of scones on the table, but I am antsy and ready to go. He looks at me in surprise.

"Well, that's a first. You're usually the one who likes to sit around and…"

"Yeah, yeah. C'mon, can we please get on the road? We've got a long drive ahead, and we still need to return the car and the train leaves at two," I remind him.

He shakes his head at me but seems resigned to our imminent departure as he takes a final sip of coffee. Grabbing a blueberry scone, he wraps it in a napkin and shoves it into my tote bag as we leave the dining room. Back up in our room, I take a last look around and declare that I am all set and ready to go. We check out, they bring the rental car around for us, and we are off.

We are making our way through the snarl of traffic in the clogged the city center on our way back to the highway, when Rob speaks up.

"Don't over-think this Jackie," he warns gently.

What?

"What am I over-thinking?" I ask, my tone frosty. *Here we go.*

"I just mean that Becca is a big girl, and there's no point in getting all worked up about her and Sean," he says smoothly.

I take a deep breath. This is not the time to have one of our bi-annual blowout arguments.

"I'm not worked up. I *am* a little nervous about how fast their relationship has, *um,* evolved." And you weren't there for most of it, Rob, I remind myself silently. "So, just cut me a little slack today, okay?" I am glad when he reaches over and squeezes my hand.

"You got it, babe," he promises, and if he notices my lack of enthusiasm for the passing scenery or the fish chowder at the inn where we stop for lunch, he doesn't say a word.

Sometimes, you have to let the person you love struggle through their issues and just watch from the sidelines. And I am clearly struggling.

Becca

The time I've spent with Sean has been amazing. We get along really well, now that we've sorted out the whole thing about what Tracie thought she saw and what I heard when he was downplaying our relationship with his brother. I can relax around him and tell him anything. He's the only person I want to talk to late at night and the first one I want to reach for in the morning. And sometimes in the middle of the night, as well. He's just great, and I've never been happier.

But now we've got a big decision to make. Can we make this work? This relationship of ours. Can it continue? I am scheduled to return home in three days. Sixty-eight hours, if you want to be exact. And I want to spend every minute with Sean. I can't even imagine saying goodbye to him. But I can't really picture myself waving goodbye to my folks, either. They are on their way back from their trip up north. I figure, in the remaining time we have, we'll check out a few more tourist attractions in and around Dublin, do some last minute shopping for souvenirs, especially Edie's teapot, and pack. And spend as much time as we can making out.

Sean was scheduled to return to work a couple of days ago. His week off flew by. Thank goodness he's got a really sympathetic boss and some accommodating co-workers. They're letting him use several days of sick time that he accrued, and a co-worker picked up his five-day tour scheduled for the week. It's weird to imagine Sean touring the country with a new set of Nomads every week.

I think about my fellow travelers a lot, especially Carrie and Ollie. They have been home for over a week now. I vow to send Carrie a text later today. And Elaine. Has she managed to mend the rift between her and her kids? I can't even imagine being separated from my folks like that. There's nothing that either of them could do that would make me choose to shut them out. Except maybe if one of them killed the other. *Ugh, where do thoughts like that come from*? My parents and I will always be close. But what if I decide to stay here? Talk about a game changer!

Sean and I talked about it again this morning. The possibility of staying together. Not just like "wouldn't it be cool?" but "how could we actually make this work?" We really talked.

Fully clothed and fully caffeinated, we sat on a park bench in the square around the corner from Sean's flat. It was pretty much vacant, except for an older gentleman with his newspaper open, umbrella at his side. We had chosen it as neutral ground with fewer distractions than in Sean's bedroom. It was time to lay our cards on the table. Sean opted to start things off.

"So, Becca, as far as I can tell, we have three choices, heh?"

Wait, three?

"You mean, I stay here, you move to the States or… what?"

"We go our separate ways," Sean said solemnly.

Wow. I hadn't been considering that last one. Splitting up was *not* an option, at least not one I was in favor of. But wait.

"Or we could try the long-distance thing and see how that goes?" I know plenty of people who… Scratch that. The only couple I know who have lasted in a long-distance relationship are my Aunt Edie and Coop. And they are both retired, have plenty of money, and the distance between them isn't nearly as far as being separated by an entire ocean.

Sean's expression left no doubt as to his feelings about that option.

"I'm not a jealous guy by nature, Becca, but I've never really been successful with the whole exclusive thing, you know? It'll be hard enough being together, even without living apart."

Ouch! I winced at that last part. Tell me how you really feel, boyfriend.

Sean tried to cover his tracks. "I'm not saying that being in a relationship with you will be all that hard, love. I just mean that… Oh Christ, I don't know. I just feel like if we're *together*, we should actually *be* together, you know? And I want us to be together."

Yeah, but how? I felt like we were on one of those house-hunting shows. Three choices. Time to narrow them down.

"So, are we taking the third option, breaking up, off the table?"

Sean nodded, and I felt a sense of relief. I don't want that, either.

"So then which is it? Do I stay here? Or do you come with me?"

Sean was silent for a while, but I could see the wheels turning. I let him ponder that one for a moment.

This is a big decision. What do *I* want? Could I see myself living here with Sean? Was grad school really my only option, if I go back home? I think Sean would really like Boston, but what about summers in Sedona?

Sean cleared his throat and reached for my hands, which were like ice.

"Jaysus, Bex. You're freezin'. Do you want to go back and get some tea?"

I shivered. The skies were overcast, but the sun was threatening to make an appearance. It wasn't the temperature that was my problem; I was chilled from the inside.

"No, I'm okay. What are you thinking?" I shivered again.

"I think we should stay in Ireland. At least for now. Do you want to know why?" At my nod, he continued. "Okay, here goes. First off, there's the whole job thing. I make pretty good money, and there's lots of perks that go along with being a guide. Some of the groups are really big tippers. Most of the time, my meals and visits to the pub are completely covered, you know? And you're, well, you're not working, so, *um*..." His voice trailed off.

His job. Yeah, about that.

"But you've told me a bunch of times that you want to quit your job, and what about the travel? You're gone so much of the time. What would I do? Sit around your flat with Dec and Sarah? Maybe I could cook all their meals and keep the place all spic and span to earn my keep, huh?" *Ugh*. That didn't sound like the kind of thing I would uproot my whole life for.

Sean's face screwed up in concentration.

"Okay, well, you're right. Long term, we probably shouldn't plan on my playing tour guide forever. And that's okay," he assured me.

"How about a job at the Nomad office then? Maybe they need someone on the phones or working on their website or something?"

Sean emphatically vetoed that option, shaking his head vigorously.

"No, no way. All the crap we drivers give the white-collar guys and vice versa?" His face darkened, as if he is picturing himself trapped in a world of cubicles. "I can't see that happening. So let's move on. What about family?"

What about them?

"Well, we both have them. How're we supposed to choose based on that?"

"Okay, so hear me out. You're an only child, Becca." At my nod, he continued. "I have two brothers and a sister." All true. "So, my family needs me more, you know? Liam is pretty self-sufficient, and Dec has Sarah and all. But Fi? Fiona needs me, Bec. I'm all she has."

Well, *that* is true. We spent a couple of days with Fi, and while her situation isn't quite as bleak as Sean led me to believe, it is true that she is struggling and really relies on him.

"But what about that? You have a dad and two brothers. Why is Fi *your* sole responsibility? Why can't the rest of them swallow their stupid pride and let her come home?"

Sean groaned.

"Well, that's not something we can solve today, but then there's the case of Billy."

"What? He needs you, too? He has three other kids, Sean. You barely see him anyway. My parents? All they have is me. What about that?"

Sean shook his head again.

"They have each other, Becca. You've told me a dozen times how happy they are together. I've seen it firsthand. The way your dad looks at your mom? Christ, he is a man in love, there's no doubt. And Jackie? Well, she just about lights up when your dad walks into the room. And besides, they can come and visit. They're gonna retire soon, and money's not an issue, right?"

He was right about that. I thought about what Sean said and had to admit that he made a pretty strong case.

"Wow, you've been giving this some thought," I marveled and got a grin in return. Actually, more of a smirk.

"Well, in between you shagging me senseless just about nonstop, I've had a few spare minutes to think on this."

I punched his arm.

"Yeah, you wish, mister." But something was missing. "So, we've considered our jobs and our families, but what about us?" At the blank look I got, I hurried on. "*Us,* Sean. Our lives. Where would we be happier?"

Sean's response was quick and very certain. He pulled me into his arms and kissed me gently, before he drew back just enough to cup my face in his hands. His hands were warm, and his voice was soft.

"Rebecca Sullivan Colby, I will go anywhere to be with you. I will come to Boston. I'll live in the desert. I'll travel to the feckin' moon. The only thing that matters to me is that I am with you."

Best. Answer. Ever. I was almost speechless. But not quite.

"I feel the same way about you. I love it here in Dublin. We could spend more time with Fi, maybe get the rest of the Donovans on board, but either way, we could have a great life here. I can put off school for a while. I've been going for sixteen years straight, you know? I'm ready to do something else for a while. I'll wait tables, I'll answer phones, whatever it takes. It'll be brilliant, as Fi says. Just so long as I get to be with you."

I barely had the chance to finish that last sentence when I was being kissed and hugged. He cherishes me, I realized happily.

And as soon as we race-walked back to his place, I was able to cherish him back. And shag him senseless, as well.

* * *

Much later, I am half dozing, lying in Sean's arms, as the light starts to fade in his previously sunny bedroom. I contemplate getting up and turning on a lamp but decide that I can't spare the energy. The man wears me out. I am spent, but we will need to get going, if we are going to meet my folks' train.

I feel Sean stir beside me, and then I hear him whisper, "Bex? Becca, you awake?"

I roll over to face him. Even in the dim light, I can see him smiling.

"*Hmmm*. I'm awake, but if you think I can go another round with you, well, you're just a bleedin' ejit, Donovan."

He groans at my awful attempt to sound like a native.

"Promise me you'll not try that again, love. But there's another option. Something we didn't think of earlier."

Wait, what?

"Do tell," I whisper.

"Best choice of all. We want to be together, but my job won't really allow us to spend much real time together. And Dublin's pricey, especially on just the one salary. I know that Dec wants Sarah to move in here soon, so I'd be looking for another rental, anyway. So what if we went somewhere else?"

"Like where?"

"Anywhere we want. We could find jobs outside of Dublin. Live pretty cheap, too. Or maybe Scotland or God, even, *ugh*... up north."

My boyfriend is a typical Dubliner. He recognizes the beauty of the country to the north for tourists but draws the line at actually wanting to live up there.

Wait, what about…?

"How about Dingle? My mom told me that you had mentioned maybe wanting to move to Dingle."

Sean looks confused at first, and then it hits him.

"Ah, Bex, I was just talking. I was telling her about how Sarah was making noises about wanting to set up her graphics shop in my bedroom. And I told Jackie that, yeah, maybe I would get out of the city, look at Dingle. I didn't mention Fi, but of course that would make the move make even more sense."

Images of Dingle's bustling waterfront flash through my brain. I start to get really excited.

"You know all those shop owners out there. You introduced me to half the town, I swear. You could give kayaking lessons or teach people how to surf. And is there a pub or inn that isn't forever grateful to the likes of Sean Paul Donovan for directing so much business their way? Surely someone from one of those places would give us jobs. We could sling drinks and serve pub grub all night and make love all day. It'd be grand, heh?"

Sean pulls back, wearing a frown. I don't think it's because I was once again trying (and apparently failing) to sound like a local. Something else is wrong.

"Yeah, I can just see how that conversation would go with your folks. Mom? Dad? I'm gonna drop out of school and move to the Emerald Isle. I'm gonna work in a pub, and so's my boyfriend. Isn't that like, cool?" he gushes, succeeding at sounding like a pre-teen girl.

I hope I don't sound like that. And his American accent is far better than my Irish one. Okay, so maybe he has a point.

"The bar would just be temporary. My folks would realize that. Sometimes you have to do what you have to, until you can do what you want to. I have heard both of my parents say that a bunch of times."

My mom came from money, but Dad supported himself parking cars at the airport and worked in a hardware store, mixing paint, after he dropped out of college. "There's no shame in earning an honest buck, Becca," Dad told me. So maybe it is my turn to work somewhere that isn't owned by my folks or their best friends. Make an honest buck.

But first, nature calls. I hop out of bed and race towards the door. "Save my spot," I tell Sean and peek down the hall. The coast is clear, so I head into the bathroom, sit, and pee for what seems like forever.

I wash my hands and splash cold water on my face. I feel good, lighter somehow. Issues are still on the table. Big ones, like where and how to live. But it feels like we've made some decisions, too. We are going to put each other first and focus on our relationship. I guess nothing else really matters so much after that.

CHAPTER TWENTY-FIVE

JACKIE

I HAVE BEEN lying here for what seems like forever, replaying the conversation from dinner, over and over. I will probably never be able to forget it.

I look over at my sleeping husband. He stirs, shifts around, and then falls back into a deep sleep. Lucky bastard. He can fall asleep anywhere, I swear. And within seconds of his head hitting the pillow, too. It can be hours until I fall asleep, unless I have the forethought to take some melatonin.

But all the sleeping aids in the world won't help me tonight. No, tonight's issues are massive, life changing, and scary as shit. It is official. My daughter is going to quit school and move here to Ireland to be with Sean.

* * *

Becca and Sean met our train when we arrived back in Dublin late this afternoon. Sean and Rob walked ahead, wheeling our luggage and chatting away like two old friends. I thought something was up, to be honest. Becca looked different somehow. Sean did, too. At first, she giggled at my efforts to figure out just how different. Then she wriggled out of my embrace and didn't make eye contact with me the whole way back to the hotel.

"What's up?" I asked her, my spidey senses tingling.

She shrugged and looked at the guys, who were still walking

just a few steps ahead of us. Then, at her feet. Then, at the busker singing and playing guitar on the street corner. Anywhere but at me. She reached around in her pocket for some change and dropped it into the open guitar case.

"Becca, what's going on?" I asked, more sharply than I intended.

"Geez Mom, chill? What do you want to know? We've been back here for a couple of days just knocking around. You know that we went to Dingle and I got to meet Fiona. She's lovely, Mom. Tiny, dark-haired, blue eyes. I felt like a gangly moose around her, but I really like her. You remember Dingle, right? All those shops and all the pubs. Such a perfect little town. We spent hours walking along the waterfront. I wanted to take out a couple of sea kayaks like you and I did, but Fi doesn't know how to swim. Isn't that so weird? I mean, here's Sean, who's just about a professional surfer, and his little sister can't even swim a stroke. You know that about Sean, right? How much he loves to surf? It's the fastest growing sport in Ireland. Did you know that? Huh? Did you?"

I actually did know that, as Sean told me during one of my turns riding up front in Bertha just a couple of weeks ago. And I knew something else, too. I knew that my darling daughter was rambling on about kayaks and surfboards and Fiona in order to keep the conversation light and breezy. She was trying to distract me. But from what?

We caught up with Rob and Sean in the hotel lobby. Robbie looked around and clapped his hands together.

"Well, I'm starving. Anyone else want to grab a bite to eat? I'm buying," he added with a grin.

Becca just about jumped for joy.

"Yeah, let's go eat, huh? Why don't you go drop off your bags," she suggested, indicating her dad and me. "We'll wait here, right Sean?"

A look passed between them. *What the hell is going on?* Rob nodded in agreement and started to walk towards the lifts.

"C'mon, Jax. Let's just drop these off and wash up, huh? I love train travel, but man, I feel like I'm covered with grit or something." With a final wave at his daughter and her boyfriend, he continued to make his way through the lobby.

I gave a last look at Becca, who was already walking towards a pair of couches by the fireplace, with Sean right behind her. I followed Rob and waited until we were back inside our room before I spoke up. We had kept the room in Dublin while we were in Belfast, in order to not have to pack up everything and take it with us on the train. Also, in case Becca needed a place to stay if things hadn't worked out with Sean.

"Looks like everything worked out," I mumbled, as I shoved my carryon bag into the tiny closet.

Rob called out to me from the bathroom. "What's gotten into you? You've hardly said a word since we got back. You tired?"

I rolled my eyes, which was stupid, as he couldn't even see me. But my uncharacteristic silence drew him out. Wiping his face on a towel, he emerged from the bathroom and walked over to where I was standing. I was looking out the window at the bustling street below.

"Sweetheart. What's the matter?"

Finally, the dam burst. I bent over, clutching my stomach, and started to sob.

"We're gonna lose her. Our girl. Something's up, I just know it," I cried.

Rob took me in his arms, and I continued to sob into his shoulder. He drew back and tried to get me to look at him. I cried even harder, as my mind raced through the possibilities. All bad. All sans Becca.

I pushed my damp face against his neck. I am *not* a pretty crier. I don't cry often, but when I do, I get all red-eyed and blotchy-faced. I can only imagine what a mess I looked like, but I didn't care. Snot dripping and tears still falling, I let him lead me over to the bed.

He sat on the edge and pulled me onto his lap. I snuck a peek at his face. Dry-eyed and dry-nosed. I love that dear, familiar face. I gratefully accepted the tissue he plucked from the bedside table and then wiped my eyes and blew my nose. *Ugh.*

"Jackie," he began tentatively. I snuffled again and tried to find my voice.

"Yeah?"

"We don't know that, okay? We don't know that Becca plans to move here. Let's wait and see what they have to say first, before we jump to any conclusions."

I shook my head at him.

"When Becca gets all chatty and rambling like that, I know something's up. I'm just trying to prepare myself is all."

Rob cleared his throat and gently pushed me off his lap to stand up. He walked back towards the bathroom, waving his towel in the air.

"Well then, let's get on with it. Maybe Sean is going to come to the States. Maybe Becca will move here *after* she finishes grad school. You don't know."

But I *did* know.

And it turned out that my spidey senses had not let me down. I found that out shortly after we settled into a booth towards the back of the pub closest to the hotel and Sean brought over a pitcher and filled our glasses. Right after we brushed off our server's attempts to take our order. A split second after Sean and Becca exchanged another glance, clasped their hands together, and leaned towards us.

That's when they told us. Calmly and resolutely. Presenting a united front. They would be living together in Ireland, probably *not* here in Dublin. Becca would not be going to grad school, at least for now, and Sean would be giving his notice at the tour company as soon as they finalized their plans. Something about his family. His little sister in Dingle.

I stopped listening. I slumped back against the vinyl booth and took a deep breath. This is what all parents dread, right? You raise your kid to be strong, independent, able to stand on their own. But Becca wasn't going to be standing alone, wasn't going to be going to school in Boston. She was going to be living in a strange country with a man she barely knew.

I looked up. Everyone was staring at me with worried looks on their faces. Robbie was holding my hand so tightly, I was starting to lose all feeling in it. He watched me closely, as if expecting me to pass out or something. Becca had tears in her eyes and was trying to reach my other hand.

"I'm sorry, Mom," she whispered.

And Sean? He was sitting back, waiting. For what? My blessing?

An angry tirade? His face was pale, and he looked scared. This glib, cocky Irishman who had led us all over his country, first in a van and then on his own, who had told us dozens of stories and jokes, who had shared so much about his life with us, and who had, except for one teeny lapse in judgment, treated Becca with love and the utmost of respect, was scared. He is the sweetest, most decent, well-mannered young man I have probably ever met. And he wants Becca and she wants him back.

I took a deep breath and let it out in a whoosh. Time to rejoin the party.

And it *was* a party. I wiggled the hand that my husband was crushing, and he let go. Becca was successful in grabbing my other hand, and Sean just sat still, grinning at me. I smiled back at him, Becca and Robbie in turn, and then I held up my glass in a toast. Who the fuck knows what will happen tomorrow, you know? You could get hit by a bus and die. You could win the lottery. You could fall in love.

"Slainte," I called out and clicked glasses with my family. Cheers, indeed.

Then we drank more beer and stuffed ourselves with fish 'n' chips and huge portions of sticky toffee pudding. Becca told me that she would learn to make it herself and would serve it to us as soon as we came back to visit. I have never seen Becca make anything more complicated than a piece of toast, so I wasn't going to hold my breath on that. But I nodded in agreement and said something like "sounds good." Rob shared the news that we were looking forward to hitting the road for a few months, probably by late summer. He called it our "semi-retirement," and I was okay with that. And we ended our next-to-last night in Ireland with hugs and plans to meet up for a late breakfast for our last day in town…

* * *

So here I am, just a couple of hours later, after the young couple made their way back to Sean's apartment and my husband fell asleep after reading just a single chapter of his latest sci-fi novel. I try, unsuccessfully, to renew the feelings of joy and optimism, however temporary, that I felt earlier. Not going to happen, not right now at least.

I manage to slow down my breathing and clear my mind, in order to join Rob in sleep. It's time to get some rest. Tomorrow's going to be a big day.

Becca

"Well, that went well, heh?" Sean sounds relieved, almost jubilant. *Hmmm,* did it go well? Did it really? I'm not totally convinced.

"Yeah, I guess so. My dad seems pretty cool, but I'm not so sure about my mom."

"What do you mean? She toasted us and asked all kinds of questions about Fi and how we might want to move to Dingle. She seemed happy."

"Sean, I know my own mother, and trust me. Right at this very minute, she is tossing and turning and mulling this over. She's thinking about a whole new list of concerns, things that didn't come up tonight."

"Concerns? Like what?"

"Like how we're going to support ourselves. If we should really be making such a big move when we barely know each other."

Sean stops walking and pulls me to him. The streets around his apartment are nearly deserted. From the sounds coming from the pubs we passed, it appears that everyone is watching a soccer game. If Sean wasn't walking home with me, is that where he would be right now?

"I think I know you pretty well, love. Let's see, your name is, *um,* Betty? No, Betsy?" he teases and then stops when he sees my expression. My glum face, even in the dim light of the overhead street lamp, tells him everything he needs to know. I have a problem, therefore *we* have a problem.

"Tomorrow, we should pull Jackie aside, okay? Explain to her what we talked about. Make her see—"

I cut him off. "See *what,* exactly? We don't have a plan. Not a real one, anyway. Where will we live? What are you going to do if you're not going to be a tour guide any longer? Can I even get a job in this country? Don't I need a visa or work permit or something? And I barely know you. I mean, do you even watch soccer? Would you be with your mates over in that pub right now, if it wasn't for me?" I realize how I must sound. Shrill, borderline hysterical.

Sean frowns at me, as he starts to respond.

"Jaysus, Bec, I don't even know where to begin. I've already paid this month's rent, so it's not like we need to leave right away. And rents are cheaper in Dingle. If we have to, we can stay at Fi's place for a couple of days again. I'll hold off giving my notice at Nomads until we have set something up. And yeah, I like soccer. Sure, I'd be watching the game right now. But I would rather be with you, arguing on a fecking street corner, than anywhere else in the world, okay? And we'll tell your ma that none of my other girls have working papers, either, so no worries, right?"

I swat at him, but he chuckles and ducks just out of my reach.

"Wow, you're a laugh riot, Donovan. Do *all* your girls think so, too?" I move in closer and run my hands lightly down his sides. That space between the armpit and the hipbone is a really sensitive zone for my boyfriend.

His breathing gets kind of ragged, and his eyes start to close in anticipation. He groans softly then grabs my hand and starts to pull me down the street towards his apartment.

"I'll show you what they think of me, love, and, if Dec isn't home, I'll have you laughing out loud in sixty seconds or less," he promises.

I let him propel me along, but I can't let that last one go.

"Sixty seconds, huh? Is that like a record for you? Your personal best?"

He growls in response and kisses me. Hard. It shuts me up. If that is his plan, well, it works. I follow him up the stairs, and we barely make it inside before he is kissing me again and pulling off my shirt and kicking off his shoes. We have the place to ourselves, which is a good thing, as he makes me laugh pretty loud, let me tell you.

CHAPTER TWENTY-SIX

JACKIE

"WILL THIS FLIGHT ever take off?" I complain as I fidget in my seat and adjust my seatbelt for the tenth time in as many minutes.

Rob places his hand over mine.

"Relax," he chuckles. "We'll be taking off before you know it. In plenty of time for you to fall asleep and drool on my shoulder."

I start to bristle at his characterization and then stop myself. He's just teasing, and I need to calm down. The flight is on time, and we will be landing in Boston in only about six hours.

Rob rebooked the second leg of our journey so that we can spend tonight with my best friend, Suze, and continue on to Arizona tomorrow. I think he feels like I can use a little cheering up from my oldest friend, and he's right. Leaving Becca in Ireland and flying home without her is not something I ever even considered when we arrived three weeks ago. Never in a million years.

A wave of panic hits me. This can't be happening. I can't do this.

"What if…?" I begin, whispering between clenched teeth.

To his credit, Rob doesn't roll his eyes at me but speaks patiently, as if I am a not-very-bright child who just can't grasp the situation we are facing.

"Honey, we've been all through this."

A dozen times in the last two days, I know. But the story is still the same. We are leaving our only daughter, who is barely a legal adult, in a foreign land with a man who is virtually a stranger.

"We have to trust our girl on this. She's smart, and she's going make this work or she'll get herself on a flight home. We've got to let her do this." He squeezes my hand and smiles at me, but it's a smile that doesn't quite reach his eyes.

I know he is scared, too, but he is trying to be brave for my sake. I will have to try to be brave for him, so I smile back.

"I know, and I'll be okay. You know me," I boast unconvincingly. He still looks worried. "And besides, we have an even bigger problem to deal with," I warn with a frown. "One of us is going to have to admit to Edie that we never located her freaking teapot." Ah, that gets me a smile from my husband. "And hey, I really appreciate how you arranged for us to spend tonight with Suze. That was so nice of you."

Really nice as, despite all my efforts to get them to bond, my best friend and my husband are just not all that friendly. I know Rob thinks Suze is a little too opinionated about everything in general and my life choices, in particular. I stopped telling him about Suze's responses to things I tell her. And I stopped sharing everything with her, as well. She *is* pretty bossy, I think with a smile, and she has opinions about everything. She'll definitely have an opinion about Becca staying in Ireland.

I settle back into my seat and tell Rob that I am going to close my eyes for a few minutes. The drink cart won't be around for while, not even up here in business class, and it is going to be a long day, especially with the time change. I lean my head back and vow *not* to drool or snore, at least not today.

Becca

"So, do you have any questions for me?"

Wow. Do I have questions? I sure as shit do.

Am I crazy for doing this? What do I know about Irish teens and their issues? Is working as a community outreach coordinator for Dingle county really the best use of my skills? What if I don't qualify for that US-Ireland Working Holiday Agreement that Fi's friend Siobahn heard about? Should I have gotten on that plane with my parents seven days ago?

"No, I'm good," I assure Bridget Finn, director of community services for Dingle county and my new boss. She is a sturdy, no-nonsense, little woman with twinkly blue eyes and a lovely peaches-and-cream complexion. I watch as she stands up and walks around her desk towards me. She shakes my hand firmly and smiles.

"We're glad you're joining us, Rebecca. You'll be busy for sure. Take the weekend and get yourself sorted out, won't you? Come find me on Monday. I'm usually at my desk at half eight or so. If you can't find me, Siobhan will be able to find me. Bring your passport so we can fill out the forms for your *working holiday,*" she adds as she walks me out of her office into the main reception area.

I suddenly panic. *What am I doing?*

Bridget sees the look on my face. Confusion? Fear?

"Are you okay, dear?" she asks me.

"Oh, yeah, sure. I'm, *um*, okay," I try to assure both of us and take a deep breath. "See you on Monday, then," I add gaily and walk out into the misty gray afternoon.

I pull the collar of my new coat up around my neck. *Brrrr*. I am glad that I let my mom talk me into a last-minute shopping trip in Dublin before they flew home. The sweatshirts and jeans I wore for the last three weeks were getting pretty tired. When I told Mom about my plans to start job searching as soon as we got to Dingle, she convinced me that I would need some new clothes.

Not that we ever need an excuse to shop. A couple pairs of dressy pants, a black pencil skirt, a tweedy jacket, a heathery soft cardigan, four blouses, two pairs of mid-heeled shoes, and an all-weather coat, and I was set for today's interview and my first couple of weeks on the job.

Or should I be wearing jeans and tees, if I am out working with teenagers? I should have asked about the dress code. *Damn.* Maybe I can text Siobhan. She is Bridget's assistant and a lot closer to my age. I will get her number from Fi.

I start down the street, and then stop as I realize that I'm not completely certain how to get back to the inn. None of the streets look very familiar. Wait, no, I am right. Two blocks up and it should be on the left.

We have been staying at the inn where Fi works for the last couple of days. I should know the way back there by now. Yeah, there it is, just before the top of the hill. A smile curves at my lips. It is a homey, friendly kind of place. Full Irish each morning, and afternoon tea, too.

I wonder what kind of delectable treats will be placed out on the sideboard today. I have never met a pastry or baked good that I didn't like, so, whatever it is, I am certain it will be delicious.

I can't wait to tell Sean that I got the job. I blush as I remember just how excited he was for me when I tried on my interview outfit for him in our room last night. And how he was even more excited for himself as I slowly stripped off each item of clothing, until… God! I sure hope that the occupants of the room next to ours are hard of hearing. That man absolutely drives me wild.

It will be great to get settled into a place of our own. I hope that Sean will have good news, too. He has been following up on leads for a two-bed flat near the center of town. Bev and Donald, the innkeepers, have been great about providing a cheap place for us to stay, but I am certain that they would love to have some customers paying full rate before too long.

We agreed that Fi would live with us right from the start, and she is determined to pay her own way. She'll continue working at the inn and will see an increase in her pay envelope, as she won't need room and board any longer.

I got my first glimpse at just how stubborn both Donovans could be yesterday. We were having a late afternoon cup of tea out on the porch. I was working on a cookie the size of my face when Sean told us how much he expected our rent might be. Fi looked a little surprised at the amount, and Sean basically told her not to be concerned.

"I've got you covered, love. Don't worry about that," he assured her.

"I'll pay my share, I will," she told her brother with an angry set to her jaw. "I'll not be living under *your* roof, mister. We're roommates, nothing more."

"So what, you think you're too grown up to accept a little help from your brother then?"

"Not if it comes with the sort of rules you've been trying to jam down my throat, I won't," Fi yelled.

"Oh, so staying out of the pubs and watching out for the blokes in them, yeah? How'd that work out for you then?"

"Fuck off, Sean. I wouldn't live with you now, not if you paid me." Fi slammed down her teacup, sloshing tea all over the lace doily covering the table, before she raced down the steps and into the street.

Sean looked at me, shock written all over his face.

"And that's why we can't have nice things," I quipped, but he cut me off.

"What the fuck is her problem?" he asked incredulously.

Hmmm. This was awkward. I shoved the rest of my cookie in my mouth to buy some time as I busied myself sopping up the spilled tea. I gestured that I would respond as soon as I swallowed a large mouthful of butter-brickle heaven.

"Well, *um,* Sean, you basically told her not to worry her pretty little head about the rent issue."

"And what's wrong with that? I'm trying to help my sister out, give her a roof over her head, and I'm the dick? Seriously?"

"Sean, that 'little' girl has been living on her own for almost a year now. She just wants to be treated like an adult. Which she is."

Sean rubbed his jaw and looked skyward as if the answers were written in the clouds. He drew a deep breath, and I could see him struggling to control his frustration.

"Okay, so what now? How do I fix this?"

"Give her some time to cool off, *huh*? Then the three of us can sit down and work out a budget. She wants to pay her share, but does she have any real idea of what that would be? It's not just the rent. We'll need to pay for electric and heat. And food."

Sean agreed to back off, and we went up to our room. We started to fool around, but neither of us was really into it, so we took a nap instead. A couple of hours later, Fi knocked on our door, and then came bursting in. She ran right over to Sean and hugged him, and he hugged her back.

"We'll figure it out, Fi," he promised her, and that was that. Crisis averted.

A short while later, I was doing my work-outfit striptease, pretty certain that his fight with his sister was the last thing on his mind by then.

So, now I have a job, and I can be an equal partner in this new domestic arrangement. My salary isn't much, but Bridget assures me that, after a three month probationary period, she will see about making my position a permanent one, provided I complete all the necessary documentation as a foreigner working in Ireland. I am an alien.

I let myself in the front door of the inn. A quick glance at the empty sideboard assures me that Bev hasn't put out the daily spread yet. Maybe I can offer to help her, I think, as I rush down the hall to our little room.

No sign of Sean. So what will it be, a quick shower or a leisurely soak? Or just grab a book and enjoy some tea while I wait for Sean in the parlor? Yeah, that. I strip down and trade my wool slacks and pink button-down for some sweats and a long-sleeved T-shirt. I decide to nix the book, as I doubt I will be able to focus on my current rom-com. I've had enough excitement for one day and lots to process.

Walking back into the parlor, I greet Bev, who is setting up the teacups and laying out the pastries. *Yum! Scones! Are those raspberry*? I have to figure out how to work some exercise into my daily routine and soon or I will need to buy my next pair of jeans in a larger size.

"So, how'd it go, then?" Bev asks, after assuring me that she has it all under control. "Sit, sit and pour yourself a cuppa, girl. I want to hear all about it." Her movements are quick and sure, as she arranges the bowls of lemon slices and clotted cream and fills the china sugar bowl. "I hope you negotiated a decent wage from that miser down at the Center," she warns with a smile on her face.

Yeah, that miser…? My new boss…? Bev's twin sister, Bridget!

"I'm really excited about the job," I assure her, avoiding the topic of wages all together. I probably could have asked for more, but, I was just so glad to be offered a job right after my first interview, I didn't even think to question the low wage. And besides, I suck at advocating for myself. My mom could have told me a million ways to up the ante, but now it will have to wait until my ninety days are up.

Her duties finally done, Bev lowers herself into the chair next to mine and lets me pour her a cup of tea.

"Thanks, dear. So tell me more. What sorts of things will they have you doing?" she asks with interest. For a split second, she reminds me of my mom. The same reddish-brown hair on its way to going gray, the same warm smile.

I squeeze back the lump in my throat and gulp down some hot tea. I really miss my mom. It has only been a week since we saw my folks off at the airport, but so much has happened since then. It feels like months.

"Well, I'll be working with teens from all over the county on life skills." I count them off on my fingers. "First, career management stuff. Writing résumés and cover letters, interviewing skills. Next, financial management. Keeping to a budget, the importance of saving, balancing a checkbook, watching your credit scores." And I will be learning how to practice all that myself, I realize with a start. "And finally, personal things. Recognizing signs of domestic abuse, birth control methods, and things like drinking and smoking and drugs." *Wow, this is a big job.* "Just say no," I finish weakly.

Then, I blush, remembering how the girls at the teen center I volunteered at in Boston howled with laughter as I attempted to fit a condom over a banana. I will have to step up my game, if I am going to reach a street-savvy group of kids like the ones I've seen these past few days.

Maybe Sean will have some ideas. I can just imagine the off-color comments he'll make, if I share my banana story with him.

Bev's bright blue eyes watch me closely as she leans over and takes my hands in hers.

"You're up to this job, girl. Don't be doubting yourself now. I've only known you for a short while, but I do know that fella of yours. Been seeing him strutting through this place for years now, bringing all his Nomads with him. He's the real deal, and if you're all that he says you are, well, that's good enough for me. That's why I told my sister about you. How you'd be right for the job. And you will be too," she adds. With a whoosh, she pushes herself up out of the armchair. "I've got some cinnamon rolls in the oven," she promises with a smile, "and they're your man's favorites. That'll be sure to get him to come running." With a final wink in my direction, she disappears back into the kitchen.

"Thank you again," I call out to her and smile to myself, as I recall how Fi took credit for paving the way for my interview today by introducing me to her "brilliant" friend, Siobhan. But Bridget's sister is our innkeeper and has known Sean for years, so she thinks *she* was instrumental in getting me hired. My mom would be proud of my networking skills.

I sit back, savoring a final slurp of tea. As soon as Sean shows up, I will have another cup. But for now, I relax and close my eyes. I have a job. I can do this. I even toyed with the idea of being a high school guidance counselor at one point. Plus, I am still young enough to remember what it's like to struggle as a teenager, and I am cool, right? I groan at that. Okay, so maybe not so cool, but I'm friendly and a good listener, so…

I am lost in thought when I hear a familiar voice.

"Come here often?" Sean whispers in my ear. I throw my arms around him and kiss him soundly, letting him pull me up into what becomes sort of a happy dance. "I've got great news, love."

"Me, too," I squeal happily.

Sean stops spinning me around and grins.

"You got it then? You got the job?" I barely nod before he spins me again. "Well, that's good, because we'll need it to pay the rent on the posh flat I found for us," he boasts. Wow, we have a lot to celebrate.

"Tell me about our new place," I demand eagerly. Sean already knows about my job duties, but I have no clue where he has been apartment hunting. He kisses me again, lightly this time, and then sits down on the chair and pulls me down onto his lap.

"All in good time, love," he promises with a satisfied look on his face. "Fi is due to get off in a bit, and I know she's excited, too."

"Excited, am I?" Fiona calls out as she rushes into the room and squeezes into the chair with us. "You bet your ass I am. Details," she demands. So Sean describes the two-bed flat that he secured for us, with a full kitchen and a spacious front room. No tub, but a large shower in the bath.

"It's close then?" Fi asks, and Sean shares the address.

I have no clue where that is, but whatever he tells Fi seems to delight her. I figure it's nearby, so she and I can walk to work. It will get lots of sun, he promises me (the former desert-dweller), and the landlord will allow Fi to get the kitten she has been hoping for. The rent is a little higher than Sean planned for, but it is partially furnished and includes utilities, so it will be easier to budget our expenses.

"You're awfully quiet, love," Sean murmurs after Fiona races off to grab her wallet, promising to treat us to a drink next door to celebrate. I am glad we will be living nearby, as I have really come to love Tir na nOg, the warm and friendly neighborhood pub that features live music most nights. "It's a lot, huh?"

Yeah, a new country, a new job, a new family, and a new place to live.

"I'm just so happy. I love you," I whisper in his ear, and he responds by kissing me just as Fi comes rushing back in.

"Not in front of the children," she screeches. "I can't leave you alone for a minute. C'mon then, let's get going." So we celebrate our new apartment and my new job with a couple of rounds. Sean tries to convince Fi to stay and have dinner with us, but she smiles and winks at us.

"Hot date, loves. Duty calls."

I squeeze Sean's hand tightly as I feel him get ready to offer her some unsolicited advice.

"Have a good time, Fi. Make good choices," I tease, as she blows kisses to us and races out of the pub. "She'll be fine," I tell Sean.

He shakes his head and grins at me.

"They grow up so fast," he murmurs and flags down our waitress. "Let's order, huh? I'm starved."

I am, too.

CHAPTER TWENTY-SEVEN

JACKIE

I ROLL OVER and groan. 6:05 a.m. I have been trying to get my body adjusted back to Sedona time, and this is the latest I have slept since we returned last week. Rob has already gotten used to the change, and the sheets on his side of the bed are still warm, so he hasn't been up for too long. Maybe I am making progress.

He is probably walking Brenda and Eddie around the neighborhood, maybe even stopping and letting them off their leashes to chase jackrabbits in the empty lot at the end of our dead-end street.

Oh crap, it hits me. Hard. Like a ton of bricks. *Becca*. She isn't down the hall, snuggled under the covers. Nor is she in Boston, living in the dorm. No, my daughter, my only child, is still in Ireland where we left her. With Sean.

Tears well up in my eyes, and I roll over and bury my face in the pillow. Becca. I more than just miss her. I long for her, pine for her. Rob knows how I feel, and he loves her as much as I do. He just deals with it so much better than me.

I try to cover up my true feelings when I tell everyone about Becca. Yeah, how she met someone and stayed behind. How she is looking for work over there. No, not going to go back to Boston. No grad school for now. Taking a break, ha-ha.

Not everyone buys it. Freaking Suze. My oldest friend flipped out when she picked us up at the airport last week. Rob and I retrieved our luggage in Boston and headed out to the sidewalk to meet her. We tossed our bags into the car, and I climbed in front. A quick hug and we took off into traffic before she looked around.

"So, where's Becca?" she asked suspiciously.

"She's *um,* staying in Ireland for a while," I admitted.

"What do you mean 'a while'?"

"She's with Sean. I texted you about Sean from the tour. How great he is. How much everyone just loves him?"

"What? Are you kidding me?"

God, I hate when people say that. *Yes, I am kidding. As if.*

"She fell in love, Suze. It happens." My husband's tone was casual, but I knew it pissed him off to have to justify Becca's actions to her.

"Yes, Rob. I know it *happens.* I also remember when your wife had the hots for a tour guide and uprooted her whole life to be…"

"It's not the same thing and you know it," Rob began heatedly.

I'd had enough.

"Stop it, both of you. Arguing about this is just plain stupid." I glared at my oldest friend. "You knock it off. Becca's fallen in love with a tour guide. Rick was a tour guide. History repeats itself. It's a great big karmic fuck you. Get over it. And you," I said, turning to face my husband. "Stop needling her. You know how she gets."

This got Suze going again, but now she was mad at me. A lot of things got said in the heat of the moment, so, after everyone calmed down, I suggested that it might be better if Rob and I stayed in a nearby hotel for the night.

Suze got off at the next exit and dropped us at the first hotel we passed. Rob ran in to make sure that we could get a room while we sat in silence. When he came back a few minutes later, all smiles, we retrieved our bags from the trunk. Suze stepped out of the car and stood silently as the pile of luggage grew. When we finished, she pointed to the back of her car.

"Over there, it's a boot, huh?" she asked in a meek, un-Suze-like voice.

What? Oh, yeah. I smiled at her, and, when she held out her arms to me, I let her hug me. When she asked if we could have breakfast together in the morning, just the two of us, I nodded.

"I'll call in the morning then. Bye, Rob," she called out and got back in her car. I watched her drive away, praying silently that telling others about Becca would not be nearly as dramatic.

So we checked in, ordered from room service, and tried to watch a pay-per-view movie, but our hearts weren't really in it. When Rob turned to me in bed later, I pulled away and told him I was too tired. For once he didn't respond with, "You can just lay there. I'll do all the work." Neither of us was in a joking mood.

After a restless night, I had breakfast with Suze while Rob took care of some work-related phone calls. Then we flew back here to Sedona, and it's been a week and I still can't adjust to the time change. I wonder if I am resisting the change so that I can be more in sync with Becca, but that's just silly. Isn't it?

Becca

"I'm just saying we need to have some sort of schedule, Fi. That's all."

Geez, she is behaving like she is eight instead of eighteen. I had to pound on the door to the bathroom again this morning. Fiona is a dawdler, although why she needs to get all dolled up just to go clean other people's toilets is beyond me. That sounds awful. But you know what I mean, right?

She shrugs as she passes me in the hallway. Only half dressed, she is drinking a cup of milky tea and looking all over for her flatiron.

"You're the one with the shy bladder, miss," she reminds me. "I've no issue with you using the loo while I'm in the shower."

I blush at that. Yeah, maybe I am a little on the shy side. I grew up in a house where bathroom doors remained closed, just as God and nature intended. Even in the dorms, there was still a stall to keep private things, well, private. But Fi is turning this around on me.

Why is this now *my* problem? Should I just hold off until Sean gets back to town on Friday? Just wait till your brother gets home, young lady. No, this is ridiculous. It needs to be addressed before things get out of hand. I take a deep breath as I follow Fi down to her room.

"It's not just the toilet, Fi. We both need to get ready in the mornings, right? I know you like to do your makeup and stuff in the bathroom, but maybe you can straighten your hair in your room, huh? That way I can use the mirror to put my makeup on. C'mon, we can do this this. And besides, when Sean is here fulltime, he's going to be getting ready, as well…"

She snorts at that.

"Yeah, that will happen right? Quittin' the best job in the world to sit behind a desk?" She notices my look of shock and relents a bit. "Now Becca, I'm not sayin' that Sean won't eventually leave the job, but you know just how posh a gig he's got, *heh*? All his meals covered, staying in grand lodgings every night, not a care in the world," she gushes.

I feel dizzy and lean against the doorjamb for support. Is it possible that Sean won't leave his job? Don't get me wrong; I am not in favor of him quitting until he has something else lined up. But I haven't rebooted my whole life to be in a weekend-only relationship. And play nursemaid to Fiona.

I kissed him goodbye on Sunday night, before he drove back to Dublin. He planned to sleep on the couch at Dec and Sarah's and then start a tour first thing on Monday. For the next couple of weeks, his boss has him booked on four-day trips so that he can finish up on Friday then come back here, probably close to midnight. He will be exhausted and probably spend most of Saturday recovering before leaving again on Sunday. It is going to suck, but I figure that we can make anything work for just a few weeks.

Oh, and the whole plan is going to hinge on his brother, Liam. More precisely, Liam's car. The only one of the three Donovan boys to have his own set of wheels, he has been pretty good about letting Sean drive back and forth the last couple of weeks, but how much longer will it go on? We thought we could make it work. What had we been thinking? Things are already starting to fall apart.

Wait. Fall apart? Seriously? A little disagreement with Fi and suddenly I am all "Doomsday?" Get a grip, I instruct myself. Fi has no idea what she is talking about. Of course Sean is going to quit his job and soon. Fi will learn to do her hair perched on her bed, instead of the sink. And I will learn to pee in front of other people.

Fi leans in for a quick hug.

"You'd best get a move on, if you're going to set a good example for all those Dingle youths," she warns and is almost at the door when she turns to me. "Oh yeah, so Becca," she calls out. *Oh, what now*? "You know that that teapot that you've been yammerin' on about?"

"Edie's teapot? Yeah, what about it?"

"One of my mates from the pub has a brother who's some big

mucky-muck at the plant, and he located one for ya. I should have it by the weekend. And you owe me twenty quid. See ya tonight." And with a wave, Fiona is gone.

I can't quite believe it. Edie's teapot—the search is over. Wait till I tell Mom! After weeks of scouring every shop across the whole country for a limited-edition bone-china teapot with a sprinkling of hand-painted shamrocks, leave it to Fi to locate it through one of her freaking pub connections. The girl is brilliant.

A quick glance at the clock by Fi's bed confirms I need to leave in five minutes. So maybe I'll hold off talking to Sean about Fi and her morning routine for now. Surely my little sister and I can work something out, and Sean has already has more than enough on his plate.

CHAPTER TWENTY-EIGHT

JACKIE

"BUT BECCA—" I can hardly get a word in.

My daughter cuts me off, again.

"Mom, you don't understand. It's a Catch 22, you know?" She is on the verge of crying. Thousands of miles separate us and it's not a very good connection, but I know my girl. She sounds exhausted and more stressed than I can ever recall.

I hear her take a deep breath. I see an opening and take it.

"Becca. You need to listen to me. You will work things out, you and Sean. You'll see that—"

"I am trying to tell you. You think everything is so perfect, that we're all la-di-da all the time." *Wait, do you know me? That's not what I—* "Sean can't take any more time off. He used all his vacation time last month, when we first got back. His boss has been great, but he's not going to give Sean more time off just so that he can look for another job. And it's not like he can set up interviews on Sunday mornings, right? And that's about the only time he's actually vertical *and* coherent," she finishes in a bitter tone.

Wow, things have gone downhill really quickly. The two have been playing house together for just less than a month, and Becca already sounds like she is ready to throw in the towel. And come home, I think. *Yay*! But no, that isn't the way it should work. If she is going to leave Ireland, it has to be her actual choice, something she really wants. But would I rather see my daughter miserable here in Sedona or try to talk her off the ledge over the phone? Has she stopped talking? Could I offer her some of my world-class advice?

Yes!

"That's why they invented phones, darling. And email and Skype. I'm not saying that it'll be easy to line up a new job that way, but at least Sean can be getting résumés out and cover letters. He can arrange for phone interviews during the afternoons, after he gets his tourists checked in. And yeah, I think the right employer would be happy to meet with him on a weekend. We're talking about Sean here. He's amazing. Anybody would be thrilled to hire him. You'll see. In a few more weeks, all this will be—"

"A few weeks?" *Uh-oh. Next stop, hysteria.* "I can't take it that much longer. You have no idea how hard it's been. Sean's gone for days at a time. I'm just now starting to figure out my job responsibilities. And the kids hate me, I know they do. Fi goes out most nights, God knows where. And every morning, we have the same fight about the bathroom. It's just awful."

Now I am starting to get annoyed. It is only 7 a.m. here in Sedona, and once Rob realized that it was going to be one of *those* conversations, he threw up his hands and left to take Brenda and Eddie for their morning walk. The cup of coffee he handed me before he left the house is long gone. "Tell Bex I love her," he mouthed on his way out the door. I need some serious caffeinating, and this conversation is, in all honesty, going nowhere fast. Time for some tough love.

"Rebecca," I growl, "listen to me. It's time to put on some big-girl panties and face the music. You knew it would be a challenge, and look at all you've accomplished. You landed a good job where you can make a real difference. You found what seems like a nice place to live. You're making some friends. And you've made some progress on that last course, right? *Uh-huh*. You know it's true." I cut off her feeble attempts at protesting. "It's only been a month. Fiona is an adult and you've told me again and again how she's been on her own for a year now. Just try to be her friend, okay? This too shall pass. And maybe start showering at night, huh? One less thing to fight about in the morning." Silence. "Becca? What do you think?"

"You're right, Mom," she concedes.

What?

"Wow, note the date and time. You're actually agree…,"

"Okay, don't get all excited now. But you raised some good points. And showering at night? Genius. Pure genius." She chuckles.

I love hearing that sound. Crisis averted.

"So, I need some coffee, and I need it now, so let's talk over the weekend, okay? I'll text you some thoughts I had on Sean's job search. Or maybe I should talk to Sean directly."

Becca agrees with that.

"All right, I'm going to get back to work and let you get going. But if you have any more advice for me on personal hygiene, just give a call. I'm all ears."

I laugh at that.

"Goodbye, my girl."

"Good morning, Mom."

And it is.

Becca

Mom is right, as usual. I am adjusting to life here in Dingle, and, overall, I really like it. I am growing into the job at the Community Center. The number of teens who attend the programs that I run doubled in the last few weeks, and more and more of them are returning with friends and siblings. I honestly think I have a future here. Siobhan jokes that I will be the "next Bridget," as it's wildly rumored to be only another couple of years before our boss is ready to turn in her papers and retire. I can't even imagine this place without her, but stranger things have happened, and, well, why not me? I crossed the first hurdle last week, when a big, official-looking envelope showed up on my desk at work. As I opened it, Bridget and Siobahn and some of the kids came in with balloons and a cake proclaiming *Congratulations Becca.* The news that I was eligible for the Work and Travel Pilot Programme, aka the Working Holiday Agreement, had spread quickly.

"But how did you know that I was approved?" I asked my boss, as paper plates with huge slabs of cake were passed around.

"The big envelope gave it away when it showed up this morning. Rejections come in a standard-size one," she told me with a wink.

"It's only for twelve months, you know? That man of yours had better make an honest woman out of you, if he expects you to stick around," Siobahn teased. *Oh great. Marriage is the last thing on my mind for now.* But first things first. In another five weeks or so, my three-month probationary period will be up, and, hopefully, I'll be able to negotiate a decent wage this time around. The extra money will really come in handy, especially if Sean gets a job here in Dingle. There is no way he'll continue to earn the same kind of money he makes as a tour guide, what with all those tips, but if that's the price we have to pay to be together more, well, so be it.

Things on the home front have settled down, as well. Fiona's shift at the inn starts an hour earlier each day, now that we're in full tourist season here in Dingle, so our squabbles over the use of the bathroom have ended. She is still a bit too much of a partier for my tastes, but since I'm in bed by 9 p.m. most nights with a hot water bottle and my laptop, I guess I'm not all that reliable of a judge.

Yes, I'm that girl. I need to look into buying a warmer comforter, as nights when Sean is gone, I tend to freeze. Heat is included in our rent, but it's never warm enough for me, and the damp ocean air keeps things pretty chilly. I grew up in the desert, remember? So I wear long underwear and bundle in with the ancient plastic water bottle that a previous tenant left behind. Fi teases me about it when she heads out most nights, and I'm getting ready for bed. In her defense, she's young, single, and really outgoing. I think she'll settle down eventually, but, as long as she pays her share of the expenses and does the chores she's agreed to do, I really can't say too much.

Speaking of chores, I did put a little chart together, more of a spreadsheet actually, and got Fi to commit to her share of the household duties. She grumbles when it's her turn for bathroom duty as she cleans toilets for a living, but that's too bad. We both agree that Sean should not have to do much of anything, since he pays more than half the rent and is never here. But he usually shops with me on Saturdays, so we have food for the week, and, on Sunday mornings, he makes pancakes for us.

Since I brownbag my lunch most days and eat home alone just about every night, I would love to go out with my hot boyfriend on weekends. After a long week, I'm raring to hit the town and go someplace nice for dinner. But Sean's so sick of eating out three meals a day all week long, he's happy to eat at home on weekends and maybe drop in at the pub for a drink or to listen to some music. So it's all about compromise, right? On the plus side, I'm just about finished with my final paper for school. I've been emailing updates back and forth with my professor, and her feedback has been very positive. It will be such a relief to get this behind me. I hope I never get myself in another situation like that again.

There's a really promising job here that Sean would be perfect for, but it has "manager" in the title, so that's freaking him out. He's so good with people and he's really organized, but he's gotten himself convinced that he's just not a "white collar" guy. Too bad, because it would be amazing.

The owner of the town's surf school just bought a company that offers kayaking year round, plus mountain biking, cycling, guided hikes, and rock-climbing. His name is Brian Kennedy, and he plans to grow "Destination Dingle" into the largest outdoor sporting complex in all of Ireland. Fi overheard some guys talking about it at the pub one night and immediately thought of Sean. The next day, she used her lunch break to go over to their headquarters and ask for an application.

"My big brother would be great at taking people out on kayak tours," she bragged to the receptionist, "and he could give surfing lessons, as well."

One thing led to another, and the next time Sean was back in town, he stopped in. As luck would have it, Brian was free to talk. Although Sean was applying for an hourly spot to give lessons or tours, Brian seemed to think that Sean would make an excellent assistant manager of the whole complex. But he needs approval of the entire management team, and it's been tough for Sean to schedule interviews, so things are moving really slowly. I don't want to push him, but it's getting really old being here all week without him.

I really miss my family and friends. And fast food and desert sunsets, but mostly my mom and dad. And my best friend, Lily. And Brenda and Eddie, my darling corgis. Oh, and Coop and Aunt Edie. I know that, if I was back in Sedona, I would be getting ready to move to Boston in just a couple of weeks, but I'm living here in another country, and it's just not the same thing, not at all.

I contemplated going back for a visit this fall, but I don't have any time off coming to me, and, besides, it would be more fun to bring Sean with me. I hope that I can talk him into spending part of the Christmas holidays back in Arizona. Mom already told me that round-trip airfare would be a holiday gift that she would just love to give us. So long as Sean isn't starting a brand new job around then, it could be amazing.

I wonder what Fi will do without us, rattling around this place by herself, but I'm sure that she will be fine. Plus, she's still talking about getting a kitten, so maybe that would keep her from feeling too lonely. I know Sean saw his dad when he was in Dublin last week. He seemed interested in hearing all about life in Dingle, particularly about me and Fi. So maybe the cold war between Billy Donovan and his only daughter is showing signs of a thaw?

CHAPTER TWENTY-NINE

JACKIE

"MOM, YOU'RE NOT gonna believe it!"

Becca's voice can sound pretty shrill at times, and this is one of those times. I was toweling off after a shower and raced out to grab my phone off the nightstand. I have an early meeting this morning and very little time right now to talk with my daughter, but this sounds important.

"You're moving back home," I guess excitedly. *Can that be it?*

Becca pauses for a second, so I probably guessed wrong. Her response is a bit less enthusiastic.

"No, Mom. I'm staying here, but it's still really exciting."

God, please don't be pregnant. Or engaged. Or both. I am still getting used to her living with Sean, I'm not ready for anything…

"It's Sean. He got that job. The one he told you about?"

Oh, this is good news. Sean interviewed for an assistant manager's position at a new outdoor sports center in Dingle. It pays pretty well and won't require any overnight travel. I worked with Sean on interviewing tips and revised the résumé that he drafted, in order to play up what I knew to be his strengths.

"Mom, Sean says thank you. Wait, he wants to talk to you."

Sean's deep voice is a welcome relief, and I have no trouble picturing the tall, strapping guy who stole my daughter's heart.

"So, Jackie. We did it, heh? Becca told you the good news. I gave my two weeks' notice to Nomads, and then Becca and I are going to take a long weekend."

To come home? I wonder. *Long trip for just a couple days, but maybe Boston?*

"She wants me take her up north. See all of the sites that you and Rob enjoyed."

I smile, thinking of the two of them scrambling over the rocks surrounding the Giant's Causeway and crossing the Carrick a Rede Rope Bridge. Yeah, that's a much better plan.

"Congratulations. I just know you'll be great. So when do you start?"

I sit down on the bed and listen to Sean's achingly familiar voice and that amazing accent, intermittently interrupted by Becca's higher-toned one. They are finishing each other's sentences, I realize, and decide right then and there that my meeting can wait.

I adjust the damp towel around me and settle in to listen to them share their good news with me from 5,000 miles away. The possibilities are endless for them, just starting out and making their way in the world. And if Sean is beginning a new job now, he'll have no problem getting some time off at the holidays. Rob and I decided our first trip will be to explore the Pacific Northwest in our brand new RV. We leave next week and plan to be back in Arizona by mid-December at the latest.

Christmas in Sedona. It will be spectacular.

JACKIE & BECCA'S FAVORITE IRISH FILMS

BASED IN OR BASED ON Ireland and/or Northern Ireland

Angela's Ashes

The Boxer

The Commitments

The Devil's Own

In the Name of the Father

My Left Foot

Once

The Quiet Man

Ryan's Daughter

The Secret of Roan Inish

Sing Street

Waking Ned Devine

The Wind That Shakes the Barley

ACKNOWLEDGMENTS

It takes a village to publish a book these days, and I would like to thank all my villagers:

To my husband Deane, for loving me and putting up with me for all these years. Every love interest and romantic male character I've ever written is inspired by no one but you, my sweetheart.

To my daughter Hayley, for inspiring me to write about the complexities and joys of a mother-daughter relationship. Our 2014 trip to Ireland and Northern Ireland was amazing, as are you, my wonderful girl.

To my son Conor, for always knowing when I need a hug or a laugh. I still haven't written a lead character with a son, but when I do, he'll have mighty big shoes to fill, my amazing boy.

To my Beta readers: Barbara Wurtzel, you are the gold standard of Betas—detailed, constructive, imaginative, and supportive. You inspire me to be a better writer, my friend. Bernadette Maycock, my Irish Beta. Thank you for helping me make the dialogue and descriptions of the Irish countryside, as well as life in Dublin, so authentic. Robin Lee, once again you have offered suggestions to improve the story, and I appreciate it and you! Joan Carney, your input and feedback improved the finished story immensely. Thank you all so much.

To Kathryn Galán, my editor, I appreciate all of your help and patience. If the devil is truly in the details, then you and Karen Alcaide, super-proofreader, are the most angelic devils ever.

Thank you to my friends and my readers and readers who are also my friends. Your enthusiasm and encouragement mean the world to me.

ABOUT THE AUTHOR

A family vacation trip to Sedona, Arizona, prompted me to start writing *Jeep Tour*, my first novel. I fell in love with the red rocks and blue skies and started imagining what it would be like to start your life over in such an amazing place.

My second novel, *Guessing at Normal*, is a rock-and-roll love story featuring dreamy poet Jill and sexy rock star James Sheridan. I am currently working on my fourth novel. A hopeless romantic, I am married to the love of my life. I am mom to two young adults and three cats, and I enjoy reading, music, and travel.

I am a professor in the School of Business & Information Technology at Springfield Technical Community College in Springfield, Massachusetts. I was the recipient of the Deliso Endowed Chair Award and was recently recognized by the Commonwealth of Massachusetts's Department of Higher Education as one of "29 Who Shine."

FROM THE AUTHOR

Did you enjoy *Driving on the Left*? I hope so, but I would love to hear from you either way. You can find me here:

On my website, www.gailolmsted.com
On Amazon, www.amazon.com/author/gailolmsted
On Facebook/GailOlmstedAuthor
Or on Twitter @gwolmsted
Feel free to email me: gail@GailOlmsted.com.

I hope that you will take the time to post a review on the website of your choice or a rating on Goodreads. Authors live and die by these reviews, so please give some feedback. It is much appreciated!

My first novel was *Jeep Tour*. Are you interested in reading about how Jackie met a hunky tour guide of her own? Here's the first chapter for your enjoyment!

Best for now,

Gail

JEEP TOUR

PREFACE

IF YOU EVER get the chance for a do-over, take it. That's the best advice I can offer you. Life is rarely predictable, so if the ball is in your court, hold on and run with it. How I got where I am today is a pretty good example. A series of random occurrences followed by a single conscious act on my part. And here I am!

Out of all the conferences I could have attended last year, I chose one held in Phoenix. Out of all the touristy activities available, we chose a Jeep tour of the desert. Does fate play a role? If one of us had asked for a third cup of coffee at breakfast or dawdled in just one more gift shop that morning, would we have been assigned to a different tour guide? Is it all about the luck of the draw? If so, is that a good thing?

I have been studying and teaching consumer behavior for most of my adult life and if I've learned one thing in all those years, it would have to be that consumer behavior is influenced by emotion and therefore it's unpredictable and, from an objective third-party point of view, often makes no sense.

I guess that's true for *all* behavior, not just in the marketplace. I can't look you in the eye and tell you that everything I've done over the past year or so has been rational. It certainly wasn't predictable, not based on my first 39 years. Honestly, it could even be viewed as crazy! But I was *not* an objective third party, *not* a casual observer. I was totally committed, in deep, up to my eyeballs actually. Life got messy and scary and then kind of sad…until it wasn't. At the time, every decision I made and every step I took seemed reasonable, and when I consider where I am today, I honestly wouldn't change a thing. Honest, not a single thing!

CHAPTER 1

TWELVE MONTHS EARLIER

"NEED A HAND?" Our tour guide was speaking to me, as I was the last one to board the brightly colored Jeep.

"Yes, thanks," I mumbled as he took my hand and helped me into the open back seat.

"You dropped this," he told me as he handed me my water bottle. Glistening with condensation, it slipped from my hand a second time and rolled under the Jeep.

"Whoops. Sorry." I can be such a klutz at times. The guide bent down to retrieve it. When he stood upright, I really saw him for the first time. I gave a small gasp. God, he was gorgeous! Tall, built, and tan, with a shock of blond-streaked hair and dazzling green eyes.

"It's okay," he said. "I always end up crawling around under the Jeep for one thing or another." X-rated images of him crawling around on me flashed before my eyes, but I quickly dismissed them. I am a middle-aged tourist, not some sex-starved guide groupie. But could I be both?

Don't be ridiculous, I told myself. Obviously, my lustful thoughts were not reciprocated. Mr. Hunk patted my hand rather absentmindedly and swung himself into the driver's seat. He turned the key and the Jeep roared to life.

"Okay then, ladies…before we set off today, I'd like to introduce myself, find out a little about you, and go over a few ground rules. I'm Rick and I'll be your tour guide. Have any of you been on a tour of the desert before?"

I looked over at the other two inhabitants of the Jeep, my colleagues Kate and Linda.

Linda spoke for the three of us, since she was riding shotgun, and since she was Linda. "No, we haven't. You're our first, Rick."

Oh grief, is she flirting with him? We've been there before, Linda and I. She gets this southern-fried thing going on and although she's never lived further south than Rhode Island, it somehow works for her. But it's wrong on so many levels.

Not now, Linda, I begged silently.

"So Rick, is this *really* the best tour in all of Arizona?" she drawled.

"Why yes, ma'am," Rick replied. "You ladies have come to the right place." He beamed at Linda, who smiled back at him like they were sharing a secret. Leave it to Linda. She always spoke up first, always got noticed, and always took center stage. *Bitch.*

"I'm Linda," she said as she extended her hand to Rick.

"Well, hello there! And who are your friends, Linda?" he responded, still grasping her hand.

"That's Kate and her camera, and this is Jax," said Linda, pointing to me.

"Hi, Jack." Rick shook my hand before turning to Kate.

"It's Jax," I corrected him.

"What?" said Rick, turning back towards me.

"It's Jax," I murmured. "Not Jack."

"Jax?" he questioned.

Knowing I should just shut up, I found myself explaining how I had been named after former First Lady Jacqueline Kennedy. What can I say? My Irish-American parents came of age in the 60s. But as a toddler, I lisped and referred to myself as 'Jackth' and the name stuck.

"But you can call me Jackie," I finished rather inanely.

Sensing my discomfort, Linda chimed in, "And you can call me Linda," and then she started chattering away about how we had been attending an academic conference in Phoenix, and had decided to visit Sedona for some R & R and a quick overnight visit.

Rick listened patiently as Linda told him that all three of us were faculty members at a small private college in New England: Linda in accounting and finance, Kate in management studies, and me in marketing. At that, Rick turned and looked at me.

"Marketing? I took a class in marketing. I remember the four Ps."

I smiled. "Yeah, I get that a lot. But it's really more about…"

"Okay, ladies, we're off," Rick interrupted. "I'll go over the ground rules on our way to the desert."

He drove through the lot and turned right onto the busy surface road. As he weaved his way through the heavy midday Sedona traffic, he began explaining some of the sights that we would be seeing. I vaguely remember him talking about keeping our arms inside the Jeep and how we should stay belted in. Something about the need to drink lots of water and that he had a cooler with plenty of cold bottles.

He might have said more, but I honestly don't remember. What he was saying was pretty inconsequential. I was still blown away by how good-looking he was. Shallow, I know. He could have been reading from a phone book for all I cared. From my current vantage point, I could only see the back of his head, the gold-streaked hair that grazed the collar of his khaki tour guide shirt, and his massive tanned right forearm as it maneuvered the steering wheel. *Yikes.* I couldn't see his left hand and I wondered if he wore a ring. *Hmmm.*

Confident that I had seen all I could for now, I started to pay attention, to listen to him. He spoke clearly and it was pretty easy to hear him over the road noise and the midday traffic. I struggled to place the slight accent that I detected. I am an amateur linguist and I have a knack for identifying where someone might have grown up.

But I also know that it's not always accents that identify your place of birth; sometimes it's the words themselves or the phrasing. For instance, if someone says their hair needs washed or their pants need pressed, you can just about guarantee that they were raised in the Pittsburgh area. It's true. But I digress. Struggling to focus, I heard Rick ask Kate about her camera and promise her some amazing shots that afternoon.

"This really is the best tour," he boasted. "Everyone loves it!"

"How long have you been giving Jeep tours, Rick?" Linda asked, accent-free.

"Almost three years," he replied. "I came here on vacation and fell in love with the blue skies and red rocks. Went back, quit my job, and here I am."

"Where?" I piped in.

"Where?" asked Rick hesitantly without turning around.

"I mean, where are you from?" I added.

"All around," Rick replied casually. "I went to college for a couple of years in Pennsylvania and lived in Ohio for a while. I worked as a computer tech, but I was miserable trapped in a little cubicle. I love it out here in the desert. I can't imagine ever leaving. Okay, we're going off road here, so hang on. This is where the pavement ends and the adventure begins!"

Over the next hour or so, Rick showed us the sights. We traveled up steep inclines and down narrow trails. We bounced over an old wagon road that used to be a cattle trail. I loved how enthusiastic he was about everything, how he seemed to delight in all the beauty and unique qualities of the desert. Also, he was very knowledgeable. He really knew what he was talking about.

"Ladies, check this out. Right over there is the prickly pear cactus. It's edible and can be used in so many different things. You should try the prickly pear jelly. We can barely keep it in stock in the gift shop," he assured us.

"Hmmm. Sounds nummy," Linda purred. *Honestly!*

At one point, we got out to stretch our legs, and Linda and Kate hurried off to take more pictures. Actually Kate was taking the pictures that Linda was telling her to take, but whatever their dynamic, it allowed me to get to know Rick a little more. Just a little bit.

Rick was a better listener than a talker, so I ended up doing most of the talking. They say nature abhors a vacuum. Well, so do I! At even a hint of a potentially awkward silence, you can count on me to jump in to save the day.

I told him about how I was up for tenure and that the decision would be announced any day now. I might have flirted a bit in my rather awkward yet endearing manner. I might have hinted that as a college professor, I had summers off. I might have even suggested that I had access to a boatload of frequent flyer miles.

I was trying to subtly communicate my potential availability without being too forward. Hey, use what you've got, right? To be truthful, those miles had been racked up by my jet-setting ex, but I am pretty certain that I have some coming to me as part of my recent divorce settlement. So I talked and Rick smiled and looked thoughtful and said things like "Is that right?" at all the appropriate moments.

A little while later, we left the mesa, somewhat reluctantly as the views were stunning for miles, but Rick assured us that there was plenty more to see. I was becoming more comfortable around him and hopefully more appealing as the afternoon wore on. He was receptive to my chatter and we really seemed to hit it off. Linda and Kate had already clambered back into the Jeep and I saw that Linda had relinquished her seat up front to me. I was thrilled to be that much closer to our engaging tour guide. And the amazing vistas. And the tour guide.

"C'mon, Jackie, we've got places to go and rocks to see!" Rick called out.

"Okay, Rick. I'm coming," I responded with probably a bit too much enthusiasm. I could get used to agreeing with him, if you know what I mean. He waited for me and took my arm to help me into my new seat upfront. It was like a date.

Okay, so *not* a date, but I felt a tingle, a really strong reaction to his touch. I think he felt it too. He smiled at me and… Wait, was that a wink? Was dating a tourist allowed or was it frowned upon by the official tour guide conduct code? And if allowed, how and when would we manage it? And if not allowed, would he be willing to sneak around or even give up his job for me?

Hold on, hot stuff, I cautioned myself. *Don't get ahead of yourself. He's just flirting to get a bigger tip*. But still.

The second half of the tour was even more thrilling. In between explaining why canyons exist (apparently rivers cause erosion—who knew?) and identifying scrub live oak and mistletoe, Rick shared bits of his life with me. Okay, with us, but honestly, I was the only one paying attention. Rapt attention!

I learned that he lives alone in a cabin in the woods, loves hiking, is a vegetarian, and that he had been working down in southern

Arizona when he first visited Sedona.

"Where in Arizona?" I asked. I'm in marketing and curiosity comes with the territory. It's an occupational hazard, as it were.

"Winslow," he replied. My face brightened. Winslow, Arizona*?* I couldn't help it. I began to hum a line from that Eagles song, *Take it Easy,* and was glad when Rick joined in. We hummed a line or two and then sang the last words, ending with a flourish.

"You two make quite a pair. You should consider a lounge act," Linda called from the back of the Jeep.

"Thank you, thank you. We're here all week," I responded.

Ignoring Linda, Rick turned to me. "Yeah," he said, gazing at me appreciatively. "Such a *fine* sight to see."

I blushed and almost dropped my water bottle again. I gulped down a large swallow before I managed something like, "Oh, I bet you say that…" when he reached across the Jeep and wiped a drop of water from my chin.

"No, actually, I never say that," he admitted candidly. *What?* Our eyes met just for a moment and I knew that what I had been feeling wasn't just in my mind or my other body parts. The attraction was mutual. We had chemistry and it was the good kind!

We were off again and Rick was deep into a lecture about tectonic plates before my breathing returned to normal. It had been awhile since I had felt such a strong reaction to anyone. Since splitting up with my husband, there hadn't been anyone else of note, not until now.

"Hang on, ladies," Rick called out and I looked up just in time to see a guy in a four-wheeler barreling towards us. Rick expertly turned us out of danger and muttered "Effin' rental" under his breath. "These guys come up here and think that they can handle these vehicles. Like it's a game or something," he complained.

Linda leaned forward. Had she been listening the whole time? When she winked at me, I knew that she had been. "How much training do you need to handle one of these babies?" she asked.

Rick explained about the process of becoming a tour guide. He really seemed to take it seriously. He ended with how you weren't able to take a tour out on your own until you had passed all kinds of on and off road tests.

"What about the rest of it?" I asked.

"The rest of it?" Rick was confused.

"I mean, you know, all the soft skills. The people skills, the knowledge of the desert, and what guests would be seeing."

"Oh, yeah, sure." Rick smiled. "Being outgoing helps. You gotta be a people person. They look for someone with some life experience. Someone who has been around a bit. Seen things. Done things. Anywhere else, my résumé would be a liability. But not here. And of course, there's classroom training too, and lots of books."

"That would be right up our alley," Linda assured him. "We love being in the classroom, especially Jackie. She's a *really* good teacher."

I colored at the sound of my name.

Rick looked at me again and said in a voice that was only meant for my ears, "I bet you would be good at *anything* you put your mind to, Jackie."

In spite of the blazing mid-afternoon sun, I shivered. This really was the best tour ever!

"Oh yeah, you too," I responded.

Have we established yet that I'm just a bit of a novice when it comes to flirting? I never got the knack. It would actually be kind of funny, if it were not so pathetic.

Rick turned our attention back to the path that lay ahead of us. The last hour of the tour was relatively uneventful, I guess, if you call watercolor vistas and harrowing descents uneventful. We drove back through the surface streets towards the tour office and were about to turn into the parking lot when Rick spoke up again.

"How long are you in town?" he asked.

"We're not," I told him apologetically. "We drove down last night and spent the morning shopping and then here. We're heading back to Phoenix now and flying home tomorrow."

Rick actually looked disappointed. "I've got another tour in a little while but maybe…"

I didn't get to hear whatever "maybe" might entail, because Kate broke in. "Another tour? Wow, no rest for the weary, huh?"

Great timing, Kate. Rick told us how three or four tours a day was standard 'in season'.

After we pulled into the lot crowded with Jeeps and started to unbuckle our seatbelts, Linda piped up again. "Can you request a certain guide? Is that possible?" she asked with more than a little flirt in her tone.

"Oh yeah, we get that a lot."

"I bet you do." Linda chuckled and discretely handed him some cash (I later found out it was $40) and promised, "Well, if I ever come back to Sedona…"

Tour duties over, Rick got busy in his role of consummate company professional and he handed her one of his cards.

"I hope you ask for me. And please, tell your friends. If you want to fill out a quick survey on our website, that'd be great!"

"Terrific. Thanks again, Rick," Linda concluded, just as Kate went in for a hug. Everyone loves Kate and she gets and gives a lot of hugs. She looked so tiny next to Rick and I think she caught him a bit off-guard, but he recovered quickly and hugged her in return.

I have never been so jealous of anyone in my life, not since my best friends all went bra shopping back in seventh grade but didn't think to invite me, citing my apparent lack of need at the time. Not much has changed, but I wished right then that I too could pull off a hug. But, no. Sadly, physical displays of affection are just not in my skill set. I would have to settle for a handshake or something equally lame.

Note to self: learn to flirt and learn to hug! Basic survival skills especially for the newly single. But for now, the tour had ended. It was time to go and my traveling companions appeared ready to depart.

"Hold on a second, Jackie." Rick disappeared around the counter. He returned just seconds later and handed me a card as well. "Hey, I really enjoyed meeting you. Have a good trip back East. And really, if you're ever out this way…"

"I'll look you up," I assured him. Would I? *Boy, would I!*

He grasped my hand in farewell and I thought he might be leaning in for a hug or something when Kate grabbed my other arm. "C'mon, Jax. Traffic is gonna be a bear."

Vowing revenge on perky Kate and all of her well-intentioned but poorly timed interruptions, I turned to wave at Rick and he smiled back at me.

"Take care," I called out. "And thank you!"

He waved and then turned and disappeared through an open doorway into what looked like a break room of some sort. *Sigh*. Oh, well. It was fun while it lasted.

Linda and Kate were already walking towards the parking lot. I hurried along to catch up, but I was too late. Kate was already in the driver's seat and Linda had claimed the front seat of our tiny rental car by the time I reached them. I was going to be squished in the back with my knees up around my ears for the two-hour ride back to Phoenix.

But somehow I didn't care all that much. The warm glow I was feeling had nothing to do with the temperature. As I struggled to make room for my long legs in a backseat designed for a toddler, I looked at the business card he had handed me. Listed beneath a brightly colored logo was *Rick Bowers, Professional Tour Guide*. The office number and website address were listed as well. When I turned the card over, I gasped. There were the digits that would change my life. He had written in a cramped hand what could only be his cell phone number, with a note.

Call me, it read.

ALSO FROM GAIL WARD OLMSTED

Guessing at Normal

Jeep Tour

# # #

Made in the USA
Columbia, SC
20 February 2018